# HELLFIRE

A Novel By Karla K. Goodhouse

## Dedication

To everyone who ever told me I should publish. I finally listened.

And for my family.

Most of all, for Kenneth. This is all for and all because of you.

## Special Thanks

Loren Purcell and The Paper Zombies Design Group
For the incredible cover art.

Barbara Goodhouse

## Author's Note:

This book contains aviation and military terminology which may be unfamiliar to the reader. For your convenience, a glossary of these terms has been provided at the back of the book.

# ~ 1 ~

10.....

Major Martina Redrick leaned back, pressing her head against the seat.

9......

She closed her eyes and opened them again.

8.......

Lying flat on her back, all she could see was the empty expanse of blue sky through the glass.

7......

*Is this real?*

6......

*Or am I dreaming?*

5......

The tension was growing in her body. Her stomach muscles were churning.

4......

She clenched her fists, gripping the arms of her chair, then relaxed her fingers.

3.....

Her eyes played over the surroundings. Everything seemed to be working perfectly.

2.....

So now it all came down to this.

1.....

All these years, all the hard work, and finally, finally, it was happening.

Ignition.

She heard the roar of the booster rockets firing beneath her. The rumbling rose up through the shuttle, shaking her entire body. She felt the sensation clear through her bones. A growing weight pressed down upon her chest—the familiar sensation of g-forces. She tensed the muscles in her legs and stomach reflexively. The years as an Air Force fighter pilot had made the action instinctive.

The space shuttle shook, hovering stationary for a moment, then slowly it began to rise, breaking away from the launch tower and climbing into the sky. The craft picked up speed as it rose until it was racing away from Earth with enough force to break free of the planet's gravitational pull.

The g-forces on Martina's chest increased. Three gs, sustained, was the force placed on astronauts. Compared with the number that could be pulled in a fighter, it was insignificant. She stared forward, watching the sky turn from light blue to a darker shade, and then finally to black. Pinpoints of stars appeared, faint at first but growing bright as the sky darkened.

"Jettison boosters on my mark," Jackson Stewart, the mission commander, ordered from the left seat. Martina moved her fingers to the computer, her gloved hands hovering over the controls.

"3... 2... 1... Mark," Stewart said.

Martina hit the button as ordered. The two solid rocket boosters, their fuel spent, fell away from the shuttle. Free from the weight of the boosters, and now powered only by the main engines of the shuttle itself, the spacecraft picked up speed. Martina felt the change as the pressure increased on her chest. She watched as the stars grew brighter and the sky became darker. She wished she could look behind her to see Earth fall away. The sky filled the cockpit windows.

Stewart seemed more concerned with watching the numbers on the computer monitor. He was studying the data on the screen intently, making sure the computer guidance system was working properly, and steering the shuttle flawlessly along its course.

"Cut engines on my mark," he commanded. "3... 2... 1... Mark."

Martina hit the corresponding button. In an instant the rumbling behind her stopped. The weight of the acceleration lifted off her chest and was replaced with a faint sensation of being pushed upward. Her space suit strained against the straps holding her in place. If it wasn't for the restraints she would float out of her chair.

"Jettisoning external fuel tank," Stewart reported. "Initiate burn on my mark."

He counted down the seconds again, and Martina flicked on the smaller set of rockets, raising the shuttle to a higher orbit. The fuel tank would fall back to Earth and burn up on reentry. A faint sensation of gravity returned, pushing her gently downward.

"Cut engines in 3...2...1...Mark."

Martina switched the rockets off. Almost immediately the sensation of weightlessness returned. She reached up and unfastened her helmet, lifting the glass dome off her head, then shook out her long brown hair, which immediately filled the cockpit due to lack of gravity.

Martina let go of the helmet. It remained suspended in mid-air. Slowly, it floated away behind her.

"Some ride, huh?" Jackson remarked.

"Yeah," Martina agreed, as she fought with the straps holding her in her seat. "That is some ride."

"Want to see something neat?" he asked, taking hold of the shuttle's controls and flipping her over so she hung upside down in space. Earth filled the front windows. Below was a swirling mass of colors— white, greens, browns, and blues. Martina gasped.

"Wow," she muttered in awe, her fingers momentarily falling away from the buckle holding her in place.

"Spectacular, isn't it?"

"I'll say," Martina agreed, returning to work on the buckles. Finally freeing herself from the constraints of the straps, she floated out of the chair and followed Stewart from the cockpit.

The sensation was incredible. She was actually floating, suspended in midair without any feeling of falling. She grabbed hold of the back of her chair and pushed off. The motion sent her flying forward. The bulkhead raced up to meet her. She stuck her hands out, gently stopping herself before she crashed into the wall. Stewart laughed.

Martina reached out and grabbed for her helmet, which was floating nearby. It went sailing in the opposite direction. She turned around and pushed off the wall with her feet. She grabbed hold of the helmet as she flew by it.

Again the bulkhead rushed up to meet her. Martina stuck her hand out, catching herself before she collided with the wall. She flipped herself over and pushed off gently, swimming back to her locker on the opposite bulkhead.

She pulled the door open and stuck the helmet inside. Slowly, she stripped off the rest of her bulky pressure suit, revealing a blue NASA flight suit beneath. She stuffed the large white suit into her locker. Closing the door, she turned back toward Jackson. He was floating beside his closed locker, his pressure suit gone.

"This way," he said.

He floated gently to the door leading to the lower

level of the shuttle. Martina followed, pushing herself carefully off the wall. She caught hold of the door and pulled herself through the passage hand over hand.

They emerged into the main compartment of the shuttle. The other crew members had already stripped off their pressure suits.

"Whoa!! This is better than the vomit comet!" Rachel Ansetti shouted. The pretty Navy pilot was somersaulting in the center of the cabin. She stopped, found the closest wall, and sprang off it into a series of back flips. Her shoulder-length golden-brown hair flipped around with her.

"C'mon, people, we've got work to do," Stewart said. The others quickly dispersed.

Martina waited until they had vanished before gently pushing off the far wall. She floated over to the far windows. For a moment she simply gazed out into the darkness. A thousand brilliant stars sparkled against a black sky. Below, Earth glowed a range of brilliant colors. Large white clouds swirled over green continents and deep blue oceans. The sight was breathtaking.

Martina gaped at it in awe. She was here, flying in a space shuttle, miles above Earth's surface. Her dream had finally come true.

Satisfied, she turned away from the window to find some way to busy herself, helping the other crew members.

✳          ✳          ✳

Rachel Ansetti gazed out the window, watching the sparkling metal satellite tumble through space toward the shuttle. At her fingers the controls of the remote manipulator arm sat waiting. Outside, wearing bulky white pressure suits, Jackson Stewart and Robert Brennan floated in the shuttle's cargo bay, waiting to begin repairs on the malfunctioning satellite. Rachel glanced back at the satellite as it drew closer. In a few more minutes it would be within reach of the arm.

"What's going on?" Rachel twisted her head around to see Martina behind her.

"Nothing yet," Rachel said. "I'm just waiting for this satellite to come in reach so we can grab it."

Martina floated up beside her to watch the spacewalk. The satellite was almost in range, hovering just above the shuttle. Rachel touched the controls of the remote arm, raising it to grab the satellite.

Suddenly, a blinding flash tore through the darkness of space. A large piece of a solar panel flew toward the shuttle, clipping the remote manipulator arm before slamming into the cargo bay. It hit the shuttle broadside, bouncing back off into space. The shuttle shook violently, throwing Martina and Rachel against the far bulkheads.

"*Discovery*, Houston," Martina's headset squawked. "What just happened up there?"

"I don't know," she stuttered.

The two women pushed themselves off the floor and floated back over to the window. The silver satellite had disappeared. In its place floated a thousand sparkling metallic stars. The top of the remote arm was also missing. One of the two space-suited figures was moving in the cargo bay, trying to orient himself. The other was motionless.

"I think the satellite just exploded," Martina said.

"What do you mean, exploded?" Houston asked.

"I mean one minute it's there, the next there's a flash of light and it's gone," she said. "Nothing left but debris. How's this ship holding together? We got shook up here pretty bad. Are we leaking anything?"

"All systems are in the green," Houston reported.

"Rob, Stew, you guys all right?" Rachel called to the two space-walking astronauts.

"I smashed my right arm pretty hard," Brennan replied. "I can't move my hand. Stew isn't moving at all."

"Stew," Rachel called. "Stew, can you hear me?"

"No answer," she said.

"Houston, give me Stewart's vitals," Martina said.

"Pressure and oxygen are fine," Houston reported. "We have a heartbeat, and he's breathing."

"He's alive," Martina said to Rachel. "He must be unconscious."

"What do you want me to do?" Brennan called.

"Get back to the airlock," Martina said.

"Will do," the injured man said. He began to move.

"What about Jackson?" Rachel asked. "We can't just leave him out there."

"We're not going to," Martina said.

"What do you mean?" Rachel asked.

"I'm going to get him," she replied. "Where's Jason?"

"He should be over by the airlock."

"Good," Martina said, disappearing from the room. Rachel stared after her in disbelief.

Martina floated to the lower deck, making her way to the airlock. Just as Rachel had promised, Jason Palmer was waiting beside it.

Martina moved over to the lockers and began to pull out a spare space suit.

"Help me get this on," she said to Palmer.

"What are you doing?" he asked.

"Stewart's unconscious," she said. "I'm going to get him. Now help me put this thing on."

She began to pull the space suit over her legs. Palmer shrugged and moved to help her.

"Rob's been hurt too, but he can still move," Martina explained as she pulled on her boots. "I told him to come inside. When he gets to the airlock, bring him back in here, then let me out."

Palmer nodded, slipping gloves over Martina's hands and fastening them to her suit.

"I'm in the airlock," Brennan's voice called.

"Pressurize it," Martina told Palmer.

Palmer nodded, floated to the controls, and hit a few buttons. Then he moved back to Martina, who was pulling her helmet over her head. Palmer locked it in place and then quickly ran through a gear check with her.

"Houston, this is Redrick," Martina called. "How do you read?"

"Loud and clear, Martina," the reply came.

Palmer opened the hatch and helped Brennan out. Martina floated over, moving awkwardly in the bulky pressure suit. Behind her, Palmer shut the door. All alone in the small white chamber, Martina floated, watching at the red and green lights above the door. Finally, the green light came on, indicating that she could open the door. Martina gripped the handle with her thick-fingered gloves and twisted it. There was a faint hiss as the hatch opened. Martina pushed it forward and floated out into the blackness of space.

She looked around. The awe that had first captivated her inside the shuttle returned with even more force. Now there was nothing but a space suit between her and the vacuum. She was actually floating in space itself. Her view of the stars and Earth was no longer restricted. For a moment all she could do was stare.

Martina shook her head, forcing herself to ignore the pure, stark beauty of Earth. She was out here for a reason: Jackson Stewart. The shuttle commander was hovering motionless at the far end of the cargo bay. Martina propelled herself to him, pulling herself hand over hand. Movement in space was slow. It took Martina longer than she expected to reach the unconscious man.

Finally, she floated up beside Jackson.

"Stew?" she asked, shaking him. "Hey, Stew can you hear me?"

Stewart didn't reply.

Martina moved around him, bringing her face to his and peering into his visor. Jackson's eyes were closed. His face was pale.

"He's out cold," Martina reported.

She wrapped one arm around Jackson's chest. The size of the space suits made it nearly impossible for her to get a decent grip around him. After a few seconds, she managed to get a tight enough hold of Jackson.

Keeping one arm around him, she pulled herself back toward the airlock with her free hand. Getting back took even longer as she struggled with Stewart. His body hung beside hers, weightless.

As she drew closer to the airlock, she could feel him slowly slipping free of her grasp. Her thick gloves were coming loose as Jackson moved upward and away from her. She half-lunged for him, pulling him back tightly to her with both hands.

Wrapping her left arm around Jackson and keeping him as close as possible, she began to move again. After what seemed like years, she reached the airlock. She shoved Stewart's motionless body inside and pulled herself in after him. Once they were both inside, she pulled the hatch closed and twisted the handle to seal it.

"We're in," she said. "Do I have a seal?"

"You're fine, Martina," Palmer said in her ears. "We'll have you out in a minute."

Martina stared at the door leading back inside the shuttle. With Jackson inside, the small airlock seemed even smaller. Finally, the door swung open. Palmer pulled Stewart into the shuttle. Martina followed.

Palmer began to strip the bulky space suit off Jackson's unconscious body. Martina reached up and pulled her helmet off. She stuffed it back in the locker and began to fight with the suit's other fastenings.

"The rest of the mission's been scrapped," Rachel announced from the door. "Houston wants us to rendezvous with the space station and check for any damage."

"Can you do that alone?" Palmer asked Martina.

"It's a simple burn, shouldn't be too hard," she replied, shoving her space suit into a closet. "Stow the rest of the gear. I'm going up to the cockpit to figure out a course."

# ~ 2 ~

Martina eased herself into the left-hand seat of the space shuttle's cockpit. Reaching down, she pulled the restraints across her waist and then drew a second set down over her chest, strapping herself into the seat. The belts kept her from floating away as she flew the shuttle.

She turned her attention to the computer screens before her, running her eyes over the green printouts of telemetry and other data scrolling along the monitors. Martina studied the numbers for a moment before reaching forward and hitting several keys on the control panel.

Almost immediately the screen before her changed, showing the flight path of the shuttle. A few more keystrokes brought up the path of the International Space Station and the trajectory and position of every other object in space in the area.

Martina typed in a few more commands. After a second, a path from the shuttle's current orbit to that of the space station appeared on the monitor. A set of numbers displayed on the computer screen indicated the specifications of the burn necessary for the two to rendezvous.

"Houston, *Discovery*," Martina said. "I've got a window in ten minutes. We shouldn't have to burn too much fuel to get there."

"Copy, *Discovery*, take it."

"Wilco, Houston," she replied. "Do they know we're coming?"

"They're waiting for you, *Discovery*," Houston replied.

"All right, burn in ten, everyone strap in back there," Martina called to the rest of the crew.

She fixed her eyes on the control panel, running through the process to change the shuttle's orbit in her mind. She had practiced this a thousand times in the simulator, on Earth. It was simple. At the proper time, turn on the engines. Hold the shuttle on course until it was in the new orbit and then cut the engines. The computer could do it. So could ground control. All Martina had to do was push a few buttons. It was nothing on the ground.

But at the moment she was not on Earth. She was floating beyond the outer reaches of the atmosphere, where one small mistake could mean the loss of the ship and her crew.

"Need any help?" a voice interrupted her.

Martina turned to see Rachel in the door between the two seats.

"It's pretty simple. I think I can handle it," Martina replied. "But if you want to sit there, you can."

"Thanks," Rachel said. She slid into the right-hand seat and strapped herself down. "I prefer being in the cockpit to riding in the back."

"What pilot wouldn't?" Martina responded, the traces of a smile outlining her lips.

"Given that view, I would want to ride up here even if I wasn't a pilot," Rachel said.

Martina looked up, seeing the sparkling stars in the blackness of space. A half moon was rising over the swirling blue and white Earth.

"You know how many people have seen that?" she asked.

"Very, very few," Rachel replied.

Martina turned her attention back to the computer screen. The shuttle was almost in position to switch orbits. She placed her fingers on the controls.

"Houston, *Discovery*. Initiating burn in 3... 2... 1... Mark." The faint roar of the orbital maneuvering engines filled the cabin. The acceleration pushed Martina and Rachel down into their seats gently. Martina watched the numbers running along the computer screen.

"Cutting engines. 3... 2... 1... Mark," she said, switching off the engines. The soft rumbling and the feeling of acceleration both vanished. "Burn successful, Houston. We should reach the space station in a few minutes."

Rachel lifted her head. Through the blackness of space, a large white structure appeared, increasing in size as they approached. She studied the huge object, picking out the Soyuz module attached and the main crew compartment.

Martina placed her hands on the controls, moving the shuttle into position to connect with the space station. The shuttle drew closer to the large structure, sliding underneath it. A small, square hatch appeared along the bottom of the station. Martina gave the shuttle a faint tap to the left. She watched the computer screen, moving the stick gently until the shuttle was perfectly aligned beneath the space station. Reaching the desired attitude, she took her hands off the controls. *Discovery* hovered exactly beneath the hatch.

As soon as the shuttle was in position, the astronauts on board the space station lowered a sleeve, connecting the two ships. The end of the sleeve sealed tightly around the shuttle's outer hatch, and air was pumped inside, pressurizing it.

"*Discovery*, this is the space station," a voice crackled in Martina's ear. "We have you. You are free to open your hatch."

"Copy that," she said as she began to undo the buckles holding her in the chair. "Somebody open the hatch," she called to the rest of the crew.

In the main crew compartment, Palmer unstrapped himself from his seat and floated over to the hatch. He quickly checked the lights beside the portal. They indicated a good seal. The air pressure in the sleeve was only slightly below that of the shuttle. Confident that the shuttle would not depressurize, he pulled down the lever to open the hatch.

The hatch came open with a soft hiss as the air pressure equalized. Palmer inhaled, noticing the slight staleness of the space station's air. He peered upward. The sleeve itself was less than three feet long. At the other end, a smiling man with shaggy blond hair was hovering.

"Hello," he said, waving to Palmer. "Welcome aboard the International Space Station. I'm Jake Hueser."

"Jason Palmer," Palmer replied, swimming up through the small tunnel.

"You in command here?" Hueser asked.

Palmer laughed. "No, I'm just a scientist. The commander's out cold. The pilot's taken over his job."

"And who would that be?" Hueser asked.

"She's right there," Palmer said, pointing back down the tunnel into the shuttle hatch.

Hueser glanced down, surprised to find himself face to face with a brown-eyed woman with long brown hair. Her face was not stunningly beautiful, but her high cheekbones and firm skin gave her a wild attractiveness, accented by the strange glint in her eyes. As he watched, she floated gracefully up the sleeve and into the space station.

"Martina Redrick," she said, extending her hand.

"Jake Hueser," he replied with a grin, shaking her hand. "Welcome to the International Space Station. How may we be of service?"

"The satellite we were supposed to recover exploded about twenty feet above our cargo bay. I need to inspect the shuttle and make sure there was no serious damage so we can safely return to Earth," she said.

Hueser nodded. "I'm sure NASA wants to avoid another disaster like *Columbia*."

"I'm in no hurry to end up dead for no good reason either," she said. "Our commander was also knocked unconscious, and we have one man with a broken arm. I understand you have some medical equipment on board."

"We have a little," he said. "I'm not sure what we can do for your commander, but we can certainly help the fellow with the broken arm. Bring them both on board."

"Thanks for your hospitality," Martina said. "We should be gone in a few hours, provided there's no damage to the ship."

"There's no need to hurry," Hueser said, grinning. "In fact, we insist you stay for lunch."

He paused, gazing in astonishment at the striking woman who had suddenly appeared through the tunnel and was floating next to Redrick.

The corners of Rachel's lips curled upward as she flicked her eyes up and down Hueser, with the look of a collector appraising a vintage muscle car. She shot a sly grin at Martina. The Air Force pilot fought hard not to laugh.

"And you are?" Hueser asked, his eyes fixated on her.

"Rachel Ansetti," she replied, smiling demurely.

Martina rolled her eyes in amusement.

⁂          ⁂          ⁂

The windows on the lower level of the space station afforded Martina a good view of the shuttle. She floated silently, staring out at *Discovery* and the swirling blues, greens, and whites of Earth. Martina ignored the beauty of the planet that was her home and concentrated on the wings of the space shuttle. Her eyes played over every single inch of the wings, looking for the slightest dent in the surface of the black silica tiles.

She remembered all too clearly how a piece of insulation had dented the heat-resistant tiling on the wing of the space shuttle *Columbia* years earlier. The damage from the impact had caused the shuttle to rip to pieces on reentry, killing her crew of seven.

A small hole in the surface of the shuttle could cause the plasma flowing over the wing during reentry to become turbulent, increasing the friction and heat over the ship, enlarging the hole. If the hole became too large, the heat would become too great and the ship would break up and burn away, just as *Columbia* had.

It was a fate Martina greatly wished to avoid.

Fortunately, after half an hour of scanning the shuttle's wings and tail, her eyes could find no holes. The exploding satellite had damaged the instruments in the cargo bay, putting several dents in the bay and the large doors. Martina had tested the integrity of the cargo bay earlier by shutting the doors and pressurizing the inside. There had been no leaks.

"How does it look?"

Martina twisted around. Rachel was floating beside her.

"Aside from dinging up the cargo bay and hurting Brennan and Stewart, the explosion really didn't do too much," Martina replied. "I can't find a single hole on the wings or tail, and none of the dings in the cargo bay were deep enough to penetrate."

"That's good."

"Of course, the only way to really be certain would be to go out there and inspect the entire wing and tail surface in a spacewalk," Martina said.

"That would make me a lot more comfortable," Rachel agreed.

"If we have time I'll try to convince Houston to let us do it," Martina said. "Do they have any idea what caused the satellite to blow up like that?"

"None," Rachel said. "The repairs were supposed to be to the navigation and communication systems. The only thing they can figure is that something broke in the propulsion system. There was no known space debris around."

"I've never heard of one just exploding before," Martina said.

"It must have either been rogue space debris or an internal issue." Rachel stated.

"Must have been, there's no other explanation," Martina agreed. "How are Brennan and Stewart?"

"Stewart's still completely unconscious," Rachel said. "They immobilized him, but that was all they could do. Brennan's better. They splinted his arm and gave him some painkillers."

"And your friend?" Martina said.

"He had some work to do somewhere," Rachel said.

"He seemed fairly interested in you," Martina said.

"Can you blame him?" Rachel asked. "Good-looking guy, been stuck up here with a Russian and that other gruff old guy for six months. He'd probably take an interest in anything female that set foot on this ship, even if she had the face of a dog and the body of a cow."

Martina laughed. "Fortunately for him you showed up."

"Fortunately for him, he meets my standards," Rachel said. "He might just get lucky."

Martina laughed again.

"He is damn good-looking."

"You're incorrigible," Martina laughed.

"You're just jealous," Rachel said.

"I had a damn good chance until you showed up," Martina said with a laugh.

"You can always try the old guy," Rachel said.

Martina laughed again. "I bet I could still seduce your friend. It didn't look too hard."

Rachel laughed. "Wasn't that hard at all. One glance and he's putty in my hands. I could have that boy anytime I want."

"That's plain to see," Martina said. "And actually, I'd take the Russian over the old guy."

Rachel laughed again. "Wouldn't blame you if you did. Foreign guys can be pretty hot. And that old guy really is awful."

"Yeah..." Martina said, her voice trailing off.

Rachel looked at her. The Air Force pilot was staring wide-eyed through the window. Rachel followed her gaze, peering outside, past the shuttle. Her eyes caught a flash of silver against the background of black sky and sparkling stars.

As the two women watched, the small object rushed for the space station, growing as it approached, until it took on the shape of an oversized missile. The body of the craft was long and slender, with a small glass cockpit bulging up behind the nose. The craft possessed no tail, only a pair of short, stubby wings. A small rocket was attached underneath each wing. Neither the rockets nor the spaceship bore any markings.

Martina and Rachel watched in horror as the missiles dropped from the wings. A small rocket on the end of each projectile ignited, spurring them toward their target. The first missile spiraled into the spare Soyuz module, impacting dead in the center. The little craft imploded with a flash of fire, which quickly extinguished itself in the vacuum of space.

The second missile arched upward, imbedding itself in the space station's bare metal superstructure, which had been put in place for future additions to the station. The resulting explosion left the metal girders twisted.

The shocks from the blasts ricocheted through the space station, first pitching Martina and Rachel against the far bulkhead, then throwing them into the large windows overlooking the shuttle and Earth beneath.

Pressed up against the reinforced glass, the two astronauts stared at the small craft as it rushed forward, revealing several small sets of thrusters on the nose and wings and along the fuselage. A human figure sat in the small cockpit, but the full pressure suit and face mask made it impossible to distinguish his nationality. For an instant, Martina was sure the pilot meant to ram the craft into the space station. She could only watch as the sleek spaceship raced at them.

Suddenly, seconds away from impact, the pilot pulled the nose up. The craft shot along the space station, disappearing into the blackness of space beyond. Martina could see the spurts of flames shooting through the thrusters and the larger rocket engine attached to the back of the craft.

"Holy fuck!" Rachel said, pushing herself off the wall and gazing wide-eyed into space. "What the hell was that thing?"

"I have no idea," Martina said, "but I don't think he's friendly. We've got to get back to Earth, fast."

She pushed herself away from the wall and floated back toward the main compartment of the space shuttle.

"No argument here," Rachel said, following.

The space station's crew was not hard to find. They had all congregated in the main control center and were rapidly checking the life support systems. Palmer and Brennan stood against the wall, their faces tight with apprehension. Brennan's right arm was pulled to his chest with a sling.

"We've got to get out of here, now!" Martina said, announcing her presence in the room.

"Don't be ridiculous," a silver-haired American named Sloane said. "There doesn't appear to be any serious damage to the space station. There's no reason to abandon ship."

"You don't understand," Martina said. "That was no ordinary explosion. We were attacked."

"Attacked?" Hueser asked skeptically.

"Yes," Rachel said. "A long silver ship fired two missiles at us. They blew up your Soyuz."

"We've got to get out of here before they come back," Martina said.

"How do you know they'll come back?" Sloane challenged.

"They want us dead," Martina said. "That was why they attacked us in the first place. We've got to get back to Earth before they return."

"Back to Earth how?" Hueser asked. "The Soyuz is gone."

"We still have the shuttle," Martina said. "It would be a tight fit, but we'd make it alive."

"It wasn't damaged?" Brennan asked.

"I've been studying the thing for the past half hour," Martina said. "I can't find any dings on the outer surface. We should make it."

"How are we going to do that without the mission commander?" Palmer asked. "Stew's still out cold."

"I guess I'll have to fly it," Martina said

nonchalantly.

"By yourself?" Rachel asked.

"Don't you need two people to fly one of those?" Brennan interjected.

"You're a pilot, right, Rachel?" Martina asked.

"Yes," the other woman said.

"Good," Martina replied. "You fly right seat, then."

# ~ 3 ~

Martina pulled herself into the left-hand seat of the space shuttle, glancing at the console before her. She reached for the buckles, strapping herself into the chair. She cinched the straps until she was held tightly in place. Rachel slid into the right seat and began to buckle herself in.

"Everyone all strapped in back there?" Martina called.

The remaining members of *Discovery*'s crew and that of the space station had all squeezed into the crew compartment of the space shuttle. Martina had quickly briefed Houston on the situation and her intentions while the seven astronauts and one cosmonaut had transferred to the shuttle. The space station's hatch had been sealed, followed by that of the shuttle. The sleeve had then been disconnected from the shuttle, while the crew had prepared for reentry.

"We're all good," Brennan's voice echoed in her headset.

"Houston, *Discovery*. We're separating from the space station," Martina said.

"Copy, *Discovery*," Houston said.

The young Air Force major placed her hands on the controls, slightly amazed at Mission Control's receptiveness. Instead of barking orders, they were following her directives, placing the pilot in control of the entire mission.

Martina pushed the nose of the shuttle down and tapped the thrusters. The shuttle moved slowly down, away from the International Space Station, until she hovered about fifty feet beneath the large white structure.

"*Discovery*, Houston," the radio crackled. "You are go for reentry. You should reach your first window in forty minutes. That will put you on course for Edwards."

"Copy, Houston, that's what the computer's telling me," Martina replied.

"Be advised that the wings and tail may have sustained some internal damage from the shocks. You might have some difficulty controlling her," Houston reported. "We're reading all systems green."

"I've got the same," Martina replied.

"Are you sure we can pull this off?" Rachel asked.

"Yeah, sure," Martina said.

"How much time do you have flying left seat?" she asked.

"About five hours," Martina said. "In the sim."

"Great," Rachel said.

"I landed once," Martina said. "It's really not that hard. The computer does most of it."

"You realize I'm only about halfway through my pilot training," Rachel said. "That's why I was flying back seat."

"That's all you need," Martina said. "It's just like landing a big cargo plane."

"Yeah," Rachel said. "A cargo plane flying Mach three, with no power whatsoever and unknown internal damage to the wings and tail."

"Shouldn't be too much of a problem," Martina said.

"Have you ever flown a cargo plane?"

"Nope," Martina said matter-of-factly. "I was a

fighter pilot. What about you?"

"You can't land a cargo plane on a carrier," Rachel said. "I flew Hornets."

"Well, this should be interesting, then," Martina said, grinning.

"Yeah," Rachel said, flashing a maniacal smile. "This should be really interesting."

"Oh no!" the Navy woman gasped. She pointed up in the blackness of space. Off in the distance the small silver shape of the mystery ship was visible, angling for the space shuttle.

"They're back," Rachel said. "And they're heading straight for us."

"There's no way this thing can outmaneuver those missiles," Martina said. Her fingers flew over the controls, calling up their position.

"We've got one chance. They don't appear to be capable of reentry. If we retrofire, they might not be able to follow us. Close the cargo bay doors."

Rachel hit the button to close the doors, as Martina's fingers continued to dance across the keys. A retrofire course appeared on the screen before her. The computer showed that the path was free of any known satellites or space debris.

"Houston, *Discovery*. That thing just came back, and he's looking to shoot us down. We're reentering now," Martina said, more to inform Mission Control of her intentions than to ask for permission to retrofire.

"Copy, *Discovery*" was the reply. Martina grabbed hold of the shuttle's controls and carefully aligned the ship for retrofire.

"It's just a big cargo plane," Rachel said, watching as the silver craft drew closer.

"Just a big cargo plane," Martina echoed.

She made a quick final scan of her instruments. The computer indicated that the cargo bay doors had shut.

"Initiate burn on my mark. 3... 2... 1... Mark!"

"Initiating burn," Rachel replied, pressing a button in front of her.

In the rear of the shuttle, the retro-rockets sparked to life. Slowly, the shuttle began to slip back toward Earth's surface.

Rachel stared up at the mystery craft. The thin sliver ship had pushed its nose down and was chasing the shuttle. She wondered what the range of the missiles was.

"Cut engines in 3... 2... 1... Mark!" Martina called.

"Engines cut," Rachel replied.

"Here we go!" Martina said.

"Let's do this!" Rachel said.

Martina turned her eyes back to the computer screen. Their progress along the descent path was holding. The numbers running along the screen paralleled the numbers for a perfect descent. The nose angle was exactly where it belonged.

She peered back out the window. A red haze of ions was creeping up over the shuttle's nose, invading the blackness of space. The small silver craft was still giving chase. Both pilots stared forward, watching as it raced toward the outer reaches of the atmosphere. Two bright fires appeared beneath the wings as the ship launched its missiles in an act of desperation before firing its engine and climbing back into space.

Martina watched as the haze covered the window. The shuttle shuddered slightly as it encountered the first particles of the upper atmosphere. The plasma shock spreading from the shuttle's wings threw the missiles approaching her off course. After a moment the friction from the hot plasma flow burned through the missiles' skin, and they exploded safely above the shuttle in two small fireballs, which ignited and died in rapid succession.

Martina and Rachel allowed themselves to exhale

as they saw the missiles vanish in twin balls of flame.

"Find me a runway," Martina said to her copilot.

Rachel typed in a few commands. "This course will put us down somewhere in eastern Russia." Her finger danced across the keyboard. "There's an airbase down there that they used for their space shuttle which should be able to take us."

"Good, program the course into the computer," Martina said.

"Done," Rachel said, hitting a few keystrokes.

The ion haze crawled up over the shuttle's window. For a few seconds, all Martina could see was the red fire, as the atoms of Earth's upper atmosphere collided with the hypersonic craft. Then the ion haze began to creep away, receding slowly over the shuttle's nose.

"Houston, *Discovery*. We're coming down in Russia," Martina said as soon as the ion haze had dissipated enough to allow radio communication. "If you could let them know we're coming it'd be appreciated."

"Will do, *Discovery*. Safe landing," Houston replied, as the last of the ion haze faded from view around the nose of the shuttle.

"We're back in the atmosphere," Martina reported.

"That's good," Rachel said "Now if we have to jump out we'll live."

"We shouldn't need to bail."

Suddenly, the ship began to shake violently and a loud warning signal started to blare. Lights were flashing rapidly on the console.

"You were saying?" Rachel prompted.

"Looks as if we did take some damage," Martina said. "There must have been a few dents in the wing, which reentering enlarged."

"Good thing they didn't get too big."

"I'll say," Martina said. "The air flow is wreaking

havoc on the computer's ability to fly her. The machine can't compensate." She looked at the screen. "Okay, this is what we're actually flying, and this is where we need to be." She reached up and keyed a few commands into the computer, then gripped the stick tightly with both hands.

"This should be fun," Martina said, taking control of the crippled ship.

"What are you doing?" Rachel asked.

"She's too battered for the computer to fly her," Martina said through clenched teeth. "We have to land her by hand."

"Can you do that?" Rachel asked, incredulous.

"If she can still fly, I can fly her," Martina replied. The shuttle jerked suddenly. Martina turned her attention quickly back to the controls.

"As long as I can keep what we're flying close to where we're supposed to be, I can get her on the strip," Martina said.

"What can I do?" Rachel asked.

"This is taking all my concentration," Martina said. "You watch everything else. Let me know if I'm forgetting anything."

"Okay," Rachel said, keeping her eyes playing over both consoles while Martina wrestled with the damaged shuttle.

It was like learning to fly all over again. The crippled space shuttle flew like no other craft. Her movements did not follow the patterns of any other aircraft, including a properly function shuttle. One wrong move, Martina knew, was likely to send her into an unrecoverable spin. To make matters worse, the shuttle was simply a glider, with no engine to give it any extra power, and it was moving ten times faster than sound.

Slowly, Martina began to gain control over the spacecraft. A movement too far to the left or right sent the ship wobbling again. It took her several minutes to cease the shuttle's erratic movement, and several more until she could get the numbers running along the computer screen to match up. Still, it was a fight to keep the ship flying straight.

The computer began to scream again.

"We're coming in too fast!" Rachel called. "Way too fast!"

"Why is that?" Martina wondered. "What am I forgetting?"

"We've got to flare her!" Rachel said. "It's the only way to slow down."

"Shit!" Martina said. "I don't know if she'll hold through that." She touched her hands to the computer. "Let's see, nose up, wings around. Okay, I can handle that."

She began to maneuver the stick gently, fighting with the shuttle to move through the proper flaring motion. Slowly, the shuttle began to bank. Martina brought her high. Suddenly, the ship started to rock. Her left wing swung low.

"Shit!" Martina called, jerking the stick to the right just in time to prevent the shuttle from slipping over into a tumble. She fought to carefully pull the ship through the rest of the turn.

"Tell me when we're back on course!" she said.

"About ten more degrees," Rachel said. "Five...Okay you've got it."

Martina attempted to level the shuttle out again. The nose dropped down as the shuttle dove to the ground.

"Fuck!" Martina called, jerking back on the stick with all her might. "Pull back, help me!" she shouted.

Rachel gripped the stick on the right console and yanked it backward. The shuttle continued her rapid descent for what seemed like ages. Then, slowly, her nose rose into the air. Martina wrestled the ship back to a normal descent attitude.

"Okay, where are we?" she asked.

"A few miles off the strip," Rachel reported. "We're coming in long and fast, though. Maybe too fast."

"Do you think we can flare her again?"

"Not enough time," Rachel said. "We're too low and too close."

"I guess this is going to be a rough landing," Martina said. "Am I still lined up?"

"Yeah, we're right on course."

"Okay," she said. "I'm going to nose her down. Tell me when we won't overshoot."

"Don't lose control again," Rachel said.

"I won't," Martina said. She pushed the stick forward very gently, easing the shuttle where she wanted it, fighting its impulse to fly from her control.

"You're there!" Rachel called. "Nose up a little, you got it."

"How we looking now?" Martina asked.

"Perfectly aligned in every way, but still way too fast," Rachel said.

"Be ready to hit the brakes when I put her down," Martina said, focusing her attention on keeping the shuttle flying straight.

"I've got a visual on the strip," Rachel said.

"Where?" Martina asked, lifting her head.

"Right there!" Rachel pointed.

"I've got it!"

Martina focused her eyes on the faint black line of tarmac stretched out across the ground. She aligned the shuttle's nose with the runway and concentrated on keeping her level and straight. The faint line was quickly growing into a thick black strip.

"How much time do we have?" she asked.

"Two minutes, no more."

"How much altitude?"

"Five hundred feet."

"Landing gear!" Martina called.

Rachel reached over and touched the computer in front of her. The landing gear began to descend from beneath the shuttle's tiled surface. The shuttle's display indicated that the gear was down and locked.

"Three green! Two hundred feet!" Rachel shouted.

"Hang on back there!" Martina called to the rest of the shuttle's crew. "This is going to be a rough landing."

Suddenly, the nose pulled to the right. The shuttle was off course again, flying toward the surrounding airbase.

"Shit!" Martina began to wrestle with the controls. The shuttle refused to turn.

"One hundred feet!"

Suddenly, the nose jerked back on line. Martina could no longer see the runway's end. They were over the tar. She pulled back on the stick slightly. The rear wheels touched once, then bounced back into the air, jostling the two pilots. Martina pushed the nose down. The landing gear slammed into the ground and stayed. The nose wheel touched the ground, throwing Martina and Rachel forward against their harnesses. The shuttle skidded erratically to the left.

"Dammit!" Martina cried, fighting her back into position.

"Brakes now!" she shouted, finally aligning the shuttle properly.

"They're already all the way on!" Rachel shouted. "We're still too fast."

"Hit the drag chute," Martina cried, fighting to keep the shuttle straight.

"Drag deployed," Rachel said, quickly punching a button on the computer. A colored parachute burst from the rear of the shuttle and spread out behind it, catching the air.

A loud noise erupted from the rear of the ship as

one of the tires burst. The rim skidded against the hard asphalt, screeching. The shuttle began to weave back and forth along the runway. Martina gripped the controls tighter, using all her effort to keep the shuttle on the tarmac.

"We're still too fast!" Rachel shouted.

Martina looked up. The end of the runway was quickly approaching. The shuttle would run off in a matter of seconds.

"Just hold on!" she shouted, pulling backward on the stick with all her might in an attempt to slow the spacecraft.

The shuttle raced toward the end of the runway, sliding to the left and right. Martina watched the buildings at the end of the runway grow closer as she held the stick against the backstop. Rachel pressed against the brakes, desperately trying to remember some other way to slow an aircraft down. The edge of the runway came closer. Only a fraction of black was visible beneath *Discovery*'s nose. And then even that distance was gone.

The nose wheel dropped over the edge of asphalt and cut through the dirt. The shuttle came to rest in a cloud of dust.

Martina looked out the window at the unmoving sky. She looked cautiously at her airspeed indicator. It read zero. Very slowly, she released the control stick. Rachel eased off the brakes. The shuttle stayed still.

Martina gazed back out the window, looking at the motionless Earth. Everything was deathly silent in the cockpit. She turned slowly back to Rachel, who was staring in astonishment.

"We did it!" she cried jubilantly.

"Holy shit!" Rachel shouted, a wide grin spreading across her face. "We actually landed this thing!"

They looked back out the window, eyes moving frantically across the landscape, the computer consoles, and each other.

"We did it!" Martina shouted again. "We really pulled that off!"

She keyed her mike "Houston, *Discovery*. We are on the ground, and intact!"

"Glad to hear that, *Discovery*," Houston said. "We heard it was quite a ride."

"Was it ever."

"Go ahead and shut down the systems," Houston said. "We'll try to get you back to the States as soon as we can."

"Thanks," Martina said. "*Discovery* out." She switched off her mike and pulled off her headset. Her hands fell down to the buckles holding her in the seat. She undid the clasps and threw the straps off. She leaned back, pressing her head into the cushioning of the seat. She closed her eyes and drew a deep breath into her lungs.

"For the first time out, that was a hell of a ride," she said.

"I'll say," Rachel said, grinning. "I'm not even supposed to be qualified to fly one of these things yet."

"I didn't expect to get a shot at the left seat for another few years," Martina said. "All things considered, that wasn't bad for the first time."

"All things considered."

"I probably could have greased that landing if the wings and tail weren't all chewed up."

"I wonder how bad the damage was," Rachel mused.

"Not bad enough," Martina said. Rachel smiled.

Martina pushed herself out of the seat and stood. "We probably should see how the others fared on that ride. Then we'll shut this thing down," she said, walking from the cabin. Rachel followed her.

Gravity had returned. Martina was no longer floating about the cabin. Instead her feet were planted on the ground. The only way to move forward was to walk.

"You know what I like about Earth?" she said, pausing on the ladder leading to the lower deck.

"What?" Rachel asked.

"When you step on the floor, you don't go flying up and hit your head on the ceiling." Martina disappeared down the ladder.

Rachel laughed and turned to follow her below.

## ~ 4 ~

General Alexendre Petrovitch stood in the middle of his airbase's radar facility, listening while the colonel in command of the center tried to impress on him just how smoothly the operation ran. Petrovitch would have greatly preferred that the little man disappear and let him conduct his inspection by himself, but he tolerated the colonel's prattling. He half-listened to the droning while he peered over the man's shoulder at the controllers, watching them work.

Suddenly, one of the men seated at a radar screen leapt to his feet.

"Sir, sir, you've got to see this!" he nearly screamed, ripping off his headset and pointing wildly at the screen.

Both Petrovitch and the colonel turned and nearly ran to the console.

"I've got a bogey you're not going to believe, sir," the controller said, dropping back into his chair. He pointed to a large, rapidly moving blip on the screen.

"It's got a radar signature unlike anything I've ever seen, sir," the man continued. "It's traveling three times the speed of sound, and rapidly losing altitude."

"What is so big that can fly so fast?" the colonel murmured in disbelief.

Petrovitch ignored him. "Where's it headed?" he

demanded.

"Straight for us, sir," the man said.

"Can you raise it?"

"No, sir," the controller replied.

"Clear any other air traffic away from its flight path," Petrovitch ordered.

"Yes, sir," the controller replied. He put his headset back on and began to shout into the microphone, hurriedly directing the few other planes in the air out of the flight path of the approaching aircraft. Since it was Sunday, there weren't many jet airborne. On the screen, the blips began to scatter.

Petrovitch stared at the mystery aircraft. There was no time to scramble his fighters and no way for them to catch a craft traveling so fast. All he could do was sit and watch as the blip drew closer and closer to the airbase.

Suddenly, the aircraft vanished from the screen.

"What just happened?" Petrovitch asked the controller.

"It dropped below our radar sir," the man replied.

"Sir!" another man shouted. "The control tower says they've got a huge supersonic aircraft lining up on the runway."

Petrovitch nodded and bolted for the door, running out of the dark radar room into the lighted hallway. His aide, who had been standing against the far wall, followed quickly on his heels. Petrovitch burst through the door leading out of the building, stepping out into the bright sunlight. He stopped dead in his tracks, looking out toward the runway.

A large white craft covered with scorch marks sat on the edge of the runway. Black tiling ran up over the nose and tail, and traced along the edges of the wings. Four high windows sat above the tiling in the front of the craft. The top of the fuselage seemed to be constructed of two large doors. Three massive black engine nozzles protruded from the rear of the craft.

The front tire had slipped over the asphalt. A huge deflated drag chute extended beyond the ship. One of the rear tires was missing, exposing the rim of the wheel. The blown-out pieces lay halfway down the runway. Tracks of burned rubber covered the asphalt.

Petrovitch's eyes fell on the black writing along the side of the craft. The word "*Discovery*" was printed beneath the windows. An American flag was painted above the wings, followed by the words "United States."

"My God," Petrovitch breathed, "an American space shuttle."

"What on earth is it doing here?" his aide asked.

"I don't know," Petrovitch replied, "but I'm about to find out." He headed for his car. "Let's get to the flight line." His aide dutifully followed.

It took Petrovitch ten minutes to drive around to the flight line and another five minutes to walk to the end of the runway, where the space shuttle sat. From a few feet away, the American spacecraft appeared even more massive.

A throng of crash trucks and emergency personnel had gathered in awe around the large craft. All stood motionless by the shuttle, gazing up at the giant, wondering just what to make of it. Most of them probably did not even know what it was, Petrovitch thought as he pushed his way to the front of the crowd, followed by his aide.

As he drew closer, the large hatch on the side of the shuttle swung open and a tall figure dropped to the ground, landing agilely on the asphalt below in a crouch, facing away from the crowd. The astronaut hesitated a moment and then stood, turning and walking toward the group.

The sight of a tall, thin woman strolling confidently over the tarmac drew several gasps. No sooner had she started walking than a second astronaut jumped to the ground. She flicked her hair over her shoulder and took a few quick steps, catching up to the taller woman.

The two astronauts stopped several feet from the crowd of Russians. The taller of the two ran her eyes carefully over the group, the crash trucks, and the base beyond.

"Does anyone here speak English?" she asked.

"I do," Petrovitch said, stepping forward. "I am General Alexendre Petrovitch, commander of this installation."

"Major Martina Redrick," the taller pilot said, extending her hand. The general shook it politely.

"And this is..." she indicated her companion.

"Lieutenant Commander Rachel Ansetti," the smaller woman said, shaking Petrovitch's hand.

"I'm sorry to drop in like this, General," Redrick said, "but we had an emergency in space which required us to reenter immediately. My government knows about this and should be communicating with yours as we speak, arranging to get us out of here."

Petrovitch nodded.

"Two of the men on my crew are injured," she continued. "One is completely unconscious. We also have three crewmembers on board from the space station who may be unable to walk after several months in zero gravity."

"I will ensure that your crew gets the attention they need," Petrovitch said. "In the meantime, I will see if we cannot put you in touch with your government and return you to your country."

"That would be greatly appreciated, sir," Redrick said.

"Please come with me," Petrovitch said, walking toward the flight line. The two astronauts followed, walking away from the runway and onto the tarmac past several rows of MiG-31 Foxhounds. The general's aide followed. Petrovitch led them into one of the buildings, which Martina assumed housed a Russian fighter squadron.

"General!" a young, blond man standing behind a desk shouted to Petrovitch. He ran up and began to chatter excitedly in Russian.

Petrovitch's face darkened.

"What's going on?" Redrick asked.

"It appears we are under attack," Petrovitch said. "We have picked up a group of Chinese fighters heading straight for this airbase."

The officer continued to chatter rapidly.

"And while we have a number of working aircraft, there are only two pilots currently on alert." The general sounded slightly embarrassed. "We're too far from any hostile borders to warrant having a large alert force. We don't fly usually fly on Sundays, so the rest of my pilots are home," he explained.

The two American pilots exchanged glances.

"I'm sorry, ladies, but I must deal with this situation."

"I take it you're going to scramble what fighters you have," Redrick said.

"Yes," Petrovitch replied.

"Is a MiG very different from an American plane?" she asked.

"I have never flown an American fighter," Petrovitch said, "but a MiG is fairly easy to fly."

"If you've got a plane, I'll fly it," Redrick said. "It's us they're after."

"I can fly too," Ansetti said.

Redrick turned her head toward the smaller woman.

"You ain't leaving me out!" Ansetti said.

"You speak English?" Petrovitch said to the man in front of him. "You can get these two suited up quickly?"

"Yes, sir," the man said, a look of surprise on his face.

"Good," Petrovitch said. "This is Lieutenant Alexi Soliev, one of my pilots. Go with him."

"Follow me," Soliev said with a thick accent. He smiled and darted into another room. The two American pilots followed close on his heels.

✳     ✳     ✳

Martina Redrick swung her legs over the side of the MiG-31 Foxhound's cockpit and eased herself down into the ejection seat. Quickly, she pulled the straps over her shoulders and buckled herself in. She pulled a flight helmet down over her head and connected up the oxygen supply as she surveyed the cockpit.

"MiG is simple," Soliev had told the two American pilots moments before as they hastily gathered the necessary flight gear. He pointed to a poster of the cockpit in the briefing room.

"Airspeed, altitude, landing gear, flaps, radio, missiles, guns." He pointed everything out on the poster as he spoke. "Engine gauges. Just make sure they stay green."

The cockpit of the MiG was considerably more worn and beaten than the crisp cockpit photographed for the poster, but Martina could easily see where everything was. The instrumentation was a combination of Cyrillic lettering and Arabic numerals. Martina could read the gauges, but not the labels.

She flipped on the battery power and keyed her mike. The Russians had not given them callsigns.

"This is Redrick, ready for engine start procedures," she said.

"Ansetti. Ditto," Rachel's voice came over the radio. There was a hint of excitement in the Navy pilot's words.

"Roger," Soliev said. He quickly ran the two Americans through the engine start procedures for the MiG. In no time, the engines on both planes roared to life.

"Follow us," Soliev instructed the Americans.

Martina watched as Soliev taxied out of his parking space. A second MiG pulled out behind him. She released the brakes on her aircraft and nudged the throttles forward. The MiG began to roll. Martina fell into place in line. A glance over her shoulder showed Rachel's MiG bringing up the rear.

The four aircraft taxied to the nearest runway. The radio crackled with chatter Martina could not understand. A moment later the two Russians taxied onto the runway. Fire shot from their tailpipes, and the jets raced over the asphalt and leapt into the air.

Martina nudged her throttles forward, positioning her aircraft just to the left of the runway centerline. She looked to her right. Rachel was already in position, giving her the thumbs-up. Martina nodded and gave the go signal.

Both pilots pushed the throttles into afterburner. The MiGs surged forward. Martina shifted here eyes back and forth between her engine instruments, the end of the runway, and Rachel's plane. The Navy pilot was holding position perfectly on her wing.

Martina felt the controls come alive in her hands. The plane wanted to fly. Soliev had given the two pilots a quick rundown of the essential airspeeds before the flight. Reaching rotation speed, she lifted her nose, and the airplane came smoothly off the runway. A quick peek showed Rachel in position beside her. Martina gave the signal to raise gear. Both aircraft lifted their wheels simultaneously. As soon as the gear was up, Rachel dropped back from abeam Martina's wing to just behind, the aircraft a mere three feet apart.

"Not a bad takeoff for a swabbie," Martina chided.

"Whaddya mean?" Rachel said indignantly.

"Didn't know they taught you how to do that in the Navy," Martina said. "Don't they just throw the plane into the air and hope you can get it to fly?"

"Shaddup," Rachel said. "I can fly this thing better than you can!"

"We'll see about that," Martina said.

Martina gazed ahead of her. The two Russians were dead ahead, with two flying on lead's right wing. Martina signaled to Rachel to switch sides. The second MiG disappeared behind her plane, a second later reappearing on her left wing.

"We're right behind you, Alexi," Martina called.

"Join up," he replied.

Martina gently maneuvered her plane into position on his left wing. The fourship was climbing fast, flying south.

"Ten Chinese fighters. Twenty miles off," Soliev said. "Lock on with missiles and shoot."

Almost instantly, the Russians fired, sending two streaks of white smoke across the clear blue sky. Martina armed her missiles. A second later the missile latched on to an aircraft. Martina squeezed the trigger. The warhead shot off her wing with a hiss, corkscrewing forward. A fourth missile came streaming from Rachel's plane.

For a moment nothing happened. Then a fireball erupted in the distance, followed quickly by a second and a third.

"Three down," Soliev announced. "The others have split. Three heading for us, the other four coming toward the base. We take first three, you get the rest."

"I got my radar working," Rachel chimed in.

"Take lead," Martina said. "As much as I hate to fly a swabbie's wing..."

"Ah, the Air Force is in their rightful place," Rachel said as the nose of her plane passed Martina's.

She quickly chopped the throttle and nosed over. Martina held her position on Rachel's wing as the two pilots swung in a wide arc. Far below, Martina saw the silhouettes of four planes racing above the ground. The Chinese MiGs passed beneath them. Martina smiled under her mask as the American pilots dropped into position right behind them.

"Keep an eye on that radar," she warned Rachel. "I don't want the other three sneaking up on us."

"Wilco."

The Chinese MiGs were only a few hundred feet away, close enough for Martina to get a good look at them. All four planes were fully loaded with bombs.

"Take a look at that," she said.

"MiG-29s," Rachel said.

"Yeah. With bombs," Martina said. "And the target is our shuttle."

"I'm not about to let them get there," Rachel said.

"Go to guns," Martina said, lining up her aircraft on the plane on the right. Rachel took the second one.

Martina threw a quick glance over her shoulder. There was nothing behind her. Looking back, she squeezed the trigger. Fire spat from the gun on her wing. Bullet holes riddled the tail of the MiG-29 Fulcrum. Fire erupted from the exhausts of all four aircraft as the Chinese MiGs went into afterburner, hell-bent on reaching their target.

Martina squeezed the trigger harder, maneuvering her plane to send the bullets straight up the MiG-29's exhaust. For a second nothing happened. Suddenly, a large explosion rocked the side of the MiG. The Fulcrum tumbled downward. A moment later the plane Rachel had been training her fire on fell from the sky.

The MiG-29s were in full afterburner, but the

MiG-31 was a faster aircraft. Martina and Rachel were having no trouble holding position on their tails. There was no way the Fulcrums could outrun them.

Martina checked back over her shoulder again. Much to her relief, her six was still clear. However, she could see the airbase just up ahead. She and Rachel might have the advantage of speed, but it would do no good if they did not stop the Fulcrums before the Chinese planes reached their target.

Martina took aim at the nearest plane and squeezed the trigger again. Bullet holes appeared in the wing and the tail of the plane ahead of her. Rachel trained her fire on the Fulcrum's left side. In the distance, the white fuselage of the shuttle was growing larger and larger.

The MiG staggered, then suddenly nosed forward, diving straight into the ground. Only one plane remained, racing the short distance to the airfield.

"This is taking too long," Martina said. "Chop the throttles and go back to missiles. Fire as soon as you get a lock on him."

She yanked the throttles out of afterburner and switched on her missiles. For a long, painful second nothing happened. The Fulcrum raced ahead, dashing over the outside perimeter of the airbase. Martina held her breath.

Suddenly, the missile locked. Martina mashed her finger down hard on the trigger. The missile hissed off her wing. She watched it race forward, a second missile a few feet behind it. They impacted the Fulcrum almost simultaneously. The Chinese plane vanished in a cloud of fire.

The two MiG-31s screamed directly over the shuttle. Martina shoved her throttles forward again and yanked back on the stick. The plane shot straight up. She pulled through until she was flying inverted. A quick stick to the left rolled the aircraft upright again to complete the Immelmann. Rachel copied the maneuver.

"They're gone," Martina said into the radio.

"Read you," Soliev said. "We destroyed the others. We are fifteen miles to south of base. Rejoin with us."

"Roger," Martina said, pointing the nose of her plane back toward the Russians. In a few minutes the two other Foxhounds appeared, flying north. Martina and Rachel swung around and slid into position on Soliev's wing.

Martina relaxed, focusing on holding her place as the four aircraft descended. Soliev was talking in Russian to someone. Martina tuned him out. They swung low over the airbase. As they did, the Russian plane on the far left broke off, circling back down onto the runway.

"You're clear to land, major," Soliev radioed. "Use the runway Vlad just landed on."

"Thanks," Martina said. She broke off from the formation and chopped the throttles, configuring the plane as it slowed. She swung the aircraft around, carefully aligning the Foxhound with the runway. She brought the MiG low over the ground and retarded the throttles. The Russian jet sailed over the strip. The rear wheels touched the asphalt, and Martina brought the nose of the plane down until the nose gear contacted the ground. Then she pulled the throttles back to idle and raised the speed brakes until the MiG came to a stop.

Martina released the brakes, allowing the Foxhound to roll slowly over the earth. Steering with the rudder pedals, she maneuvered the plane off the runway and taxied to the tarmac, where the long row of MiGs sat.

She parked her jet beside the first Russian pilot's and quickly powered down the engines. Unstrapping herself from the ejection seat, she raised the canopy and removed her helmet. Leaving the helmet on her seat, she dropped agilely to the ground.

Martina looked around. Soliev's plane was gliding to a stop on the runway. Rachel had parked her Foxhound next to Martina's, and the Navy pilot was in the process of extracting herself from the ejection seat. Vlad had also climbed from his jet and was walking toward Martina.

The Russian reached Martina just as Rachel swung herself over the side of the cockpit and landed beside the plane. She crossed to the other two pilots in a few long strides.

"Those Russian planes aren't too bad," she said with a grin.

"Please come with me," Vlad said in very broken English. "General wants see you."

The two American pilots shrugged and followed the Russian. He led them across the tarmac to the second, larger runway, where *Discovery* sat. The Russians were in the process of unloading the still unconscious Stewart, along with the two astronauts, and the cosmonaut from the space station, who were incapable of walking because the months in space had caused their muscles to atrophy. Brennan and Palmer stood beside General Petrovitch, watching.

Vlad walked up to Petrovitch, saluted, and spoke quickly to him in Russian. Petrovitch nodded and made a reply the Americans could not understand. Vlad saluted again and then turned away, heading for his squadron.

"Major, Commander," Petrovitch said to the two American pilots, "I have spoken to my superiors, who have contacted your government. They want you to return to the United States immediately. A jet is inbound to fly you to Moscow. There you will be met by a United States Air Force plane, which will return you to your country."

"Yes, sir," Martina said.

"Is there anything you need from the shuttle?" Petrovitch asked.

The two astronauts exchanged glances.

"I can't think of anything," Rachel said.

"What about the rest of the crew?" Martina asked.

"NASA is sending a plane to take them back to Houston," Petrovitch replied. "They will be quite safe here until that aircraft arrives. And I will see to it that your injured men receive the medical treatment they need."

"Thank you, sir," Martina said.

"It is the least I can do, Major," Petrovitch replied. "Especially after you helped defend my airbase. Thank you."

"Just doing our job," Martina replied. Rachel nodded in agreement.

"It is a good thing you can do it well," Petrovitch said. "Is there anything else?"

"I think we're good to leave," Martina said.

"Can I have one minute of their time, General?" Jason Palmer interrupted.

The Russian general and the two pilots turned to face the young mission specialist. He was holding a camera in one hand.

"I want a picture of the two pilots who saved us," he said.

"I don't see why not," Petrovitch said, stepping aside.

Martina looked at Rachel and shrugged. The crash trucks had pulled away from *Discovery*, leaving the shuttle alone on the tarmac. The two pilots stood in front of the damaged space shuttle, put their arms over one another's shoulders, and smiled brightly. Palmer raised his camera and snapped a picture.

"Thanks," he said.

"I want a copy of that," Martina said.

"My aide will drive you to your plane," Petrovitch said, stepping forward and shaking both women's hands. "Safe trip, ladies, and thank you again."

"Goodbye, sir," Martina replied. "Thanks for your hospitality."

The two astronauts followed the general's aide to a car sitting at the side of the tarmac and climbed inside.

# ~ 5 ~

"What's the final count up to?" David Webster asked, leaning back in his chair and staring at the Secretary of Defense.

"Five, Mr. President," Justin Hayworth replied.

"Give me the specifics."

"Three secure communications satellites and two spy satellites," Hayworth reported. "And we almost lost the space station and a space shuttle."

"I know. I read about that," Webster said, tapping a copy of the morning paper.

"Rookie Pilots Save Shuttle." He read the headline aloud. Beneath it was the blurred black and white image of two women.

"So what happened?" Webster asked. "Did the satellites just stop working?"

"All communications stopped, and the satellites disappeared from radar," Hayworth said.

"Did any of them have previous problems?"

"Only the satellite the astronauts were about to work on. We'd been having some trouble with communications. The others were functioning perfectly."

"Any guess as to why our satellites are just vanishing?" Webster asked.

"Why, no, but we may have some idea as to how."

Hayworth paused. Webster made a "come on" motion with his hands.

"The shuttle provides an interesting clue. The satellite was about to be hauled in for repairs when it ceased working. Apparently, it simply exploded over the shuttle, causing some damage to the spacecraft. NASA caught the whole thing on tape. And we have four eyewitnesses: the two spacewalking astronauts and two inside the shuttle. I'm having the tape analyzed as we speak.

"Following the explosion, the space shuttle docked at the space station to assess the damage. NASA reported that the two pilots witnessed a small manned craft that came out of nowhere. It fired two missiles, which destroyed the Soyuz escape module and damaged the space station."

"My God," Webster said. "Is there any way to get a good look up there?"

"The only way would be to use a space shuttle," Gordon Smith interjected. "And that's out of the question."

"Why is that?" Webster asked the Secretary of State.

"If this isn't some freak accident," Smith said, "and someone is actually systematically destroying our satellites, we would just be giving them another target. A space shuttle is slow, not very maneuverable, and gives off a huge radar signal. She would be a sitting duck."

"What about the Hellcats?" Hayworth said.

"Those hi-tech space fighters the Air Force has been developing?" Webster asked. Hayworth nodded.

"Those are barely off the drawing board," Smith said. "There's no way they can be ready to fly."

"We have two working prototypes out at Edwards," Hayworth said.

"But have they ever been tested?"

"Only a few atmospheric flights and some wind tunnel time," he said, "but they're ready to be tried in space."

"And what about pilots?" Smith countered. "Are there astronauts ready to fly these?"

"Not out at Edwards," Hayworth said. "That's why they haven't been tested in space. The pilots would have to come from NASA."

"We need pilots," Smith said, "trained pilots, and they'll have to be brought up to speed on the situation. That will take far too much time."

"Not necessarily," Hayworth said. "We have two perfect candidates in mind."

"Who?" Webster asked.

"Your 'Rookie Pilots,'" Hayworth said, tapping the newspaper on Webster's desk.

"Those two?" Smith said.

"You really think they're qualified?" Webster asked. "After only one flight?"

"The Hellcats have more in common with the F-22 Raptor than with the space shuttle," Hayworth explained. "We need fighter pilots, test pilots, not shuttle pilots. Redrick and Ansetti are two of the best fighter pilots we have, and they are both fully qualified astronauts and test pilots. Would you like to hear the specifics on them?"

"Please," Webster said.

Hayworth reached down, pulled a picture from his briefcase, and passed it to Webster.

"This is Major Martina Redrick," he said.

Webster studied the picture. It showed a tall, thin woman with long brown hair and almost cold brown eyes. Her face was not strikingly beautiful, but possessed a certain rugged attractiveness.

"She looks awfully young for a major," Webster said.

"She is," Hayworth said. "One of the youngest ever. She's a graduate of the Air Force Academy and was first in her pilot training class. She earned herself a Raptor right out of undergraduate pilot training. She was the top pilot in her fighter squadron. She spent two years as a test pilot at Edwards and joined NASA several months ago after being promoted to major. She had just completed training as a shuttle pilot prior to the most recent flight. When the commander was injured, she immediately took over the mission and landed the shuttle from the left seat."

"Is there a difference?" Webster asked.

"Yes," Hayworth said. "The pilot performs certain tasks, the commander performs others. Redrick had only a few hours flying from the commander's position, but she managed to land the crippled shuttle. She had to fly it in manually because the computer couldn't compensate for the damage, which is very impressive."

"And the other pilot?"

Hayworth passed Webster a photo of a very pretty woman with blue eyes and shoulder-length golden-brown hair.

"Lieutenant Commander Rachel Ansetti is an Annapolis graduate. She flew F/A-18 Hornets and is a highly decorated pilot. She also spent a few years test-flying aircraft. Her skills are second only to Redrick's. She had only been with NASA long enough to complete astronaut training and was halfway through her pilot training. She was a last-minute addition to the flight due to a lack of personnel. She was only supposed to be riding in the backseat. After the incident she took over the pilot's position in the shuttle and helped Redrick land it."

"So these are our top fighter pilots," Webster said.

"Yes, sir," Hayworth said. "I have more specifics on their careers in fighters if you wish to see them."

"I trust your judgment," Webster said.

"They were also the only two to see the craft that attacked the space station, so they may be able to provide us with some information concerning it."

"Excellent," Webster said. "Where are they now?"

"En route to Moscow. As soon as they land, we have a plane ready to fly them to the States. They should be here sometime tomorrow morning."

"All right," Webster said. "I want to debrief Redrick and Ansetti when they land. Then send them to Edwards and get them flying the Hellcats."

"You're sending two junior O-4s to fly a highly secret test plane?" the Secretary of State asked, incredulous.

"Is there something wrong with that?" Webster inquired.

"That's an awfully low grade for such a mission," Smith said. "You should have at least a lieutenant colonel, if not a colonel, flying those planes."

"So promote them," Webster said.

"Promote them?" Smith said, nearly choking.

"I can do that, can't I?" Webster said. "The Constitution gives me the power to commission officers in the armed forces. If I want to promote a couple of pilots, I can do that. Promote Redrick and Ansetti."

"Sir, couldn't we just pull some more experienced senior pilots from NASA?" Smith said.

"Redrick and Ansetti have seen combat. And they've seen what we're chasing up there," Webster said. "I want them flying the Hellcats."

"Yes, sir," Smith said.

"Do you have anything else for me, gentlemen?" Webster asked. The two cabinet members shook their heads.

"That will be all, then," the President said. "Inform me of any new developments."

✳          ✳          ✳

"Do you want a drink?" Rachel asked.

"No, thanks," Martina said, relaxing back in the

leather seat of the small Russian jet. She turned her head to stare out the window into the night. Rachel couldn't tell if she was lost in thought or simply tired.

Standing in front of the small bar, Rachel frowned.

"Damn Russians," she muttered under her breath. "There's no scotch."

She shrugged and poured two inches of vodka into a glass.

"Not even water?" she asked Martina.

"Water's fine," Martina said. "With ice, if any's over there." She gazed out the window. The lights of the earth were slowly falling away.

Tired, Rachel decided as she plunked three ice cubes into a second glass and filled it with water. Closing the bar, she picked up the two glasses and walked across the small room, dropping into a chair across from Martina. She handed Martina her glass.

"Thanks," the Air Force pilot said, taking a deep drink. The cool water felt good as it trickled down her dry throat.

Rachel sipped her drink and fixed her eyes on the Air Force woman.

"How close do you think we were to buying it?" she asked.

"Not too close," Martina said, looking up at her. "I had a pretty good hold on her most of the time."

"I suppose if it got really hairy we just could have jumped," Rachel said.

"Yeah, but it didn't get that bad. I've come much closer to drilling a hole in the ground," Martina said.

"So have I," Rachel said, half laughing. "You flew in combat?"

"Many times." Martina's eyes seemed to spark. "What about you?"

Rachel nodded. "You ever have to bail?"

"No. Have you?"

"Only once."

Martina nodded and peered back out the window. Rachel took another drink. The small cabin fell silent.

"Why did you try to land her?" Rachel asked finally.

"Hmm?" Martina said, turning her eyes back to the other woman.

"It would have been a lot easier to just jump," Rachel said. "So why'd you try and land?"

"I wanted to save the ship if possible," Martina said. "And it still seemed possible."

"And what if you hadn't been able to?"

"Then we could have jumped," Martina said. "It's better to die trying than not to try at all."

"You think so?" Rachel said.

"If you have to go out, there's only really one way," Martina said, "and that's to go out with a bang."

Rachel stared at Martina. She did not know the Air Force pilot well. Martina had joined NASA several months before Rachel and had completed her astronaut and pilot training ahead of the Navy woman. Their paths might not have crossed at all had Rachel not been a last-minute add-on to *Discovery*'s crew. During the training for the mission, the women had been far too involved in preparing for their respective roles to do more than exchange names. Rachel realized that she had learned more about Martina during the return flight than in the entire time since they had met.

"I guess you might as well go down in flames," Rachel said. Martina fell silent for a moment, studying the Navy pilot. Rachel felt Martina's eyes looking deep beneath her skin.

"What would you have done?" Martina finally asked.

Rachel smiled.

"I would have tried to land," she stated.

Martina grinned.

"What made you decided to join NASA?" Rachel asked.

"It was my lifelong dream. The thought of flying in space fascinated me. Go faster and higher, I guess."

Rachel nodded. "When I was young I always used to stare up at the moon and pretend I was walking up there with the Apollo astronauts. I guess that old dream never died." She looked out at the moon shining in the sky, a faint smile on her lips.

"I would love to walk on the moon," Martina said, turning her head back to the window.

"What's so interesting out there?" Rachel asked. "You've been staring out that window since we took off."

"The stars," Martina said, not turning.

"They are nice to look at," Rachel admitted, "but you must really be into astronomy to look at them for that long."

"You can tell a lot from the stars," Martina said. "If you know the constellations and the time of year, you can navigate by them." She turned her head back toward Rachel. "Did you know we've been flying south for the past fifteen minutes?"

Rachel twisted her head around, pressing her face to the glass and peering out into the darkness. Had the airplane been on a westerly course, headed for Moscow, the North Star would have been clearly visible off the starboard wing. Instead, the setting constellation of Cygnus appeared on the horizon.

"Holy fuck! You're right," she said, turning around to face Martina. "They're taking us to China!"

"I don't know about you, but I'm not too thrilled about the idea of a trip to Beijing," Martina said, standing.

"Me neither," Rachel said, rising. "What do you plan to do about it?" she said, a look of confusion washing across her face.

"Two pilots can't be that hard to overpower," Martina said, heading for the cockpit.

"You're going to hijack the plane?" Rachel said. She downed the rest of her drink and followed.

"Why not? It's a little jet. We shouldn't have any trouble flying it," Martina said.

"You armed?" Rachel asked.

"I've just got this," Martina said, pulling a red Swiss Army knife from her pocket.

"A jackknife with a two-inch blade," Rachel said, clearly unimpressed. "The more time I spend with you, the more I'm becoming convinced that you're crazy."

"Yet you still tag along," Martina observed.

"Yeah, well, if I wanted to be bored, I never would have left home," Rachel said. "Besides, someone has to make sure you don't get yourself killed."

Martina laughed. "Let's hijack a jet, then," she said, pulling open the door to the cockpit.

The two pilots twisted around in surprise as the door behind them swung open. The two female passengers were standing behind them, one leaning on each side of the doorway. Their arms were crossed over their chests, and they glared coldly at the pilots.

Martina swept her icy eyes over the two men. Both were small, with dark hair and eyes. Their faces had a distinctly Asian appearance. They were attired in identical Russian Air Force flight suits.

"Where are you taking us?" Martina demanded.

The two men glanced at each other nervously.

"Moscow," the man on the left finally said in thickly accented English. His accent was clearly not Russian.

"Either you've got terrible navigation skills or you're lying through your teeth," Rachel stated coolly.

"We take you to Moscow," the man repeated.

"Moscow is west of here," Martina said. "You're

flying south. See?"

She reached forward and tapped the compass. The needle was pointing south.

The little man did not answer. Instead he twisted in his seat and agilely leapt over it, crashing into Martina. The Air Force pilot rolled backward with him, using his momentum to toss him over her. He landed sprawled on his back in the center of the passenger cabin.

The copilot began to scream frantically into his radio. Rachel was no linguist, but she knew enough to tell that the stream of words flowing from his mouth was not Russian. It was clearly an Asian dialect. She reached forward and unplugged his headset from the radio.

The man twisted around to face her. As he turned his head, her fist collided with his check, snapping his head back. The blow knocked the man from his seat, and he crashed into the yoke, pushing it forward. The small jet began a frantic nosedive.

Martina leapt to her feet just as the plane pitched forward, throwing her against the bulkhead. The man on the floor slid toward her. Martina raised her foot, jamming it into his face. The man skidded away from her, landing against the opposite wall.

Rachel dove for the airplane's controls, pulling upward with all her might. For a moment the little luxury jet continued its downward plunge. Then slowly the nose began to creep up, and the plane leveled out.

The copilot jumped onto Rachel's back, looping his arm around her throat and yanking her backward. The motion pulled the yoke back, pitching the nose up momentarily before Rachel released her grip on the controls and toppled backward, landing on top of her assailant as the plane again leveled out. He wrapped his hands around her throat and began to choke her.

The sudden pitch threw Martina to the floor. As the plane leveled out, the pilot jumped off the floor. He landed agilely on his feet only inches from Martina. Before she could move, he raised his foot and slammed it into her stomach, sinking all his weight into the strike.

The blow caught Martina just below her breasts, forcing the air from her lungs. She heard a loud, sickening crack as her ribs snapped. A wave of fire raced through her chest, nearly immobilizing her with pain.

The man raised his foot and prepared to kick her again. Martina rapidly rolled to her left as he brought his boot down toward her neck. The blow grazed her shoulder. Before the pilot could advance, she leapt to her feet, ignoring the pain dancing in her chest as she moved.

The copilot dug his fingers deeper into Rachel's throat. The Navy pilot wriggled against his grasp, but his grip did not loosen. Twisting to the side, she thrust her elbow into his stomach with as much force as she could muster. The blow seemingly had little effect. His grasp only tightened.

The edges of Rachel's vision were beginning to darken. Slowly, she slid her hand underneath her body, lifting herself slightly off the copilot. She tightened her hands around his groin, squeezed her fingers as tightly as she could, and pulled.

The man squealed and released his grip on her. Rachel leapt up, swinging her boot into his side. The small man rolled over and climbed to his feet. Angrily, he lunged for Rachel, pushing her onto the right yoke, which immediately rotated counterclockwise, rolling the left wing down.

The sudden motion flung Martina against the left bulkhead. The pilot crashed into her, his shoulder colliding with her chest and sending another cascade of flame rippling through her ribs. Pinning her against the bulkhead, the man wrapped his hands around Martina's throat. She dug her thumbs into his neck and pushed up, shoving him off her.

The rolling motion threw the copilot off Rachel. The Navy pilot fell away from the controls, and the small jet immediately leveled its wings. Rachel managed to keep her feet. She thrust her fist directly into the copilot's face. His head flew backward, hitting the bulkhead.

As the jet righted again, Martina found her feet back on solid footing. Keeping her thumbs imbedded in the pilot's neck, she stepped forward, throwing him over her hip and onto the floor. She released her grip before he landed.

Martina dropped to her knees and rapped her knuckles against the man's temple, dazing him. In an instant Martina's Victoronox was open in her hand. She brought the knife down across the man's throat in a quick slash. Blood gushed from his neck, spurting from the arteries, and the man lay still.

The copilot shook his head and stepped forward, driving his knee into Rachel's stomach, followed by a quick uppercut to the chin that knocked the Navy pilot backward. She crashed into the instrument panel between the two yokes. The man leapt on top of her, digging his fingers into her throat with all his might.

Suddenly, the little man went stiff. His hand's fell away from Rachel's throat, and he slumped to the ground, blood trickling from a small hole behind his right ear. Martina stood over him, holding her bloody knife in one hand.

"What was that about making sure I don't get myself killed?" she asked.

"If you had given me another minute I would have

had him," the Navy pilot said indignantly. "I didn't need any help."

"Right," Martina said, rolling her eyes. She wiped her knife along her leg and closed the blade, returning it to her pocket.

"I see your little sticker is good for something after all," Rachel said.

"You'd be surprised how often that little thing comes in handy," Martina said, sliding into the left-hand seat. She winced as another shower of sparks danced through her chest.

"Are you all right?" Rachel asked, sitting down in the other chair.

"Yeah," Martina said. "I think that fucker just cracked a few of my ribs. It's not bad."

"If you say so."

Martina played her eyes across the controls. As in the MiG, the lettering was Cyrillic, but the numerals were Arabic. The panel was similar to that of most airplanes.

"Let's get the fuck away from China," she said, taking hold of the yoke and putting the jet into a smooth turn to the west, and Moscow.

"Shit, Martina, you better listen to this," Rachel said. The Navy pilot had plugged the headphones back into the radio. Martina snatched up her headset and looped them over her ears.

"I'll be damned if that isn't fighter pilot chatter," Rachel said. "And it ain't the Russians."

"You ever get the feeling somebody really doesn't like you?" Martina asked, half grinning. She pushed the throttles to their stops.

# ~ 6 ~

"How much time do you think we have?" Rachel asked.

"Depending on where they're coming from and if they're flying in full afterburner. Maybe ten, fifteen minutes at the most till they're in range," Martina said. "We can't outrun them."

"I'd kill for radar right about now," Rachel said. "Or even just a clear view of our six."

"No flares, no chaff, no fucking missile warning, and no weapons. Our only shot is to outmaneuver them," Martina said.

"That won't do us much good," Rachel said.

"We've just got to keep them off our tail until help gets here," Martina said.

"Help?" Rachel said, looking at Martina as if she were half crazy. "Where the fuck are we going to get help?"

"Hopefully someone friendly's listening out there," Martina replied. She reached forward and twisted the radio to the emergency broadcast frequency for the United States armed forces.

"Mayday, Mayday, Mayday," Martina called. "This is a Russian jetliner on guard. We are under attack by Chinese forces. I repeat, I am a Russian jetliner under attack by Chinese forces."

Martina turned to Rachel. "Try and figure out where we are."

"On it," the Navy pilot replied. She pulled her phone from her pocket and opened up the GPS.

"MAYDAY, MAYDAY, MAYDAY," Martina repeated. "This is a Russian jet. We are defenseless, and we are under attack by Chinese fighters. Someone please help."

"You don't sound much like a Russian to me," a voice replied almost casually.

"I'm an American, flying a Russian jet," Martina said.

"I bet that's an interesting story," the voice said.

"Yeah, but I don't have time to tell it," Martina replied. "Who are you?"

"A twoship of F-22s over Afghanistan," the voice said. "Where are you?"

"Don't know exactly. Roughly..." She looked over at Rachel. The Navy pilot shoved her cellphone under Martina's nose. Martina immediately relayed her coordinates and altitude.

There was a pause on the other end of the radio.

"Hang on," the Raptor pilot said. "We're on our way."

"Told you help would come," Martina said to her copilot.

"I'm more concerned as to when the help will get here," Rachel said.

"Help me try to figure out the nav instruments," Martina said, changing the subject. "Specifically, does this thing have terrain radar or alerts?"

"You want to get down on the deck?"

"Yeah. If we can get low enough maybe we can drop below their radar. That might buy us a little more time."

Rachel grabbed a nearby aeronautical chart.

"I'm guessing the lowest altitude we can drop down to safely is that." She pointed to a large number on the chart. There was one in the center of every grid.

"Okay," Martina said. She chopped the throttles and nosed over. The jetliner began to descend rapidly.

The small business jet had no chance of outmaneuvering fighters at altitude. To stay in straight and level flight was sheer suicide. The Chinese MiGs would quickly find the jet and shoot it down before the two American pilots even knew they were there. Martina hoped that by hugging the ground she would make herself harder to find, and maybe harder to hit as well.

Martina's eyes flicked over the instrument panel. She quickly found the transponder and switched it into what she guessed was the off position. She flicked off several more switches, which she hoped were the aircraft lights.

She watched as the altimeter wound down. Reaching what Rachel guessed to be the minimum safe altitude, she pulled the nose up and shoved the throttles forward.

Martina keyed her mike. "Raptors, you still there?"

"Yup," the answer came.

"We're heading west. My transponder's off," Martina said. "We're going to stay low. We'll remain on this freq."

"OK," the Raptor pilot replied. "We'll see you soon."

"I need terrain," Martina said to Rachel. "I want to put this thing as low as I can."

"Use this as best you can for now," Rachel said, handing Martina her phone and the charts.

"We're there," she said, thumping her fingers on the chart.

"Why didn't I learn Russian?" Rachel muttered under her breath as she began to fiddle with the instrument panel. "I can't understand a damn bit of the gibberish."

Martina ran her eyes over the chart, quickly

surveying the terrain. She compared the GPS position on Rachel's phone to the map. A pair of mountain ranges, running east to west, were dead ahead of them. She turned the plane slightly to fly between them.

The moon was high in the sky. It was just past full, casting a pale light on the surrounding terrain. The land below was barren and desolate. Martina could not see any sign of civilization at all. To either side of the plane, tall, shadowy mountains rose.

"Are you nuts?" Rachel asked. "We're lower than those mountains!"

"The MiGs will kill us same as hitting the ground will," Martina said. "We've got a better chance of survival dodging hills than against the fighters."

"You're nuts," Rachel said. "I think I may have the alerts working."

She pointed to a screen on the right side of the cockpit displaying colored terrain. The map clearly showed that the plane was well below the tops of the mountains.

"Good," Martina said. "Go to the back of the plane. Look for lights from those Chinese fighters."

"You actually think they'll be stupid enough to be running lights?" Rachel asked.

"Maybe," Martina said. "They think this is just a luxury jet. They don't know we're fighter pilots. They probably won't think we know those tricks."

"I take it you've already killed ours?" Rachel said, standing.

"I sure hope so," Martina said.

"I'll shout as soon as I see something," Rachel said, vanishing into the back of the plane.

Martina waited a few moments to let Rachel reach the back of the aircraft. She kicked the rudder back and forth, yawing the plane to the left and right in hopes of giving the Navy pilot a view of what was behind the plane.

A few seconds later Rachel reappeared.

"There are lights back there. Better get low and fast," she said.

"The radio's still dead, so it's not our Raptor friends," Martina said. "Strap down. I'm going to see what this thing is capable of doing."

She pressed the throttles forward and lowered the nose, hugging the terrain as tightly as she dared. Rachel dropped into the right seat and rapidly buckled herself in. Martina tossed the map and her phone back to Rachel.

"Keep an eye on everything else," she instructed. "Try to keep those friendlies updated on our position."

The jet streaked over the ground, racing over the barren earth below. The plane's white skin shone pale in the moonlight against the dark rock. To either side of the little aircraft, craggy peaks stretched toward the sky. High above, four Chinese MiGs closed in.

Martina could not see the planes behind her. She had no idea how many fighters pursued her or where they were. There was no way to look behind her aircraft. Nor was it equipped with any warning systems or radar. She was flying blind, hoping she could maneuver the little jet to prevent the MiGs from getting a clear shot at her.

Overhead, the MiGs spotted their quarry and dove for it. The lead MiG dropped in line behind and slightly above the jet. The other three stayed in a diamond formation on him as he took aim at the plane in front of him.

Suddenly, the little plane banked steeply to the left in a climbing turn. The jet hugged the mountainside as it climbed, nearly skimming the tops of the rocky outcroppings. Clearing the ridge, it disappeared over the edge, once again dropping down below the mountain.

Startled, the MiG pilots pulled up, searching desperately for their prey. Spotting the white jet on the other side of the mountain, the lead MiG again descended into position and prepared to shoot.

Martina held the little plane level with the ridgeline. She could see several peaks of the mountain range ahead of her. She quickly pulled to the right, snaking around the mountain directly in front of her. Almost immediately, she turned the plane back to the left, rounding the opposite side of the next mountaintop.

This time, the lead MiG dropped lower, trying to place himself directly behind the jet. The other three held their positions in formation. The lead clung to the jet's tail as it rounded the mountain. The MiG flying lead's left wing slammed into the mountains, the jet smashing to pieces on the rock.

The lead MiG held his position. Seeing their wingman disappear, the other two MiGs immediately pulled up, clearing the mountain range. After a few seconds they dropped back down, this time in trail behind lead, flying his exact course as he chased the little jet in front of them.

Martina continued to weave back and forth through the mountaintops. The three MiGs followed closely, but none could get a clear view of the jet for long enough to shoot. Martina held the little plane as near to the earth as she dared.

Rounding a peak, Martina dropped the jet's right wing, sliding back down the side of the mountain. The two mountain ranges narrowed. Their sides rose high into the night, the rocks only a few feet from the plane's wingtips. The aircraft swept over the barren earth below, underbelly nearly touching the ground as it raced through the night.

The narrow channel curved to the right. Martina held the jet through the curve. The mountains sloped upward on either side of her. The three MiGs held their position behind her, still unable to get a clear shot at the weaving jet.

Martina rolled wings level again, the little plane racing above the earth as fast as it could. Ahead the gap between the mountains widened. The mountains to the left of the plane began to die out. Martina swept up the rock face to the right, dropping behind a ridge.

The three MiGs clung tightly to her tail as she dashed along below the mountaintops. The little plane dropped down below a ledge, disappearing from the MiGs' sight for a moment. The Chinese fighters followed blindly, unwilling to let their quarry escape.

Martina pulled upward, cresting the ridge, once again racing toward the summit of the mountains. The MiGs hung in position, trying to get a clear shot at the jet ahead of them. It was useless. The small plane was too close to the ground and moving too erratically.

In frustration, the lead pilot squeezed the trigger, firing a missile without a lock. The projectile launched from his wing in a blaze of fire, momentarily blinding him as it lit up the ground beneath him. The missile shot underneath the little luxury jet, narrowly missing it.

Martina saw the fire trail of the missile as it flew beneath her wing. Immediately she pulled to the left. The missile hit the side of the mountain and exploded in a bright blossom of fire. Martina felt the shock wave from the explosion hit the plane, lifting the right wing up.

She pulled hard to the left, yanking the plane up and over the top of the mountains, and sliding back down the other side. She continued to weave back and forth, pressing the little plane lower to the ground in hopes of evading the MiGs.

"They're definitely still back there," Rachel said.

"I noticed," Martina replied.

She kept her eyes focused straight ahead, trying to read the moonlit terrain as best she could. She held the jet close to the ground, maneuvering around every obstacle she could as she dashed back and forth across the tops of the mountains.

"We're about to lose this mountain range," Rachel said. "The chart is showing a canyon to the north. You crazy enough to try it?"

"Are you?" Martina asked.

"I wouldn't have mentioned it if I wasn't," she replied almost nonchalantly.

"Let's see if these MiGs are," Martina said.

The mountain range died out abruptly. Martina rolled to the right, racing down the sloping hill. Just below her she could see a crack in the earth. She raced across the open plain, smoothly dropping down into the canyon. The walls were barely wider than the wings of the jet. The three MiGs held their position on the little jet's tail.

The walls of the canyon blocked the moon's light. All Martina could see beneath her was a dark black abyss. The edges of the canyon were still illuminated. She held the little plane just below the rim, hoping there were no outcroppings hidden below the surface.

Martina followed the twisting course of the canyon, yawing the jet to the left and right to negotiate the tight turns without clipping her wings. The rim seemed mere inches from the wingtips, waiting to grab the plane at the first chance. The MiGs stayed close behind.

The canyon snaked to the left and then back to the right. Martina hugged the turns, managing to keep the little plane in the center of the canyon. She couldn't see the MiGs, but she knew they were still right behind her.

The lead MiG switched his armament to guns and depressed the trigger. Bullets shot forward, racing toward the little jet. He tried to center the plane in his gun sights, but it was moving too erratically. The bullets hit the canyon walls harmlessly. The lead continued to fire, hoping that a stray shot would hit the little plane and bring it down.

Martina kept the throttles pressed to their stops as they raced through the winding canyon. She was constantly jerking the stick to the left and right, careful not to overcontrol. Too sharp a movement would send the little plane into the cliff.

Out ahead, a white rock loomed in the moonlight. Quickly Martina pulled back on the yoke. The little jet popped up, barely clearing the rock. The lead MiG didn't see the rock until it was too late. He flew head on into it, exploding in a fireball. The other two Chinese fighters immediately pulled up.

Martina rapidly dropped back down into the canyon, racing along inside the narrow passage. The two remaining MiGs followed her, keeping a little more distance. The three planes raced above the narrow abyss, the moon glinting off their wings.

The jet twisted back and forth rapidly. Martina tried to keep her wings directly in the center of the canyon. Rocks jutted from the right and left, threatening to rip the little plane apart. The canyon was growing narrower by the minute.

"This canyon ends in a couple more miles," Rachel said, "and after that it's flat for about fifty miles."

"Completely flat?" Martina asked.

"As far as I can tell from the charts," she replied.

"Fuck," Martina said. "If I level off, we're dead fuckers."

"If we stay here, we'll hit the rocks," Rachel said.

"I know, I know," Martina muttered. "Maybe

there's something else we can use for cover."

Ahead the canyon narrowed. Martina pulled up. The plane rose out of the canyon, skimming over the earth a few feet over the ground. The rim of the canyon ran along just under the plane's wing until it closed up completely.

Martina looked around as the jet crested the edge of the canyon, hoping to see some formation of earth that she could use to shield herself from the fighters on her tail. There was nothing. The earth beyond was completely barren, devoid even of trees. The moon shone on a long, empty plain that seemed to stretch endlessly before them.

# ~ 7 ~

"I'd like to know what the hell an American pilot is doing flying a Russian jet," Major Chris Vella said to his wingman.

"You and me both, Desperado," Major George "Apache" Pershing replied. "You and me both."

"However they got up there, it's up to us to go bail them out," Desperado said.

"The good guys to the rescue," Apache said as the two Raptors raced northeast in full afterburner. Twin plumes of fire shot from the two Raptors' tails into the black night as they dashed through the sky, leaving a beautiful pattern of blue and red Mach diamonds behind them.

"Lucky for her we were up here," Desperado commented.

"She'll be lucky if we get to her before the Chinese do," Apache replied.

"You see anything on the radar yet?" Desperado asked. "We should be nearly on top of them."

"Not yet. Give it another minute."

"There!" Desperado said. "On the deck."

Apache glanced down. Ten miles ahead, a small white jet was racing across the ground, weaving as if it were out of control. Two MiGs followed tightly. They were almost in position to fire.

"Let's go," Apache said. He chopped his throttles and dove toward the MiGs.

*          *          *

"Fuck," Martina said.

She and Rachel stared blankly out at the flat stretch in front of them. There was nowhere to hide. Martina continued to bank the plane to the left and right, flying erratically in hopes that it would make it harder for the MiGs to line up a shot.

"You got any good ideas?" she asked Rachel.

"Land and run?" the Navy pilot suggested.

"That might be our best option," Martina said. "I think we are officially fucked."

Suddenly, a dark gray shape shot across the cockpit, spewing blue fire in its wake. A second later a loud explosion shook the plane. The sky to the right lit up in brilliant flames, then vanished in an instant.

"What the fuck was that!?" Rachel shouted.

"The U.S. Air Force!" Martina said with a grin.

"You can go ahead and climb now," a voice crackled in Martina's ears. "We'll take out this last fucker if he's too stupid to run."

"Wilco," Martina said. She pulled the nose of the plane into the air.

"Turn to a 290 heading," the Raptor pilot said. "You're about eighty miles from the Kazakhstan border. The Russians are waiting for you there."

Martina turned the plane to the northwest as she climbed. She kept the throttles wide open, wanting to reach the border as soon as possible.

"Go get 'em," she whispered to the Raptor pilots.

*          *          *

The business jet began to climb. Apache had quickly taken out the first MiG with a missile. Desperado made a quick pass over the last remaining MiG. The Chinese fighter stayed tightly on the little jet's tail.

Desperado yanked back on the stick, pulling the Raptor over on its back. Once inverted, he smashed the stick to the left, quickly righting the jet. The MiG was now dead ahead of him, several hundred feet below him. Desperado chopped his throttles and dove toward it, arming his Sidewinders. The heat-seeking missiles instantly locked onto the MiG.

The Chinese fighter immediately banked hard to the left. Desperado followed him, closely holding his position on the MiG's tail. As the MiG turned into him, Desperado depressed his guns, chewing the MiG to pieces as it flew through the barrage of fire.

Apache lined up his plane behind and to the left of the business jet. A moment later Desperado joined him. Just as his wingman leveled off, a warning blared in his ears.

"Someone's painting us, Desperado," he said. "Just got lit up by radar from the southeast."

Desperado immediately broke out of formation. He rolled up and over Apache, turning his nose to the south and activating his radar.

"I've got another flight of four planes coming from the heart of China," he said. "I guarantee they're not friendly."

"We destroyed the two MiGs that were chasing you," Apache told the pilot of the jet. "But there are four more incoming. You just keep running to the border as fast as you can. We're going to take care of the others."

"You got it," she replied.

"Let's get 'em, Desperado," Apache said.

The two Raptor pilots shoved their throttles past the detent and into afterburner, racing toward the MiGs.

"Twenty out," Desperado said, stating the distance to the approaching fighters.

"Those other two must have called for reinforcements a while ago," Apache said. "These guys are close."

"And I guarantee they didn't see us cross into their territory," Desperado said.

"Paint 'em and let 'em know we're here," Apache said. "If they don't turn back, we'll knock 'em down."

Desperado and Apache both armed their AMRAAM missiles, which quickly locked on to the two lead MiGs. The four MiGs immediately broke formation, two twisting to the right and two to the left. They all continued to race toward the business jet.

"Okay, you've had your chance," Apache said to the MiGs. "Fox Three Desperado!"

Both Raptor pilots squeezed their triggers, loosing a pair of missiles. The air-to-air missiles raced toward the Chinese fighters, each leaving a brilliant trail of red flame in its wake. An instant later two fireballs blossomed in the sky. One of the MiGs disappeared from Desperado's radar screen.

"We got one," he told Apache. "The other must have got off some chaff."

The three remaining MiGs screamed past the Raptors.

"They're still trying to shoot down our jet," Apache said. "Either these guys are suicidal or someone's told them not to come back if they don't finish their mission."

"Maybe they just don't realize who they're up against," Desperado said.

"Let's go finish them off," Apache said.

The two Raptors pulled up, reversing course in an Immelmann. Desperado held position on Apache's wing through the maneuver. The two Raptors descended, dropping down on the MiGs' tails. The Chinese fighters were racing toward the little jet.

The business jet was speeding away as fast as it could, but the MiGs were still faster. At the current rate of closure, the Chinese would be within firing range of the target in a few minutes.

Desperado armed his Sidewinders. The heat-seeking missiles immediately locked onto the exhaust of the jet on the far right. The Chinese pilot rapidly pulled up, looping up and over the two Raptors. Desperado quickly yanked back on his stick to follow.

"I'm going to get this guy," he said.

"I'll try and take out the other two," Apache replied.

With its thrust vectoring, the Raptor could easily outturn the MiG. Desperado held his F-22 in place on the MiG's tail as the pilot pulled through a loop. The Chinese plane leveled off with Desperado still right behind him.

Apache armed his cannons and opened fire on the far left MiG. The Chinese pilot broke away, twisting to the left. The remaining MiG rolled sharply toward the ground, dropping a few thousand feet before righting himself again. Apache let him go. He turned after the first MiG, continuing to pelt the Chinese plane with fire.

Desperado loosed a Sidewinder at the MiG in front of him. He watched the missile track toward the plane. Suddenly several points of fire appeared behind the MiG. Fire and smoke filled the sky ahead of the missile. The Chinese fighter immediately pulled up, twisting to the left. The missile continued to fly straight, exploding in the middle of the flares the MiG had dispensed.

The MiG Apache was chasing quickly reversed his course. The F-22 pilot continued to pelt the Chinese plane with bullets, staying in position behind him. The MiG dove toward the ground in a frantic attempt to escape the Raptor. Apache chopped the throttles to follow him and nosed down.

Suddenly the missile warning growled in his ears. Apache turned his head to see the third MiG closing in on his own six. The Raptor pilot pulled up, twisting back to the right. Quickly he hit the button to release his own flares.

Desperado cursed as he watched his Sidewinder explode harmlessly behind the MiG he was chasing. He pulled upward, tracking the MiG as it tried to evade him. The Chinese plane twisted back for the business jet. Directly ahead of it, flying back toward him, Desperado saw Apache's Raptor.

"Apache, pull up!" he shouted, quickly banking his own aircraft away in a tight turn.

Apache didn't question his wingman's command. The two pilots had flown together for years, leading Apache to trust Desperado completely. He immediately pulled back on his stick and shoved his throttles forward, standing the Raptor on its tail.

G-forces pressed against Apache's body. He instinctively tensed all the muscles in his legs, back and stomach as the g-suit around him filled with air to prevent him from passing out. The F-22 screamed into the sky, gaining several thousand feet of altitude almost immediately.

Beneath Apache, the two MiGs flew head on into one another. A huge fireball lit up the sky as the aircraft collided. Pieces of metal rained down, tumbling toward the ground. Desperado had looped back around, giving the two MiGs a wide clearance. He smiled under his mask as the planes vanished.

High above, Apache retarded his throttles. He pulled back further on the stick, pointing the nose at the business jet. Rolling the aircraft upright, he chopped the throttles further and began to dive at the jet. He switched on his radar. The screen showed the last remaining Chinese MiG still limping after the plane.

Apache lined his plane directly on the MiG. He swooped down over the Chinese fighter, depressing the trigger on his gun as he did. Bullet holes riddled the upper fuselage of the MiG from the tail to the nose.

The fighter dropped its nose and began to spiral out of control, slamming into the ground below. Apache pulled his nose up and maneuvered back toward the business jet. Behind him, Desperado watched the remaining MiG plummet into the earth.

"He's down," he informed Apache. "And I'm not showing anything else on radar."

"We're almost to the border," Apache said. "We'll be out of Chinese airspace before any more MiGs can reach us."

The two Raptors leveled off behind the business jet. Slowly, they edged forward, each taking up position on one of the jet's wings. The three planes dashed back toward friendly territory, their wings gleaming in the moonlight.

✳     ✳     ✳

The two Raptor pilots slid their aircraft slowly into position on either side of the Russian jet. Martina watched as the two silver planes slipped in and out of view on her wings, their sleek noses poking into the air.

"The Chinese are gone," the lead Raptor pilot said. His voice sounded somewhat familiar.

"Thanks," Martina replied.

"We'll stay on your wing until we reach your Russian escort," he said.

"How long till we're back over friendly airspace?"

"We'll cross over in about five minutes," the Raptor pilot replied. "What have you got for instruments in that thing?"

"Can't really tell. The numbers are all Arabic, but everything else is Cyrillic."

"All right," the Raptor pilot said. "You ever flown in formation?"

"Countless times."

"I'm going to pull out in front of you. Take up position on my wing. I'll take you over the border to your escort."

"Wilco," Martina said.

Slowly, the Raptor on her left accelerated, sliding out ahead of the jet. Martina watched the plane move into view, the dark skin pale in the night sky. Small slits at the back of the plane glowed blue where the engines exhausted into the air.

Martina moved the yoke forward, positioning her own aircraft along the Raptor's wing as she had done so many times in her Air Force career. She smoothly followed the plane's movements, using his lead to determine her course and speed. The second Raptor remained to the right of the small jetliner, holding his position on the wing.

For the first time since taking the controls of the aircraft, Martina allowed herself to relax. She felt comfortable flying on the wing of a Raptor. It was an old trick she had mastered years ago. She let herself slip back into the mode of formation flying, relaxing from the thrill of combat.

"So how'd you end up piloting a Russian jet?" the Raptor pilot asked.

"They were supposed to be flying us to Moscow," Martina said, "but somehow our pilots got switched to a couple of Chinese, who started heading in the wrong direction. When we realized it, we overpowered them and took the controls. That's when they sent the fighters after us, and we called you guys."

"Good thing you knew how to fly," he said.

"Yeah," Martina said, looking out at the Raptor ahead of her.

"Those fighters really wanted you dead," the Raptor pilot said. "They weren't about to stop. We shot down all of them. The last guy was half shot up and still trying to knock you out of the sky."

"Damn," Martina said. "Thanks for the help."

"Anytime," the Raptor pilot replied. The radio fell silent.

"That was insane," Rachel said.

"We got out of it," Martina said.

"I've never been so happy to see an Air Force plane."

Martina laughed. "They'll probably turn back soon. They've got to be pretty low on gas. From then on it will just be MiGs."

"As long as they're Russians, I don't care," Rachel said.

"You might as well see if there's any coffee in the back," Martina said. "This is going to be a very long flight."

✳     ✳     ✳

Apache dropped to the tarmac at his forward base in Afghanistan. His Raptor sat silently behind him, engines cooling. Beside him, Desperado was extracting himself from his jet. After turning their escort over to a pair of Russian MiG-29s, the two F-22 pilots had made tracks for their home base, landing just after midnight.

"I've seen some crazy things in this job," Desperado said, walking over, "but that one takes the cake."

"Damn straight," Apache agreed.

The two pilots turned and began to walk toward the small building that housed their squadron.

"What are the chances she even knew how to fly?" Desperado said, "let alone be an experienced pilot?"

"Very slim. I bet she was ex-military," Apache said, shaking his head slowly. "A couple of Americans take over a Russian luxury jetliner because some Chinese are trying to kidnap them."

"There's only one person I know who's crazy enough to try something like that," Desperado said.

"Or actually pull it off."

Apache laughed. "There's no way. She's back in the States, training. Although I definitely could see her doing that," he added.

"That pilot didn't sound a little familiar to you?" Desperado asked, pushing open the door to the squadron.

The main area of the building was packed with the other members of the squadron, all staring up at a color television set to CNN. The image on the screen showed an American space shuttle sitting on a runway. Apache and Desperado stopped, looking at the television. The announcer was saying something about the landing.

"You guys see this?" a captain standing by the door said.

"No, what happened?" Apache asked.

"Your old wingman made an emergency landing in the space shuttle," a major said. "Set it down in Russia a few hours ago. It's all over the news."

Apache turned back to Desperado. Both pilots' eyes slowly widened in shock.

*        *        *

They flew through the night for what seemed like ages. Not long after the strange threeship formation crossed the border into Kazakhstan, two MiG-29s had appeared. The Raptors rolled away and headed for home as Martina followed the MiGs toward Moscow.

The MiGs led them onward, switching out every hundred miles or so, until Martina lost count of how many escorts had flown with them. The earth beneath was dark except for the occasional lights of a scattered town or city.

The two pilots chatted idly throughout the flight in an effort to keep each other awake. They took turns flying, each holding formation with an experienced hand. The earth slipped slowly by beneath the small jet.

The sky to the east was beginning to lighten when the MiG leading the jetliner began a gradual descent. Martina nosed the aircraft down, following him. She watched as the ground grew closer. She saw the lights of a city out in front of the plane. A few minutes later, what looked like runway lights appeared on the ground.

"The runway is straight ahead," the lead MiG pilot said in broken English. "You are set up to land."

"Thanks, I can see it," Martina replied.

"We are going to leave then," the Russian said.

"All right, thanks for your help," Martina said.

Rachel had found the flight manual for the jet, and the two pilots had managed to decipher the approach and landing speeds from the book. That gave Martina the information she needed to set the jet down safely.

She easily aligned the small luxury jet with the runway, and lowered the landing gear and the flaps. The jet swooped low over the asphalt, touching down gracefully under Martina's experienced hand. It rolled to a stop at the end of the runway.

A follow-me truck was sitting on the end of the strip. It started up its engines and drove slowly onto a taxiway. Steering with the rudder pedals, Martina guided the jet across the pavement and brought it to a stop on the tarmac. She powered down the engines as a few maintenance workers rushed up to put chocks under the wheels.

Martina and Rachel unstrapped themselves from the seats and walked slowly out of the cockpit. The Navy pilot opened the door and lowered the steps, and the two astronauts disembarked. The fresh air of the morning, mingled with the smell of exhaust and jet fuel, greeted them as they stepped out onto the tarmac.

"Major Redrick, Commander Ansetti?" a distinctly American voice asked.

The two pilots turned to see a tall, somewhat lanky man in an Air Force flight suit standing a few feet away. He stood a few inches over six feet tall. His thinning, slightly curly brown hair was cut short. Captain's bars adorned his shoulders. His lips turned upward in a friendly smile, which his light blue eyes echoed.

"Captain Matt Hopkins," he said, sticking out his hand. "I'm your ride back to the States."

"Glad to see they sent an Air Force pilot," Martina said, shaking his hand. "How soon do we leave?"

"As soon as you ladies are aboard, ma'am," Hopkins said, pointing to a C-21 Learjet sitting on the tarmac twenty feet away. Martina was pleased to see the Stars and Bars painted plainly on the side of the aircraft.

Hopkins led the two astronauts across the asphalt toward the small plane.

"Where are we headed?" Martina asked.

"Washington," he replied. Martina and Rachel exchanged glances, the Navy pilot arching her eyebrows in curiosity, but neither spoke.

"After you," Hopkins said, motioning to the stairway leading up to the Air Force plane. The two astronauts climbed aboard the jet, and he followed, stopping in the doorway to retract the stairs and close the door.

"Let me know if you need anything," he said before disappearing into the cockpit.

Martina surveyed the cabin. The jet had been fitted with several large plush leather chairs, similar to those in the first-class cabin of an airliner. Rachel had already collapsed into one seat, pulling a blanket over herself before reclining the chair. The Navy pilot's head dropped off to one side, and her eyes closed in sleep.

*I wonder how long I've been awake,* Martina thought, falling into a chair beside one of the windows. It had been well over a day since she'd slept. By her time, Houston time, it had been after midnight when the shuttle landed, but only mid-afternoon in Russia. The flight to Moscow had lasted most of the night.

She checked her watch, still set to Houston time, but after a moment realized that the numbers meant absolutely nothing. She was far too tired to try to make any sense of them. Instead, she turned to the windows and gazed out at the breaking dawn.

No sooner had she settled down than the plane began to roll forward, moving from the tarmac and taxiing out to the runway. It paused on the edge of the strip as the engines spooled up to full power. Then Hopkins released the brakes, and the jet surged forward, leaping agilely into the sky.

Martina was asleep before the wheels lifted from the ground.

# ~ 8 ~

The thump of the landing gear against the runway stirred Martina back to consciousness. She opened her eyes and blinked, trying to get a sense of where she was. She could feel the rapid deceleration of the aircraft as the pilot activated the speed brakes and reversed thrust to stop the racing plane.

She peered out the window, watching the buildings rush past. The sun was shining brightly across the airfield, and Martina was sure that if there was any grass, it would have been a deep green. But all she saw was tarmac, hangars, and military transports, all painted gray. After a moment, she realized where she was, remembering her destination. They had just landed at Andrews Air Force Base.

The small passenger jet rolled to a stop, then turned slowly and taxied to the transient ramp. The pilot brought the plane to a halt and shut down the engines, filling the cabin with silence. Through the window, Martina saw the ground crew rushing out to place the chocks beneath the wheels.

She turned from the window and shook her head, trying to clear it. The thick fog of exhaustion still clouded her mind. Not quite free of the deep sleep that had claimed her on the trip across the Atlantic, she moved slowly, reaching down to unbuckle the straps holding her in place.

Across from her, Rachel was looking out the

window. The Navy pilot was trying to make sense of her surroundings, but her still half-asleep brain was far too slow to process any of the images her eyes sent. Instead she stared forward, trying to figure out just where she was and how she had gotten there.

Hopkins stepped out of the cockpit. The young captain stretched to his full height, extending his long limbs to relieve the stiffness from the hours of flying. He appeared as awake and friendly as ever.

"Welcome to Andrews," he said with a smile.

"Thanks," Martina said, her voice thick with sleep. "What time is it?"

"Zero eight hundred hours," he said, walking over to the door and opening it.

Martina looked at her watch in confusion and then turned her eyes back to Hopkins.

"What day is it?" she asked.

"Monday," he replied, lowering the stairs to the tarmac. "Your ride is waiting at the bottom of the steps. I don't think you want to keep them waiting."

"I guess not," Martina said, pushing herself out of the plush chair and crossing to him. Rachel followed.

"Thanks for the lift," Martina said.

"Anytime," Hopkins said. "You were probably the best passengers I've ever had. No whining, no complaining, nothing."

"That's because we passed out the moment we got on board," Rachel said, half smiling.

Hopkins laughed.

"Thanks again," Martina said, walking down the steps and onto the tarmac. Rachel followed. They spoke briefly with a man standing beside a black sedan, and then both astronauts disappeared into the car. The vehicle's engine sparked to life, and the car pulled away from the plane.

Hopkins turned back to the cockpit to finish shutting down his jet.

\*          \*          \*

"What the hell are we doing here?" Rachel whispered in disbelief.

"I'm as clueless as you are," Martina replied quietly.

"Obviously, he wants to see us," the Navy pilot said, motioning to the door. "But I can't begin to imagine why."

Martina nodded, glancing at the thick wood doors leading to the Oval Office. She turned, catching a glimpse of herself in the mirror. While she had known that, being in the military, she might one day meet the President, she had never imagined it would be like this.

She was attired in a simple set of Air Force blues, which fit very loosely despite Martina's best effort to tuck the shirt in. It felt odd being in a blues shirt that was not tailored to fit her trim figure. She wore a set of pilot's wings over her left breast and a major's gold oak leaves on her shoulders. Her hair, still wet from the quick shower at Andrews, had been swept up and tied tightly behind her head. A pair of brand-new Korframs were on her feet.

Across from her, Rachel was similarly attired in an even more ill-fitting white uniform. How the people at Andrews had managed to produce a Navy uniform was beyond Martina, but somehow they had. Likewise, that uniform was adorned with only pilot's wings, and gold bars across the shoulders, indicating Rachel's rank as a lieutenant commander.

The whole situation seemed absurd to Martina. She should have been wearing well-tailored service dress, decorated with the ribbons she had earned, with her astronaut wings and jump wings above. Instead she was wearing blues that were so loose they looked sloppy. They fit her so badly she wouldn't have even considered wearing them in a fighter squadron.

But nothing else was available save a flight suit, and no one went into the Oval Office in a flight suit.

Stranger even than her appearance was the rank on her shoulders. She was a major, and a very junior one at that, having pinned on not six months ago. The President had generals to advise him. Why on earth would he want to see a major?

She glanced back at her reflection in the mirror. While her face appeared as it always did, and her hair was neatly tied back, her eyes betrayed hints of exhaustion. Being awake for almost two straight days, combined with switching time zones so frequently, had greatly upset Martina's internal clock. She had no idea what time it was or what time it should feel like to her. She simply felt tired, strange, and out of sorts.

"The President will see you now," his secretary announced in a bored voice, stepping into the antechamber and pushing the door to the Oval Office open.

Martina made a few quick adjustments to her uniform, trying to tuck all the excess fabric from her shirt into her pants. Then she lifted her head and strode into the Oval Office, with Rachel by her side. The two women crossed the Presidential seal and stopped six inches from his desk.

Martina raised her hand in a salute. "Sir, Major Redrick and Commander Ansetti reporting as ordered."

Webster returned the salute casually and watched as the Air Force pilot dropped hers sharply. He was a thin man with light brown hair. His face was just beginning to show the signs of aging. Martina judged him to be in his forties.

"Please have a seat, ladies," he said, waving them toward a few chairs beside his desk. Martina noted the presence of several other men in the room, recognizing the Secretary of State and the Chairman of the Joint Chiefs.

"For the past forty-eight hours we have been losing satellites," Webster said, turning to face the two pilots. "To date we have lost six communications satellites, four military, two civilian. We have also lost five spy satellites. NORAD reports that satellites are disappearing at a rate of one every two to three hours. The civilian sector has lost two or three others, and our allies in Britain and Russia have also lost several. The only things that haven't disappeared are our GPS satellites. We suspect this may be deliberate, but we don't know why."

The two pilots nodded, slightly surprised.

"I understand you are the two pilots who brought *Discovery* safely to the ground," Webster said. "NASA reports that you landed the shuttle after the space station was damaged, believing you were under attack. Do you have any knowledge of what is doing this?"

"Yes, sir," Martina said. "We both saw the craft."

"It was a spacecraft?" Webster said in surprise.

"Yes, sir," Martina said. "Commander Ansetti and I got a close look at it. It was shaped like a rocket, long and streamlined, with two small wings near the center. It had a missile on each wing, which it fired at the space station. No guns, as a far as I could determine. The craft was powered by a rocket engine, and maneuvered through the use of thrusters positioned along the body, much like our spacecraft. It had a small bubble cockpit, similar to that of an F-16, near the front, and the pilot was clearly human."

"Fortunately, it is not capable of reentry," Rachel added. "It appeared just as we were breaking away from the space station, and tried to attack again. We reentered the atmosphere, but it couldn't follow us."

"How can you be so sure they didn't let you get

away?" the Secretary of State asked before Webster could reply.

"The craft fired at us as we reentered," Martina said. "Fortunately, the missiles burned up when they hit the plasma flowing off the shuttle. There didn't appear to be any type of heat-absorbent material anywhere on the body for reentry. An aircraft with that design could not function in the atmosphere, nor did it have any control surfaces for maneuvering in the air."

"And they tried to kill us three times after that," Rachel said. "First, they sent jets to bomb the base where we landed. Then they attempted to kidnap us by switching the pilots flying us to Moscow. When we realized that, they tried to shoot us down. If that ship could have reentered and destroyed us, it would have done so."

"If what you say is true, then whatever this thing is, it must be based somewhere in space," the President said.

"NORAD has not reported anything unusual," the Secretary of Defense said, "and they can detect every launch into space."

"It's quite possible that they could be using some sort of stealth design," the Chairman of the Joint Chiefs said. "We've developed the necessary technology; someone else may have done the same. NORAD did not detect the craft that attacked the space station, but it clearly existed, as these pilots saw it."

"There are only three nations that we know of that can place a human in space: us, the Russians, and the Chinese," Webster said. "We know this is no creation of ours. I think we can also rule out the Russians, as they also had crew members aboard the space station, and safely harbored our shuttle and astronauts. Had they been responsible for this, Major

Redrick and her crew would have vanished without a trace upon landing. That leaves the Chinese."

"Sir, the MiGs that attacked us were Chinese on both occasions," Martina said. "The men who tried to kidnap us were attempting to fly us to China, and they were clearly Asian."

"Interesting," Webster replied. "I'll see what the CIA can unearth about their space program. Is there any other information you can give us?"

"That's all we know, sir," Martina said apologetically.

"Very well," Webster said. "I have a request. I need your piloting skills for a mission of the utmost importance. Unfortunately, I can't tell you what it is until after you've agreed to it."

Martina and Rachel exchanged glances. Martina could tell from the glint in the Navy pilot's eyes that her curiosity had clearly been piqued. Slowly, she turned back to Webster.

"I'll do it, sir," Martina said.

"So will I," Rachel said.

"Thank you," Webster said. "*Marine One* is waiting outside to take you to Langley Air Force Base. A pair of fighters is waiting for you there. You will fly to Edwards Air Force Base in California, where you will be briefed on your mission."

"Yes, sir," the two pilots said, standing.

"Before you go, ladies, there is one other thing," Webster said. The pilots turned to face him, a slight look of curiosity on their faces.

"Congratulations on your promotions," the President said, handing each a sheet of paper.

Martina looked down at the sheet in her hands. She immediately recognized it as a set of orders. Skimming the writing quickly, she discovered that she had been promoted to the rank of lieutenant colonel, with her effective pin-on date being the day before. She managed to keep her mouth from dropping open, but her eyes widened with a surprise that bordered on shock.

"Thank you, sir," she nearly stammered.

"Thanks, sir," Rachel said, her lips spreading wide into a grin.

"That will be all, ladies," Webster said. "Safe journey and good luck."

"Yes, sir, thank you, sir," Martina said. She raised her hand in a crisp salute. "Good afternoon, sir."

"Afternoon, Colonel, Commander," he said, waving his fingers in the direction of his eyes. The two pilots stepped back and spun around, then marched from the room.

"Wow," Rachel said as the door closed behind them. For a moment she simply stared back toward the Oval Office.

"Didn't think I'd be a full commander for a few more years," she said as the two pilots walked out of the antechamber.

"I take it you're now a colonel?" she said.

"Only a light bird," Martina replied.

"Good, I was afraid you outranked me for a minute there," Rachel said, with a smile.

Martina laughed. "I wonder what other surprises he has lined up for us."

"No idea," Rachel said. Suddenly, her face darkened. "Can you fly?" she asked, lowering her voice. "With your ribs?"

Martina shrugged. "If Chuck Yeager broke the sound barrier with a couple of cracked ribs, I can make it across the country." She spoke softly. There were only a few people in the hall, and it was large enough so that most were out of earshot, but she didn't want to chance being overheard.

"Yeah, but what about after that?"

"I should be all right," Martina said. "It really only hurts when I twist that part of my chest."

"I hope you're right," Rachel said.

"You'd still fly," Martina stated.

"Yeah, but I'm really stupid like that," the Navy pilot said as the two women stepped from the door out into the bright, warm afternoon. Sitting on the White House lawn, its rotors slowly spinning, was a large black helicopter marked with the Stars and Bars.

"I guess that's our ride," Martina said, walking down the marble steps and starting toward the helicopter.

"Guess so," Rachel said, following. The two pilots dashed across the grass and ducked beneath the spinning rotor blades, climbing into the helo. A moment later it lifted off the ground and headed west.

# ~ 9 ~

Martina's combat boots hit the asphalt of Edwards Air Force Base's transient ramp. She reached up and pulled her flight helmet off her head. Her long brown hair tumbled down as she cast her eyes along the dry lakebed surrounding the base. The Mojave Desert stretched out around her, the white sand broken only by the hangars and buildings of the air base and the numerous paved runways and taxiways.

Martina reached up, tying her hair back. She knew the base fairly well, having gone through test pilot school there a few years earlier. Rachel had never been to the California high desert. The Navy pilot stood beside her aircraft, surveying the land.

The two pilots had flown from Langley Air Force Base in Virginia, crossing the entire country in full afterburner. They had only throttled back to refuel their aircraft before powering back to maximum velocity. Less than two hours after taking off, the two astronauts had landed at Edwards.

It had become very obvious to Martina during the initial flight briefing that Webster wanted her and Rachel in California as soon as possible, and was willing to get them there at any cost. But she still had not been able to discern the nature of the mission which demanded such speed. Now, gazing around the base in the bright afternoon sun, she could still find no answers to that question.

"Colonel Redrick, Commander Ansetti?" a voice called. It took a moment for Martina to realize she was being spoken to. The word "colonel" in front of her name sounded utterly foreign to her. She turned around to see a young man with captain's bars on his shoulders approaching.

"General Peters' compliments, ma'am," he said. "Please come with me."

The two pilots followed the captain as he walked from the flight line to a staff car parked beside one of the buildings housing a test pilot squadron. A man of medium height and build with graying hair waited beside the vehicle. A single star decorated his flight cap. He regarded the two approaching pilots with interest, but said nothing.

The three junior officers saluted the general as they approached. He returned the gesture casually, then nodded to his executive officer, who immediately climbed into the driver's seat of the car. Peters turned to the two women facing him.

"Colonel, Commander," he said. "Welcome to Edwards."

"Thank you, sir," Martina said.

"Shall we?" Peters said, motioning to the car. He pulled open the door to the front seat as Martina and Rachel slid into the back. No sooner had the doors closed than the captain put the car into gear and began to drive away.

"I suppose you want to know why you're here," Peters said, turning around and giving the two astronauts a grin.

"Yes, sir," Martina said.

"That's what I'm about to show you," the general said. "It will take us a few minutes to reach the hangar. It's necessary to keep these things separate from the rest of the base to ensure they stay secret."

Martina nodded, glancing out the window. Already the main area of the base was fading into the distance as the car moved across the lakebed on a deserted paved road. After a moment, a small hangar appeared in front of them. The captain drove up to the building and killed the engine.

Peters got out of the car and motioned for Martina and Rachel to follow him. The captain remained seated at the wheel as the three senior officers began to walk toward the hangar.

"Ladies, what you are about to be brought in on is what is known as a black project," Peters said. "It's so secret that the government denies it even exists. Very few people know anything about this. Needless to say, if you breathe a word of this to anyone who is not authorized, you can be shot for treason, no questions asked. Do you understand?"

"Yes, sir," Martina said. Rachel simply nodded, watching Peters raptly.

"You ladies are both astronauts, so you must know that the United States government has been talking about developing an aircraft that could take off and land as a conventional aircraft, but fly straight into orbit." He pushed open the door to the hangar. "I am very pleased to inform you that we have succeeded."

The two astronauts did not reply. Both were frozen in their tracks, staring forward with looks of shock on their faces. Rachel's jaw had dropped open as she gaped at the sight in front of her. Martina was motionless and wide-eyed.

Two sleek fighters sat inside the well-lit hangar. The identical craft were slightly smaller than an F-22 Raptor, but similar in design. The wings swept back gracefully from the fuselage. Twin tails slipped outward at an angle. Gun ports were visible along the edges of the wings, but no munitions mounts appeared underneath. The fighters' underbellies were covered with black, which crept up along the edges of the wings and tails and swept entirely over the nose. A series of small holes appeared along the nose, wings, and tail. Two large jet intakes angled back from beneath the canopy, also completely covered in black. A pair of black strakes ran from the nose to the inlets.

"These are the Hellcats," Peters said, motioning to the aircraft. "They are designed to operate as fighter aircraft in the atmosphere and in outer space. Their performance is nearly identical in both regions, and they can seamlessly transition from one environment to another."

For a moment, neither pilot replied. They continued to gaze forward at the aircraft, taking in every detail of the sleek planes.

"How?" Martina finally managed to stammer.

"A combination of materials, computers, and some very fancy engine technology," a voice inside the hangar said.

Martina turned to see a tall man with dark brown hair leaning up against the corrugated metal wall. He wore jeans and a t-shirt, which revealed the muscles in his tanned arms and shoulders. His handsome face was also a deep tan.

"Ladies, this is Bill Durant, Lockheed's head engineer for the Hellcat project," Peters said, closing the hangar door after Martina and Rachel stepped inside.

"And you are?" Durant said, walking up to Martina.

"Lieutenant Colonel Martina Redrick," she replied, barely catching herself before she said "major."

"Colonel Redrick and Commander Ansetti are our pilots," Peters said to him. "I'd appreciate it if you could answer their questions about the planes."

"Fire away," Durant said, flashing Martina a smile.

"How on earth do you get this into space with those engines?" she asked, walking to the plane and peering in the jet intake. "You'd need a scramjet to achieve orbital velocity. It looks to me as if all you've got in these babies is a normal low bypass turbofan."

Durant grinned, walking up behind her. "That's because the power plant is a low bypass turbofan, comparable to that of an F-22's, with a few modifications."

Martina turned to him and arched an eyebrow.

"I take it you are familiar with afterburning jet engines," he said.

"I've spent my entire Air Force career either studying airplanes or flying them," Martina said evenly. "I know how every major system on an aircraft works."

"That's good," Durant said grinning. "Getting the plane into space is rather simple. The Hellcat takes off like a normal aircraft. It then flies to the maximum allowable altitude for sustained flight. At that point it goes nose up, trading all the kinetic energy for height."

"A zoom climb," Martina said.

"At the top of the climb, the pilot, who would be you, throws a little switch in the cockpit. A panel slides in front of the inlet, sealing it off." He moved past Martina, putting his hand in front of the inlet to demonstrate the process.

"A second panel seals off the afterburner from the rest of the engine. Fuel and oxidizer are then injected into the afterburner chamber and ignited, effectively turning the engine into a rocket. A minute or two later, you're in orbit, using much less fuel than a conventional rocket launch."

"And has this ever been tried before?" Martina asked coolly.

Durant straightened his back and stepped up to her.

"Isn't that what you're here for?" he said with a smile.

"Not only is the mission Top Secret, it's also potentially suicidal. Nice," Rachel said, a broad maniacal grin across her pretty face. The Navy pilot stood at the edge of the Hellcat's wing, watching Martina and the engineer.

"The aircraft has gone through several wind tunnel tests," Durant said. "We don't anticipate any problems."

"Ah, something is definitely going to fail, then," Rachel said with the same sarcastically excited tone in her voice. Durant shot her a cold glare.

"Would you like to see the cockpit?" he said to Martina, reaching past her and touching a button which raised the canopy.

"Need a hand?" he asked, offering her one.

"I've been flying fighters for almost ten years. I think I can get in one," she said, placing her hands on a ladder beside the plane and pulling herself to the cockpit. She stopped at the top rung of the ladder and leaned forward, surveying the inside of the Hellcat.

"It's really pretty standard," Durant said as she looked around. "Heads-up display, glass cockpit with all the normal instruments. Stick on the right, throttle on the left. The computer up there is very powerful. I'll explain it to you later, in the simulator. Note that little jet-rocket switch. It's how you convert the engines and the flight mode. Rocket for space, jet for the atmosphere."

"I take it in space it tells the thrusters to maneuver, and switches to the regular flight controls in the atmosphere," Martina said, starting down the ladder.

"Exactly. The seat is an ejection seat which can

be used in the atmosphere," he continued. "We're working on a way to bail out while in space."

"So if you have trouble in space, you're fucked," Rachel said.

"Are all Navy pilots like that?" Durant asked Martina as she dropped off the ladder, landing agilely in front of him.

"She's the only one I know," Martina said. "Tell me about the tiling. How good is it?"

"Fifty times better than that of a space shuttle," Durant replied. "Materials technology has come a long way since those were built. This stuff is much stronger, and much better at radiating heat. And it won't melt away with a little ding, like the *Columbia* did. It's designed to take multiple reentries in a short period of time. Basically, you have nothing to worry about."

"And the seals around the engines and anything else?"

"The seals work incredibly well," he said. "We've tested all the material."

"I take it all weapons are carried internally."

Durant nodded. "Two fifty-millimeter cannons. Four weapons bays. Both work in space and in the atmosphere."

"You fly it in space exactly like you fly it in the atmosphere, in terms of pilot input?" Martina asked.

"It's identical," he said. "The computer works the thrusters, and it responds. Of course, changing orbital path or radius requires a burn, but the computer can do that too. Maneuvers like that are very similar to the shuttle's procedures."

Martina nodded and let her eyes play across the Hellcat, taking in the sharp contrast of the black tiles and the silver skin.

"Stealth design?"

"Of course."

"It has radar?"

"In the nose."

"And countermeasures?"

He nodded.

Martina looked back at the plane, sweeping her gaze across it, studying the wings and tails, the control surfaces and the thrusters. She was trying to take in every inch of the aircraft.

"Any other questions?" Durant asked.

"How soon do I get to fly it?" she asked, turning to Peters.

"It will take a day or two to bring you up to speed in the simulator," the general said. "As soon as that's accomplished, you fly. The President wants you in space immediately."

"Sweet," Rachel said, smiling up at the plane.

"Very," Martina said, nodding in agreement.

"If you want to head over to the simulator now, Mr. Durant can start training you on the flight controls and the computer," Peters said.

"Absolutely," Martina said. She began to walk toward the door. Rachel followed. Durant trailed close on their heels.

✳     ✳     ✳

"Holy shit," Rachel whispered after the waiter at the officers' club had walked away from the corner booth where she and Martina were sitting.

"This is crazy," the Navy pilot said. "I mean, fuck, this is something out of some sci-fi novel or something."

"I wonder how the hell we ended up here in the first place," Martina said.

"They needed pilots. We're the best they've got," Rachel said.

"You know how many thousands of fighter pilots there are in the Air Force?" Martina asked.

"Yeah, but there aren't that many in NASA," the

Navy woman replied. "We have astronaut training, that's what sets us apart. We know how to fly in space. The rest of those people don't."

"I suppose," Martina said, falling silent as the waiter returned and deposited a glass of water in front of her, then handed Rachel a beer. The two pilots watched as he walked away. It was still early in the afternoon, and the officers' club was mostly empty. Despite the quietness, it still maintained the dim lighting, giving it the atmosphere of a bar.

"I can't believe what those things are capable of," Rachel said softly once the waiter was out of earshot. "If they can do half as well as that engineer brags, they've got to be the most incredible planes ever built."

"And we get to fly 'em," Martina said, smiling.

"Damn," Rachel replied.

"Yeah," Martina agreed.

"Speaking of that engineer, he seemed pretty interested in you," Rachel said.

Martina shrugged.

"He never took his eyes off you," Rachel said. "I call that interested."

"That's because he didn't see you," Martina said. "Any man in his right mind would pick you over me at first sight."

"I could have been standing in front of him naked and he still would have gone for you," Rachel said. "That guy didn't even notice me because he was so fixated on you."

"Maybe he was dropped on his head as a kid," Martina said, taking a sip of her water.

"Please, Martina, you can't tell me you weren't interested in him."

"Nope," she replied.

"He's good-looking," Rachel said. "And did you see those muscles?"

"If you say so."

"C'mon. You have to at least admit he's hot."

"You like him, you can have him."

"He doesn't want me," Rachel said. "That man was wholly absorbed with you."

"That's his problem, then," Martina said.

"You can't tell me you don't find him attractive," Rachel said. The Air Force pilot simply gave her a deadpan stare.

"Martina..."

"All right, he was good-looking. Are you happy now?"

"Very," the Navy woman said sarcastically.

"I was more interested in the planes anyway," Martina said.

"There are thousands of planes in this world."

"Not like those," Martina replied. "And there are far more cocky pretty boys out there. You can't tell me you were more intrigued by the engineer than by the planes."

"Of course not," Rachel said, "but that doesn't mean I didn't look at him too. You know what really got me about him?"

"I don't think I want to know, but what?" Martina said.

"How he was completely fascinated he was with you," Rachel replied. "I can get almost any guy to drool over me if I want, but he never even saw me because you were standing there."

"You're that good, huh?" Martina said.

"That's not the point I was trying to make," Rachel said. "And yes, I am that good."

Martina laughed.

"Seriously, Martina, that guy is head over heels for you."

"So what if he is. I don't care."

"Bullshit."

"All I want is to fly those planes. I couldn't care

less about the damned engineer."

"Right," Rachel said sarcastically.

"Just because a guy is good-looking doesn't mean I'll fuck him," Martina said flatly. "I have to at least feel something for him. I don't even know this guy. There is nothing more than physical attraction there."

"So you do find him attractive. I knew it," Rachel said triumphantly.

"This is pointless," Martina sighed. "I don't know why I even bother having these conversations with you."

"You know anyone else around here?" Rachel asked.

"I might. I did go through TPS here," Martina said.

"Know anyone who's bad at poker?" Rachel asked.

"What, out of the three other people who are in this room who I've never seen before?" Martina replied.

"Damn," Rachel cursed.

"Why the random change of subject?"

"I was hoping I could find a few Air Force hotties to take some money from," Rachel said.

Martina laughed. "Cards, beer, and men. You really are a swabbie."

The Navy woman shrugged. "At least I don't deny that I'm interested in men, unlike some people."

"Let's just say I do find you a few poker players. What's in it for me?" Martina said

"What do you mean?" Rachel said.

"If I find you some chumps, I get in on the poker game, deal?" Martina said.

"Sounds good to me," Rachel said. "You play poker?"

"Of course," Martina said. "There's nothing else to do when you're deployed to a remote bare base."

"That sucks," Rachel said.

"Oh, and it's really better than spending six months on a ship surrounded by nothing but ocean,"

Martina said.

"Aircraft carriers are actually pretty big."

"Not big enough," Martina said. "You're still trapped in the same area."

"There are advantages to tight quarters," Rachel said, grinning.

"Oh, brother," Martina groaned, dropping her head to cover her eyes with her hand.

Before Rachel could comment, the waiter returned carrying two burgers, which he set on the table before vanishing. The Navy pilot twisted her head around, looking at the door as a group of officers in flight suits walked in. One flashed her a smile. Rachel grinned demurely.

"This might turn out to be a good night," she said, raising her beer and tossing a drink back.

"What are you going to do, walk over there and say, 'Hi, are you bad at cards, cause I want to take your money and fuck you'?" Martina said

"Not a bad idea," Rachel said.

"My God," Martina muttered, turning her attention to her burger. Rachel simply laughed.

# ~ **10** ~

Zhan Chow stepped from his office, closing the door behind him. He checked the clock, which read a few minutes to five. He was leaving work a little early, but as the head of China's space department, he felt no remorse about granting himself such luxuries.

"Heading out for the day, sir?" his secretary asked, glancing up from her desk.

Chow turned and smiled at her. Li Won was a striking woman in her mid-twenties. She possessed a curvaceous figure, which Chow could not help but marvel at. He wondered how she managed to stay so trim when most women, including his own wife, only let themselves go.

"Yes," he replied. "Lock up for me, will you?"

"Yes, sir," she said.

Chow picked up his coat and placed his hand on the door.

"Oh, Li," he said, turning back to her, "my wife is visiting her family for the week. I was wondering if you wanted to come over for a drink. Say about eleven."

"Certainly, sir," Li replied, smiling. She watched as he stepped outside, closing the door quietly behind him. She had found that in her profession there were numerous advantages to sleeping with the boss.

She ran her eyes quickly over her desk, looking for any unfinished work. Satisfied she had completed the necessary tasks for the day, she logged off her computer and stood. She made sure everything in her boss's office was in order before shutting the door and securing the bolt. Crossing the room, she pulled up her long black hair, tying it into a high ponytail, which still draped almost halfway down her back.

Grabbing her coat and slipping it on, she made her way from her office on the top floor of the building down to the streets of Beijing below. Gray clouds hung low over China's capital city, threatening rain. A cold breeze was blowing. Li turned up her coat as she stepped onto the sidewalk, blending into the throng of people moving from their workplaces to their homes. Bicycles, trucks, rickshaws, and everything in between packed the roads, crawling forward slowly, as walls of humans choked the sidewalks.

Li moved with the crowd until she came to her own apartment building. Reaching the door, she slipped out of the bustle of the streets into the relative silence of the building. Allowing her coat to loosen, she climbed the stairs to her flat and unlocked the door, stepping inside.

The apartment was small but functional. The door opened to a small living room, with a kitchen and bedroom through two separate doors. The décor was sparse, and the furniture was as old as Li herself, but it was comfortable.

Li dead-bolted the door behind her and shrugged off her coat, tossing it on the chair. She flipped on a light switch, and after a moment a bare bulb in the center of the room sparked to life. Li weaved around the furniture and slipped into the bedroom.

The small laptop computer that sat on the desk seemed strangely out of place in the run-down apartment. Li reached down and flipped it open. The screen flashed to life as she slid into a chair in front of the computer. Li's fingers danced over the keys as she connected to a satellite above and quickly downloaded her email. Almost immediately an urgent message flashed on her screen. Li clicked on it. A string of numbers was the only thing the message contained: a phone number.

Li quickly dug a small satellite phone out of the top desk drawer. To the casual observer it looked like any other cellphone. She dialed the number on her screen. The phone rang once in her ear.

"Section A control center," a voice said.

"This is Dragon Lady. I'm secure," she replied, indicating that the line she was using was not being tapped and her cell signal was being encoded.

"Dragon Lady, your assistance is required. We need to know immediately if the Chinese government has any plans for constructing a secret space station armed with space fighters. This is of incredible urgency. These orders come from the highest division."

"Dragon Lady will comply," Li said.

"Inform us as soon as you know anything," the voice said. The line went dead.

Li cursed under her breath as she lowered the phone. Immediately meant tonight, and she had to be at her boss's house by eleven. That did not give her much time, but she could not disobey orders that came directly from the President.

Despite Li's distinctly Asian features, she had been born and raised in Hawaii. Her parents were Chinese immigrants who spoke very poor English. As a result, Li had learned to read and write Mandarin flawlessly.

She left Hawaii at eighteen and traveled to California, where she had studied computer science. Her programming skills had been nearly unmatched. Almost immediately after graduation, she had been approached by the CIA. Her ability to pass easily for a Chinese native and her hacking talents made her the ideal choice for a field agent.

After several months of training, she had been smuggled into China, where the agency had placed her as a secretary for the head of China's space program. She had been reporting on the actions of the agency ever since.

But she had never come across anything which indicated that China had built a space station, let alone spacecraft to defend it. If she had, the American government would already know of its existence, and they would not be sending her on this mission.

Li cursed again. Her position and her boss's faith in her allowed Li to snoop the space agency's network almost at will. Given another day, she would be able to get the information they needed easily, with almost no chance of being noticed. But the control center wanted the information tonight, which meant she would have to sneak back into the building, risking getting caught and blowing her cover. The Chinese did not take well to spies.

*This must* really *be important,* Li thought. The CIA was willing to lose one of their best sources in the Chinese space program in order to get this information. The agency hated to lose people in deep cover. They would not give her such a task unless it was urgent.

But then again, this had come from the President.

Li sighed. Cursing the agency's bad timing would get her nowhere. It was time to go to work. She quickly scanned her email for any other significant messages. Seeing none, she closed the laptop's screen and leaned back in her chair, staring out at the soft rain running down her dirty window and at the gray city beyond.

Her mind raced furiously. She knew almost every inch of the building where she worked, how the security system was set up, and, probably most importantly, which computers would have the information she would need. Sneaking around after hours was a contingency she had always planned for, but she wanted to make sure she did not make any mistakes entering the building.

Li pushed her chair back and stood, quickly discarding her work clothes. She stepped over to the closet and pulled the door open. She pushed all the clothes to one side, pulling out a pair of black pants from the last hanger. She stepped into them and pulled them up over her hips. The clothes fit tightly. Reaching into a nearby drawer, she snatched up a black sweater and slipped it over her head. Like the pants, the shirt was snug. She dug a pair of black boots from the closet and pulled them on.

Zipping the boots up over her ankles, Li stood and walked back to her desk, wrapping her long ponytail into a bun as she did. She reached into the bottom drawer and removed a small lockbox. She set the nearly square box on top of the desk, pushing her computer to the side. She quickly punched in the combination, and the box opened easily at her touch.

Li reached into the lockbox and pulled out a small silenced Russian-made pistol. She set the gun on the desk and removed four clips of ammunition. She slid one magazine into the gun, chambering a round, and placed the gun in a small holster.

She pulled a black leather belt from the box and slid it through her belt loops, slipping the holstered gun onto her right side. The magazines of ammunition fit perfectly into several loops on the left side of the belt.

Li turned back to the lockbox, pulling out a four-inch knife, which she slipped into her right boot. She wrapped a thick band around her left wrist so that four liquid-filled needles rested on the inside of her arm, then pulled her sleeve up over the band, concealing it beneath the thick black cloth.

Finally, she removed a small black bag from the box and set it on the table. Then she locked the box and replaced it in the lower desk drawer. She disconnected her laptop and placed it on top of the box, then shut the drawer.

Reaching over the desk, she unlocked the dirty window. She gave the room a quick final survey just to make sure she hadn't forgotten anything. Satisfied she had everything she needed, she grabbed her bag and walked from the bedroom, leaving the light on.

She crossed the shabby living room in three steps and slipped through the door, careful to lock it behind her. Sliding her key into her boot, she made her way down the stairs to the city streets below, pulling on a pair of black gloves as she did.

The rain and the encroaching darkness had evaporated the throngs of people who had crowded the sidewalks earlier. The Beijing roads were nearly deserted. Most of the hard-working population had returned to their homes, leaving only those who frequented the town's seedy bars, and those who had no home to go back to.

Li slipped quietly into a side alley. She didn't want anyone trailing her to the space agency's building, preferring the back streets where she could hide in the darkness. Most people avoided the alleys at all costs, afraid of the people who lurked there. But Li was well armed, and she feared being caught by the Chinese government much more than she feared any hoodlum lurking in the shadows, whose death would go unnoticed.

Fortunately, Li had no need to use her weapon during the short walk to the agency's building. Not a single soul appeared as she crept along the back alleys through the pouring rain. Either the scum of the city were elsewhere at the moment, or they decided not to trouble her.

She paused in the shadow of the alley to survey the building. From the outside the space agency's headquarters looked no different from any other of the large buildings of China's capital city. The two guards in the main lobby weren't visible from where Li stood. Sometimes they waited outside, but the rain had driven them indoors. Li smiled. That made her life a little easier.

Had she wanted to, Li could have simply gone up to the lobby and walked inside. All she had to do was show the guards her identification and they would let her in. Most people who worked at the agency knew she was Chow's personal secretary and knew to stay on her good side. She quickly dismissed the idea. It would look suspicious if she were to show up here this late, and if something went wrong, the Chinese could easily accuse her of snooping.

Li gave the front entrance one last glance, just to make sure the guards were well hidden, before slinking quietly across the alley. Reaching the back of the building, she grabbed hold of the fire escape's lower rail and agilely swung herself up onto the platform. For a moment she crouched in the darkness, watching the dark alleyways surrounding her. The streets remained as dead as ever. The only sound her ears detected was that of the softly falling rain.

Satisfied she was alone, Li slowly climbed up several flights of stairs, moving as quietly as possible. She stopped every few steps, watching for any interlopers, but to Li's delight no one appeared.

Reaching a large black door on the third floor, Li stopped. All the building's windows and doors were protected by a security system. If any were to be forced open after hours, an alarm would sound, calling out the guards. A small keypad hung on the heavy steel door in place of a handle. Entering the right code would unlock the door and deactivate the alarm.

Li pulled a small electronic device from her bag and attached it to the keypad. She activated it, watching as a series of red lights danced across the keypad. After a moment the numbers stopped scrolling and the bolt slid back audibly. Li slipped her gloved fingers around the edges of the door and pulled it open. Quickly, she disconnected the electronic device and dropped it back into her bag. Then she slipped into the building, shutting the door behind her.

The hallway in front of her was bathed in dim light. Rows of offices lined either side of the hall. The entire section of the building was devoid of life. Li's eyes flicked over the hall. This was a fairly unimportant area of the space agency. There were no motion sensors or other detectors, and the guards rarely patrolled here. However, the computers on this level were not capable of accessing the most highly classified information Li needed. To get to that, she would need to sneak into Chow's office.

Li walked as silently as possible down the empty hallway, stopping at the door to the stairs about a third of the way down the hall. She carefully cracked the door and pressed her ear to it, listening for footsteps. Like the hallway, the stairwell was deadly silent. Confident she was still alone, Li slipped through the door, gently shutting it behind her.

Slowly, she made her way up the stairs, careful not to make a sound. She moved cautiously, ever alert for the sound of footsteps or voices. But she heard nothing as she climbed toward Chow's office on the top floor.

She was two flights of stairs from her destination when she heard the door beneath her swing open. Footsteps rang up through the stairwell. Li froze momentarily, quickly surveying her options. She was caught between floors with nowhere to safely conceal herself.

With no other options, she raced up the remaining three steps, trying not to make noise despite her hurry. The sound of her footsteps would alert the guard, but if she was quiet enough, the ringing of his own boots would drown out her footfalls.

Li reached the landing and pulled the door open, sliding through into yet another abandoned hall. She closed the door quietly behind her, glancing at her surroundings. The hall she found herself in was fairly similar to the one she had snuck through minutes before. However, these computers could access certain classified information, and therefore the security was higher, and Li did not have time to break into one of the offices without activating an alarm.

Instead she quickly ducked into a small bathroom across the hall. She left the door ajar, peering through the small crack at the empty corridor and holding her breath.

A moment later the door swung open and one of the uniformed security guards walked out. He casually peered down the hall toward where Li hid. Then he turned and began walking in the opposite direction, moving through the hall as he glanced at the closed office doors.

Li let out a sigh of relief as the guard disappeared around the corner. She stepped from her hiding place and quickly crossed the hall back to the stairs. Silence once again permeated the stairwell as Li cracked the door open.

She slipped back into the stairwell, carefully shutting the door behind her. She hurried up the next flight of steps, to the top floor. Most likely the guard was doing a routine walk-through of every floor, and the top would be next. Given time, Li simply would have waited him out, but time was something she did not have. Chow would be furious if she was late.

The door to the top floor had a keypad similar to that of the door on the fire escape. Li knew the code, but she still attached the device to open the door. Picking the lock would make it look like a stranger had broken into the building. She did not want her snooping to look like an inside job.

The bolt slid back easily. Li quickly disconnected her decoding device and reached back into her bag, removing a piece of opaque tape. With agonizing slowness she slid the door open several inches and reached up, feeling for the motion sensor that hung there. Carefully, she wrapped the tape over the sensor.

Slowly, Li slid the door open further and slipped inside, keeping her slow pace. Once inside, she looked up at the motion sensor. The tape had completely covered it. She shut the door silently behind her and quickly crossed her own office to Chow's door.

One final keypad stood between Li and her goal. Again, the little electronic decoder was quick to decipher the code, allowing Li to slide the door open and disarm the final motion sensor. She slipped into the director's office, sliding the door shut behind her.

Chow's computer sat on one side of his massive desk, which faced the door. A dark window looked out at the streets below. The city lights shone dimly through the window, outlining the objects around the room.

Li placed her bag on Chow's desk and walked around it, dropping easily into his chair. She pushed the button to turn on the computer, and the machine hummed to life. As it did, Li reached into her bag and pulled out a blank CD, which she dropped into the disk drive.

The computer screen flashed from a progress bar to a small box requesting a password. Li bypassed it with several quick keystrokes. The main operating system came up. Li accessed the space agency's internal network

She began typing rapidly, programming the computer to run a search of all the information on the network. Li's fingers once again danced across the keyboard as she programmed the requirements for her search. She called up the parameters for a broad search, scanning for mention of a space station. From here, she could scan not only every file on the network, but also those on the workers' personal machines.

During the normal workday, such a search would take hours. Li would have to be discreet, using only her own computer to power the search. But this late at night the building was empty except for a few security guards. Every single computer was logged off for the night, but still powered on to receive necessary updates. That meant Li could use the maximum computing power of every single machine on the network.

Hitting "enter," Li initiated the search. The computer's hard drive began to whirl. Li sighed and leaned back, watching as the search progressed. Despite the massive amount of power she was using, it still seemed to move with agonizing slowness, forcing Li to wait.

She hated the feeling of sitting motionless in the darkness, unable to leave until the program finished its search. The longer she stayed in one place, the greater her chances were of being detected, and the more likely she was to be late for her rendezvous with Chow. She wished there was some way to speed up the search, but she was powerless to do so. The engine was already using all the power it could draw.

A faint series of short electronic beeps drifted to Li's ears. The keypad outside! The guard must have completed his search of the floor beneath her and was making his final sweep of the top floor. A moment later she heard the door to her office creak open. She caught the sound of the guard's footfalls as he walked into the room and stopped, shining his flashlight about. The dim beam flashed back and forth, shimmering through the cracks around Chow's door.

Li's hand fell slowly to her hip. Moving quietly, she pulled the pistol from its holster and withdrew the small weapon. She flicked the safety off and pointed it at the door. A quick check of the computer screen revealed that her search was almost complete. Li held her breath and waited.

She heard the sound of the guard entering the key code on Chow's door. The door swung open just as a faint chime announced that the search had finished. The guard stepped inside and stopped dead in his tracks, amazed at seeing the dark silhouette of a figure sitting in the director's chair, staring back at him.

# ~ **11** ~

For a moment the guard simply gaped, as Li's eyes dashed to the monitor. Her search had not uncovered anything. Li glanced back to the guard. He dropped one hand to his radio and screamed that there was someone inside as he raised his own weapon with the other hand.

Li's gun discharged with the faint zip of a silenced pistol. The bullet caught the guard dead in the chest, and he fell backward, his own gun firing into the ceiling. Li logged off the computer. She ejected the empty disk from the drive, dropping it back into her bag. She shut the bag quickly and threw it over her shoulder, holstering her pistol as she did.

Any hope of silently making her way out through the building was gone. Li knew that a swarm of guards were currently charging up the stairs toward her, effectively sealing off that route. Her only hope of escape was the window behind her.

Li turned, pulled the window open, and swung herself out. A brick ledge ran around the window. Li grabbed the top ledge with her fingers and pulled herself upward, standing on the windowsill. She did not dare look down. It was a good ten stories to the ground below.

Taking a deep breath, Li pulled herself upward. As her feet lifted off the sill she reached up with her left hand, grabbed the edge of the roof as tightly as she could, and pulled with all her might.

Beneath her Li heard the loud report of gunfire. Bullets began to whiz around her. She looked down to see two guards pointing rifles up at her. Their figures looked small so far beneath. For an instant the sheer drop made Li dizzy.

She clung to the wall as the bullets began to hit the brick around her. Li pulled herself higher, lifting her left foot to the spot where her hand had been and grabbing onto the roof with her right hand. She raised her right foot, but her boot slipped off the ledge, and her leg dropped down.

Flecks of brick and dust from the gunfire ricocheted off Li. She held onto the wall with all her might, raising her leg once again. This time she found a foothold. With a small leap, she pulled herself up, rolling over onto the roof and lying flat on her back so that the gunmen beneath no longer had a target. Much to Li's relief, the chatter of gunfire ceased.

Li took a deep breath and rolled onto her stomach, crawling to the center of the roof. The stairs below could access the roof from the top floor, and she knew it wouldn't be much longer before the guards reached her. Slowly she stood. The buildings in this part of Beijing were close together. Li glanced around, finding the one closest to the space agency building. It was an office building of roughly the same height.

Li took off at a dead sprint, leaping into the air as she reached the edge of the agency's building. She easily crossed the two-foot gap between the buildings, landing lightly on the other side. She twisted her head back to see ten guards come pouring onto the roof of the agency. A moment later, gunfire again filled the air as bullets started to zip around Li.

She began to run again, pulling her gun from her holster and turning back to fire as she did. One of the men on the building dropped to the ground. Li continued to run. She jumped off the building, dropping about five feet before hitting another roof. Li landed hard, falling forward as she did. She easily somersaulted across the floor, quickly regaining her feet.

As she dropped out of sight the gunfire stopped, only to be replaced by the sound of numerous heavy footfalls. The men were chasing her. Li looked around again. She had to move quickly, before the guards came within range of her a second time. To simply vanish would be best, but she could see no easy way down to the alleys below. Instead she turned and ran to the left, jumping a small gap to another roof.

She heard a loud thud behind her. Looking behind her, she saw one of the guards drop onto the roof where she had been. Two more quickly followed. The gunfire immediately resumed. Li fired off a few rounds from her own pistol. One bullet caught a guard squarely in the chest, while another projectile sliced through a second man's shoulder.

Li stuck her gun back into its holster as she took the last few steps across the roof. She easily jumped a three-foot gap, catching hold of a metal ladder which served as a fire escape for another building. She scrambled upward, ignoring the bullets ricocheting off the wall around her, and pulled herself onto the roof above.

Climbing to the top of the building, she swung her legs over and lay on her stomach, facing the approaching crowd. Unable to see her, the men had stopped firing. She pulled her pistol from the holster again and took careful aim. One of the men in the front stumbled and fell as the silenced weapon discharged. Another quickly joined him.

The small group of guards ignored their fallen comrades and continued to rush forward. They began to rake the area above the ladder with bullets, hoping one shot would hit their target. Li rolled away from the edge of the roof and stood again, starting off at a run toward yet another nearby rooftop.

Once again the air fell silent as Li disappeared from sight. A second later she heard the rattling of metal against brick as one of the guards leapt onto the ladder and began to pull himself to the top of the building.

Li twisted to the right and leapt downward, falling nearly seven feet before her boots hit the roof of the building below. She lost her footing and tumbled forward. Rolling over quickly, she came up running, trying to put as much distance as possible between herself and the guards chasing her.

She could hear the men shouting behind her, and more footsteps approaching rapidly. The man who had climbed the ladder after her had seen her disappear and was screaming to the others, trying to point them in her direction.

The night erupted with the sound of gunshots again. Li turned her head around to see one of the guards drop to the roof behind her. The weapon in his hand spat fire into the night. He landed on the roof with a thud but managed to keep his feet. Still firing, he charged for Li.

The young spy looked around, scanning her surroundings for an escape route as she tried to increase her pace. Bullets began to whiz by her, coming closer by the moment. The fire only intensified as more of the guards dropped to the roof and joined in the chase.

Li glanced around frantically. To her right, the building dropped off nearly eight stories to a large road. The building in front of her was a good two floors higher than the roof where she now stood. The building on her left was the same height as the one she was running across, but there was a gap of at least ten feet between the two roofs. She knew she would never make it.

The horror of being trapped struck Li like a blow. She nearly faltered, but managed to keep her pace, watching the edge of the building approach. The gunfire grew ever closer. She could hear the pounding of feet over the chatter of fire.

Her only chance was to draw her own weapon again and fight. Li was an expert shot, but the odds were against her. There were at least six men behind her, and several had semiautomatic weapons. The instant she presented a stationary target, the bullets would rip her to pieces. At best, she would be able to take out one or two before the hail of fire found her.

Li desperately surveyed her surroundings again, looking for something to hide behind. If she could place a barrier between herself and the guards, she just might be able to survive long enough to stop them. But the roof was completely empty, affording Li no shelter whatsoever. She was trapped in the open.

Suddenly, three steps from the edge of the roof, she spotted an open window in the building ahead of her. Twisting to the side, she launched herself at it, barely managing to catch hold of the windowsill. As her body slammed into the wall, the bricks beneath her right arm gave way, tumbling to the ground below her.

Li lunged forward in a desperate grasp as she felt herself begin to fall. Her hand caught the edge of the window. The bullets began to hit the wall mere inches from her body. Li scrambled forward, pulling herself through the window and dropping onto the wood floor beneath.

She crouched down so as not to make herself visible to her pursuers, and drew her own gun. Twisting back around to the window, she raised her weapon and fired, dropping one of the men on her far right. The others were nearly to the edge of the roof. They would be inside in a matter of minutes.

Li turned away from the window and stood. In the dim light, she could see two small faces staring up at her from a pair of beds. The children regarded her with a mixture of astonishment and utter fear.

"Lie still and don't make a sound, no matter what happens," she whispered to them. Out of fear, the two quickly lay down again and tried to make themselves as small as possible. Li dashed from the room as the first of her pursuers leapt onto the window and began to pull himself through.

Li found herself standing in what appeared to be a small living room. She realized that she must be in one of Beijing's many apartment buildings. She could make out a door on the far side of the room, and she ran for it.

She could hear the footsteps of her pursuer as she reached the door and flung it open, stepping out into a long hallway bathed in pale light from several naked bulbs hanging every ten feet. A window was at each end of the hallway. Li ran for the far window, knowing the one closer to her would only bring her back to the guards chasing her.

"Freeze!" Li heard a voice behind her shout. She turned around immediately, firing as she did. The bullet caught the guard in his right arm, causing him to drop his weapon. He yelped but continued to chase her.

Li stuck her pistol back in its holster as she reached the window. She stopped and pulled it open, ducking her head out. She twisted her body around so that she was sitting on the windowsill. Slowly she brought her right leg up and lifted herself upward, grabbing onto the edges of the window for support.

Suddenly, she felt someone grab her left foot and

pull her back toward the building. Li peered through the window to see the guard tugging at her boot, oblivious to the blood running down his arm. Li allowed herself to fall back to a sitting position and lashed out with her right foot. The blow caught the guard squarely in the chest, but he kept his grip on her ankle, pulling her leg further inside.

Li raised her right foot and kicked again. This time the heel of her boot smashed into his nose. The man released her as he fell backward, blood gushing from his crushed nose.

Li scrambled, putting her feet back on the ledge and standing again. She could see the guard climbing to his feet. Li scanned her surroundings. A rusty metal frame fire escape hung three feet to her right. She leapt for it just as the guard lunged for her. She felt the tips of his fingers brush against her pants as she jumped.

Li's hands caught the metal rail of the fire escape, and she quickly pulled her feet up, resting them on one the rungs beneath her. Instead of ducking through the rails and racing up the steps, she simply began to pull herself upward, rapidly scaling the outer rails of the fire escape as if it were a ladder.

Reaching the top of the fire escape, Li pulled herself onto the upper landing, which was level with the roof. Looking back down, she saw the bleeding guard standing on the ledge of the window that she had crawled from. He was reaching across to the fire escape, intent on following her.

Li pulled her pistol and fired. The bullet smashed through the man's skull. His body went limp, and he fell downward, limbs flailing as he tumbled to the alleyway below. His body disappeared into the darkness before Li saw it hit the ground.

Suddenly, bullets began to zip past her head again. She peered downward to see another guard leaning out of the window, firing up at her with a semiautomatic rifle. Li quickly ducked away, swinging herself onto the roof and running away from the road.

The gunfire ceased again. A moment later she heard the clattering of boots on the fire escape. The chatter of semiautomatic fire resumed just as Li reached the edge of the roof. She quickly leapt the distance to the adjacent building.

Dropping to a crouch, Li carefully drew a bead with her pistol. The silenced weapon fired with a soft zipping noise, and the man closest to Li fell to the ground. The remaining three men jumped over his body and ran for her.

Li stood, turned, and leapt the two-foot gap to the building on her right. No sooner had her feet touched the roof than she began to sprint, firing back toward the men. One bullet caught the guard on the right in the shoulder, but all continued to charge at her, firing nonstop as they did. The men jumped to the building where Li stood and ran for her.

Li ran to the edge of the roof. A six-foot gap stretched between her and the next roof. Ignoring the distance, Li launched herself into the air, falling as she did. As she dropped downward, she caught onto one of the fire escape rails. Her feet hit hard on the platform beneath, and she began to swing herself downward toward the alleyway below.

The three guards dashed to the edge of the building, where they stood and peered downward. Their quarry had seemingly vanished into the night. The alley was completely deserted, and the only sound was the soft patter of rain. The men gazed around in bewilderment.

"Look!" one of the guards shouted, pointing to an open window on the third floor of the building across from them. A light shone dimly inside.

"How do we get down there?" a second asked.

"This way," the third man said, pointing to a ladder on the side of the building.

The first man slung his rifle, and the other two holstered their pistols. They scrambled rapidly down the ladder, then raced up the fire escape of the second building. Unslinging his weapon, the first man stepped through the window into the room.

A long-haired woman in a short green dress that revealed more of her chest than it covered stared at him in complete and utter shock and then began to scream uncontrollably.

"Don't shoot me, don't shoot me!" she wailed, dropping to her knees as her hair flew around her face.

"I don't want to hurt you, miss," the guard said, surprised. "Did anyone come in here?"

"No!" the woman screamed. "No one came here. There is no one here but me. Please don't shoot me. Don't shoot me!" she cried in fear, burying her face in her hands.

The guard shrugged and stepped back out onto the fire escape, leaving her sobbing on the floor.

"Must have run off through the alley," he said to his two companions. The three started down the stairs to the ground.

Li lifted her head as the man stepped from her apartment, a faint smile crossing her face. The man had believed her frantic act. She remained motionless until their footsteps faded. Then she stood and closed the window.

Picking up a hairbrush, she smoothed her long black hair and dabbed a spot of perfume on her neck. She slipped on a dark coat, picked up her small purse, and once again walked out of her apartment.

∗          ∗          ∗

Zhan Chow cursed as he hung up the phone.

"What's wrong?" Li asked as he turned back to

her.

She moved closer to him, running her hand over his bare chest. Although Chow's height and broad shoulders made him a large man by Chinese standards, he was still smaller than many of the Americans Li had known in school. He was not a muscular man, but neither was he flabby. He was older than Li by at least twenty years, but she had never found that distasteful.

Sleeping with Chow was a pleasant experience for Li. Despite his power within the space agency and the government, he had always treated her kindly, especially since she was willing to give him favors. That willingness had allowed Li to gain his trust and improve her own stature in the agency. It also gave her increased access to Chow and whatever secrets he knew.

Li had been in bed with Chow for nearly an hour when his phone rang. The space agency's director had reluctantly answered the call, and from the look on his face and the tone of his voice he had not liked what the caller had to say.

"Someone broke into my office at the agency earlier this evening," he said.

"My goodness!" Li said in shock. Her hand froze on his chest. "Do they know who?"

"Russians, most likely," he replied. "Whoever it was had a Russian weapon."

"They didn't catch him?" she asked.

"No." Chow replied. "Some of the guards chased him halfway across the city, but they never caught him."

"Fire those imbeciles," Li snorted. "What good are they if they can't run down one stupid Russian?" She slid over beneath the blankets, pressing her chest to Chow's.

"The head of security already did, love," he said,

kissing her.

"Good," Li replied, pressing her lips against his. She rolled easily off Chow and picked up two glasses of wine that had been sitting on a table beside the bed. With a gentle slip of her hand, she slid a small white pill into one glass, then handed it to Chow.

"Forget about that stupid Russian for now," she said, slowly sipping from her own glass.

"That shouldn't be too hard," Chow said, running his eyes over her trim, naked body. He smiled, then drained his own glass. Li set hers down and moved back to him, kissing him again. Chow ran his fingers over her breasts as she did, then traced his hands over her stomach and around her hips, then finally down between her legs.

Li simply continued to kiss him, sliding her tongue in and out of his mouth. His motions became slower and slower, until he stopped moving altogether. Li smiled and rolled off him again. The small pill she had given him placed him in a semiconscious state. It would also completely erase his memory of the next four hours. When Chow woke up in the morning, he would simply think he had fallen asleep.

Li stood and walked over to her handbag. She removed a small hypodermic needle filled with truth serum. Uncapping the needle, she injected it into Chow's arm. She was careful to return the used hypodermic to her bag.

She sat down beside Chow again, gently patting his face to wake him up. The space agency's director looked at her through glazed eyes.

"What do you know about space stations, Zhan?" she asked.

"The Americans and Russians have built them," he said slowly.

"Have the Chinese?" she said.

"No," he said.

"Have you heard about any plans for one?"

"There has been talk of building one in the future, but no definite plans," he murmured.

"Have they made any secret plans to build a space station?" she asked.

"No," Chow said, sounding half-drugged. "No plans."

"What about armed spacecraft?"

"Never heard anything about that," Chow muttered.

Li sighed. Clearly, this was not her night.

✳     ✳     ✳

"Section A control center," the voice on the other end of Li's satellite phone said.

"This is Dragon Lady. I'm secure," Li said, as she gazed out the window of her apartment at the alley below. "Initial search results are negative. There is nothing about a space station or armed spacecraft in the space agency's database or in the director's personal files. I even drugged him up and he knew nothing. I will perform a more thorough search of the databases tomorrow."

After interrogating Chow, Li had searched his house and personal documents for any evidence of the space station. She had found nothing.

"Thank you, Dragon Lady," the controller said. "Carry on."

"Dragon Lady will comply," Li said, flipping her phone shut. Then she flopped down on her bed, not even bothering to remove her slinky green dress.

# ~ 12 ~

"What do you have?" David Webster asked the Director of Central Intelligence.

"Nothing," he replied. "I've had every agent within China snooping around for information on this. There is no record of a space station anywhere within the space agency, nor does its leadership have any knowledge of it. I have an agent very close to the space program's director who could not find a single shred of evidence. Whatever is going on, the Chinese government knows nothing of it."

"So you don't think this is based in China?" Webster asked. "Even though Chinese MiGs attacked our pilots on two separate occasions?"

"China's a large country," the Director said, "and the western regions are sparsely populated. It is quite possible whoever is destroying our satellites is working from that area of the world. As for the MiGs, anyone who can finance such an endeavor can certainly afford a few MiGs. But as far as we know, the Chinese government, and certainly the space agency, has no knowledge of such a program."

"So nothing concrete," Webster said, frowning.

"No, sir," the Director said.

"Tell your people to keep their eyes open," the President said.

"Yes, sir."

"What about you?" Webster said, turning to the

Secretary of Defense.

"The bad news is that we've lost all our surveillance satellites and about ninety percent of our communications," he said.

Webster scowled.

"Fortunately, we still have our secure satellite phone network," the Director of Central Intelligence added. "It's disguised as a civilian company and has not been heavily targeted yet."

"But I do have some good news," the Secretary of Defense continued. "NORAD has analyzed the data on when and where our satellites were lost, backed out potential orbits for the attacks, and used that to come up with a general idea of where this space station is."

"Good," Webster said. "What about the Hellcats?"

"Edwards reports they're ready to fly."

"Excellent," Webster said. "Tell them where to find this thing, and get them up there. We don't need to know who's behind this space station to knock it down."

"Yes, sir," the Secretary said. "They'll launch first thing in the morning."

"Good," Webster said. "I want a report as soon as they're on the ground."

"Of course, sir."

"Hopefully we can crush this thing once and for all," the President said.

*     *     *

Martina stood in front of the mirror in the bedroom of her visiting officers' quarters, staring at the silver oak leaves on her shoulders. Less than half a year ago she had been wearing captain's bars. Now she was a lieutenant colonel. She had barely adjusted to being called "major." Being called "colonel" sounded like something out of a dream.

Somewhere in the back of her head, Martina half expected to wake up, only to find herself lying in her bed in Houston with her cat curled around her feet. The time-zone changes and lack of sleep had made the events following the shuttle's landing in Russia seem dreamlike. Then again, jet lag had always had that effect on Martina.

The Hellcats certainly seemed like a figment of her imagination. Yet they existed. Martina had spent the entire day in a simulator, learning the nuances of the plane and its complex computer system. They were a fighter pilot's wildest fantasy, a space fighter that performed just as well in the atmosphere. She still didn't quite believe they were real.

And she couldn't believe that *she* had been selected to fly them.

She gazed back at the silver oak leaves on her shoulders. Four days ago, she had just been another rookie major at NASA. Now she was a light bird colonel. She outranked not only everyone in her Academy class, but everyone in the three classes above her as well. The thought of showing the oak leaves to some of the upperclassmen in her freshman squadron brought a smile to Martina's face. They'd be the ones saluting her now.

Martina grinned, then looked at the oak leaves again, shaking her head in disbelief. Lieutenant Colonel Redrick. She wondered how long it would take for her to get used to hearing that. Her life had certainly taken a strange turn in the past few days.

No matter how impossible it seemed, she was a light bird, the Hellcats were real, and she was about to fly them. She could stare at those oak leaves all day, she knew, and it wouldn't change a thing. Pushing her thoughts of recent events to the back of her mind, she reached up and pulled down the zipper of her flight suit. Slowly she peeled off the loose garment, letting it fall to the floor around her ankles before kicking it into a corner of the room.

She stood in a black t-shirt that she wore beneath her flight suit. Her combat boots and socks were gone. She had removed them before catching sight of herself in the mirror and pausing to contemplate her rank.

Slowly she raised her right hand above her head, eliciting only a few small whimpers from her broken ribs. Martina had found that if she didn't twist or bend her chest, she could function with almost no pain. Using her left hand, she pulled her t-shirt over her head and flung it on top of her flight suit.

She now stood in front of the mirror in nothing but a white bra and a pair of red cotton string bikini underwear. Her dog tags hung down past her breasts, lying against her flat stomach. Her figure was tall and lean, curving out slightly at the hips, then back in at the waist. Wiry sinews traced across her arms, shoulders, and back, hinting at the power hidden in her muscles. Her height came from a pair of long, tapering legs.

Martina looked at the bruised area just beneath her right breast. She reached down slowly with her left hand, gingerly running her fingers across her ribs. They seemed to be healing slowly. The bruise was fading away, no longer the stark blue it had been two days earlier. The area hurt less when she moved, although lightning pain still raced through her chest if she twisted it.

It should be healed in a week or two, Martina thought, as she gave the area one last look. Slowly she turned away from the mirror. She'd take a quick shower, then go down to the dining hall and grab a takeout dinner. After that, she planned to just watch a movie or something, and crash early.

*If I can sleep at all*, Martina thought, reaching back to unclasp her bra. *We're flying those planes tomorrow. The sheer excitement of that will keep me awake all night.*

A knock on the door stopped Martina just before she snapped off her bra.

"Fuck!" she spat. What did that crazy swabbie want now?

"Hang on!" Martina shouted, grabbing a pair of jeans she had bought at the base exchange the day before and attempting to pull them on. As she bent over, a wave of agony washed through her chest, nearly causing her to yell out from the pain.

"Fuck, fuck, fuck," Martina muttered, quickly pulling the jeans up over her hips and buttoning them.

*I should just answer the door in my underwear*, she thought, finding a t-shirt and pulling it over her head. This time she was careful not to aggravate her cracked ribs. It was probably just Rachel, wanting to go to the O-club or something. Martina was fairly sure that the Navy woman wouldn't even bat an eyelash if she showed up at the door half-naked.

*She'd probably just make some crack about interrupting me when I was fucking someone,* Martina thought.

Pulling her long brown hair out from under her t-shirt, she walked over to the door and pulled it open, fully expecting to see Rachel standing there.

Bill Durant was leaning against her doorframe.

"Hi," Martina said, trying to conceal her surprise.

"Hi," Durant said, straightening up and smiling. "Mind if I come in?"

"No," Martina said, stepping back and motioning for him to enter.

Durant strode in, closing the door behind him. Martina leaned up against the counter of her small kitchenette and stared at him, unsure just what to make of his sudden appearance.

"Do you have any plans for dinner?" he asked.

"I was just going to grab something from the dining hall," Martina said. "Why?"

"I was wondering if I couldn't interest you in some pizza and a movie," Durant said.

Martina gazed at him skeptically. That was about on par with what a freshman stuck at the Academy could come up with, provided he had some contraband DVDs.

"It's the best I could do, seeing that you can't leave the base," he said apologetically. In order to ensure the secrecy of the Hellcats and their mission, the pilots were being kept at Edwards until after the flight.

"That depends," Martina said.

"On what?" Durant asked.

"What kind of movie are we talking about?" she asked, half smiling.

"I saw there was an old Vietnam flick coming on in a few minutes," he said.

"That sounds good," she said, her lips curling upward into a grin. She pushed herself off the counter and walked over to the couch, dropping down on it.

"Cool," Durant said, walking over to the television set and turning it on. He flipped through the channels until he reached the one he wanted. Then he stepped back and sat down on Martina's right, wrapping his arm around her shoulders.

"So how long you been in the Air Force?" he asked, leaning in to her.

"Ten years, give or take," she said as the television flashed a picture of several Hueys flying over rolling hills. "I started basic training at the Academy a week or two after graduating from high school. I was seventeen."

"So you're, what do they call them?" Durant said. "A ring-knocker?" He gently fingered her large class ring, touching the skin on her hands.

"Yeah, that's where I got that," she said.

"And after that?" he asked, moving still closer.

"I went to pilot training, got myself a Raptor, flew those right up until I got into test pilot school. Then I got picked up for NASA."

"And that's how you ended up here?" he said, bringing his face to within an inch of hers.

"Yeah," she said, her lips brushing against his as she spoke. Before she could continue, he gently pressed his lips to hers, kissing her softly.

Martina went stiff with surprise for an instant, then she relaxed, allowing Durant to slide his tongue inside her mouth. She certainly had no strong emotions for him, but his touch didn't feel wrong, so she let him continue. It had been a long time since someone had held her...

She twisted toward him, running her tongue along his lips as she wrapped her arms around him. He tightened his arms around her back, leaning into her and pushing her back onto the sofa as he kissed her. She could feel the comfortable weight of his chest against hers.

Suddenly, a stab of pain raced through her as his body pressed against her ribs. Martina went rigid, shoving him off her abruptly. Durant leapt back in surprise as she sat up, her left hand instinctively curled around the injured area.

"Are you all right?" he asked.

"Yeah," Martina said, almost gasping.

"Are you sure?" he said.

"I'm fine," she repeated, keeping her hand against her chest. "I don't think that's such a good idea."

"All right," he said, slightly unsure of how to react.

"But we can keep watching this, if you want," she said, sliding back over to him and giving him another quick kiss on the lips.

"Just no rough stuff, okay?" she said, smiling.

"Okay," he replied, wrapping his arm back around her shoulders as she settled down against him. On the television a battle scene began to play out. The fire in Martina's chest had died, and she allowed herself to relax as Durant gently moved his hand over her bare arms. She half-focused on the movie, unable to push the thoughts of the next day's mission from her mind. She still couldn't believe she was about to fly the Hellcat.

*          *          *

The early morning light was creeping slowly across the land, turning the sky from black to pale, pale blue and fading out the stars. A cool breeze blew softly across the desert, spinning a few grains of sand over the tarmac. Edwards was deathly silent in the predawn light.

The Hellcats had been pulled from their hangar. They sat motionless on the asphalt, their silver skin pale against the faint blue sky. The ground crew had already preflighted the unmarked aircraft, leaving the planes sitting in the cool morning air, cockpits open, awaiting their pilots. One crew chief remained standing in front of each plane.

Martina studied the two aircraft as she stood by the edge of the ramp, flight helmet in hand. The soft wind blew across her skin, chilling her slightly. The thin pressure suit she wore kept the air away from her body, but she still felt the breeze on her face and down her neck. She paid no attention to the feeling, keeping her eyes fixated on the two aircraft sitting in the dim light, and only sensing the eerie silence of the base.

She glanced to her left, where Rachel stood. The Navy pilot waited quietly beside her, taking in the sight of the aircraft. The feel of early morning seemed to calm even Rachel. She turned to Martina and nodded. The two pilots stepped silently onto the tarmac and walked slowly to their aircraft.

Reaching her plane, Martina climbed into the cockpit, lowered herself into the seat, and carefully strapped herself in. She connected her helmet to her oxygen supply, pulling it over her head. She completed the seal between her helmet and pressure suit, and checked her life support systems. Reaching down, she strapped a checklist to one leg and a kneeboard to the other.

Martina closed the canopy and locked it down before running through the pre-start procedures. Despite the complexity of the plane, it took only a few minutes to prepare for engine start, running through the list from memory. Martina quickly reviewed the checklist strapped to her leg to ensure she hadn't missed any steps, then set her radio and keyed her mike.

"Hellcat check," she said.

"Two," Rachel's voice echoed in her ears.

Martina looked out and gave the crew chief the signal that she was about to start the first engine. The left engine caught smoothly, leveling at idle power. She started the right engine. Beside her, Rachel was bringing the second plane's engines to life.

The roar of the jet engines sparking to life filled the early morning air. Martina ran her eyes over the gauges and instruments. The computer was reading all systems green, with a pressurized seal around the cockpit.

"Edwards ground, Hellcat one, request taxi to the active," she said. Ground responded with her taxi instructions.

Martina gave the crew chief the signal to pull chocks. Rachel did the same. The crew chiefs ducked under the planes, pulling away the blocks that prevented the wheels from moving. Martina's crew chief walked back to the front of her plane and began to marshal her forward.

Releasing the brakes, Martina nudged the throttles slightly. Slowly the plane began to roll. Martina tapped the brakes, then pushed the throttle up again. She turned toward the taxiway. As her Hellcat slipped past Rachel's plane, the Navy pilot began to taxi out of her own parking spot. One behind the other, the planes taxied slowly to the runway, stopping short of the approach end. Martina signed a frequency change.

"Hellcat check."

"Two."

"Edwards tower," Martina replied, "Hellcat one. Holding short of the active, ready for takeoff."

"Hellcat one, Edwards," the control tower replied, "you are cleared for takeoff." The controller quickly relayed the winds and the flight's desired departure heading and altitude before adding, "Safe flight."

"Hellcat one," Martina answered. She repeated the takeoff clearance.

She released the brakes, and the Hellcat began to roll forward. Steering with the rudder pedals, she moved the aircraft into position on one of Edwards' remote runways. Rachel lined up her plane behind and to the right of Martina's.

Martina pushed the throttles to their stops. The Hellcat surged forward, racing down the runway with ever increasing speed. Reaching her rotation speed, Martina eased the stick back. Beside her, Rachel did the same. The Hellcats' wheels lifted off the ground as the sleek craft caught the air and rose smoothly into the sky. The two planes left the ground as one, leaping into the air together.

Signaling to her wingman, Martina raised the landing gear and put the plane into a wide turn, swinging around to the east. Rachel hung on her wing, flying in perfect formation. The two craft climbed into the pale morning sky.

Leveling out at cruising altitude, they kept their throttles shoved forward, pushing the planes to maximum velocity. The sky to the east was growing lighter as the two airplanes pulled nose up in unison, streaking into the outer reaches of the atmosphere.

Martina watched as the altimeter spun in circles. Her airspeed bled away as she traded every bit of her speed for height. Despite the coming dawn, the sky around her began to darken as she slipped into the outer reaches of Earth's atmosphere. The aircraft continued to slow.

"Hellcat two, Hellcat one. Fire rockets in 3... 2... 1... Mark," she said, flipping the small switch on the console to rockets and hitting the ignition.

The kick of the rocket engines was like nothing Martina had ever experienced before. One moment she was barely moving, the next the Hellcat was accelerating forward at incredible speed. The g-forces pressed against her body. Reflexively, Martina tensed the muscles in her body as a flash of pain raced through her cracked ribs.

Martina stared forward, focusing her eyes on her heads-up display. She attempted to turn her head to see Rachel's plane, but another wave of fire danced through her chest. Keeping her body nearly rigid and facing forward seemed the only way to minimize the agony from her ribs. Her radar told her that her wingman was in position and her instruments showed her aircraft was right on course.

"Hellcat one, Hellcat two," Rachel said, using the shortwave radio frequency that enabled the two planes to talk exclusively to each other. "How you holding up?"

"I'm all right, Hellcat two," Martina replied, hoping the pain in her voice wasn't too evident.

"If you say so," Rachel said, her tone indicating she clearly did not believe Martina. The airwaves again fell silent.

"Hey Rachel," Martina said after a moment, "let's ditch this Hellcat stuff. Nobody's going to hear us anyway. You got a callsign?"

"Yeah," the Navy pilot replied. "The boys called me Moondog. What about you?"

"Panther," Martina said, glancing at her computer. "Cut engines in 3... 2... 1... Mark," she ordered.

She reached over and switched off the engines. The air around her immediately fell silent, and the pain in her chest vanished. She felt her body lift in the absence of gravity, held down only by the straps connecting her to her ejection seat. Through the blackness of space surrounding her she could see the rising sun. The Hellcat seemed to hang motionless in the darkness as Earth spun slowly beneath her and the stars sparkled above.

"Okay, Moondog," Martina said, "let's go get these bastards."

"Hell yeah!" the Navy pilot shouted.

Panther switched on her radar, turning it to the maximum range. A vast array of signals appeared on her screen. All the echoes looked very strange to her. She was seeing satellites, she realized, not aircraft. Having never read satellites' radar signatures, she found it difficult to decipher what she was looking at.

"Keep your eyes open," she said to Moondog. "This thing doesn't show up on Earth, so our radar might not pick it up either."

"Right," the Navy woman said.

Martina leaned back, scanning the sky around her slowly. Beneath her she saw the vast blue of the Atlantic Ocean. All around the stars sparkled, and the sunlight danced off the metal of the satellites flying by her. She could see Moondog's Hellcat, hovering just off her right wing. The silver plane shone in the light, contrasting starkly with the darkness of space around her.

The complete and utter silence that surrounded Martina seemed entirely foreign to her. There had always been noise in the cockpit of an aircraft—the roar of the jet engines, the whistle of air around the plane, the constant chatter and static on the radio. But here, out of Earth's atmosphere, with the engines completely shut down and no one but Moondog for miles around, the world was totally silent.

Despite the strange lack of sound, Panther could still feel the old familiar sensation of a combat mission surrounding her. The adrenaline was already trickling through her veins, heightening her senses and alerting her to everything around her.

The world continued to slip by slowly beneath her. The Hellcats crossed silently over Europe. Martina kept her eyes peeled, studying every object that passed her, every glint in the darkness that caught her eye, no matter how small. But she saw nothing. Slowly Martina began to wonder if she had been given the right orbit, or if the space station even existed.

"Panther! Two o'clock," Moondog called suddenly.

Martina twisted her head to the side. In the distance she could see an object, growing larger by the second. Even at such a great range, she could tell it was far too big to be a satellite.

"Let's go," she said, placing her hand on the stick and moving it to the right. The thrusters along the Hellcat's nose sparked to life. Small flames shot into the blackness with a soft hiss. The sleek craft responded seamlessly, maneuvering easily through the vacuum.

Martina rolled out smoothly, pointing her nose at the space station. A quick check over her shoulder showed that Moondog was in perfect position.

Although her face was hidden beneath her mask, Martina was sure she was smiling.

Martina shifted her heads-up display to combat mode and armed her guns. Keeping her fingers wrapped around the stick, she waited for the space station to slip within range.

"Let's show these assholes they picked the wrong people to fuck with," she said to Moondog.

"Mess with the best..." Moondog said, grinning.

"Die like the rest!" Panther said.

# ~ 13 ~

Martina watched the space station grow until it nearly filled the Hellcat's canopy. It was a massive circular object, nearly two hundred feet in diameter. Each section was made of large panels, which were laid at odd angles to one another. She made out at least three different levels. Large, thick-paned windows were interspersed throughout the structure. The silhouettes of people moving about the station were visible through the glass. The remainder of the station was composed of thick paneling.

Martina immediately recognized the sleek silver craft that had attacked the space shuttle several days earlier. The small ship was docked on the side of the station, connected to the structure by a large sleeve extending from the canopy. At least five identical craft hung beside it, making a circle around the space station.

Martina touched a button her control panel, taking a quick picture of the station with her gun camera.

"How on earth do they keep that thing hidden from radar?" Moondog said in disbelief.

"I don't know, but they're not going be up here much longer," Martina said. "Let's strafe the thing. Hopefully, we put a few holes in it, the whole thing will depressurize and kill everyone on board. Then we won't have to worry about tangling with those fighters."

"Let's do it," Moondog said.

Panther tapped her throttles and dove at the space station. The engines fired briefly, shoving the Hellcat forward. She felt herself being pushed down in her seat from the force. The pressure caused by the small maneuver was gentle. She depressed the trigger as she dashed at the station. The guns on the Hellcat's wings opened up with a staccato pulse. She raced toward the space station, firing all the while.

Much to Martina's horror, the bullets simply bounced off both the metal and the glass, leaving only a series of dents in the station. Merely feet from the surface, she rolled to the left and skimmed along the large structure. She could again feel herself being pushed down into the seat. Moondog followed close behind her.

"These handle like a dream," the Navy pilot said as she slid back into position. "But I don't think those bullets did a damned thing."

"That paneling must be a foot thick," Martina said, putting her plane into a turn.

"Rockets this time?" Moondog asked.

"Yeah," Martina said, rolling out and pointing her nose back to the space station.

"Oh, shit, we got trouble," Moondog said.

Martina watched in disbelief as one of the small silver craft detached from the station and headed straight for the Hellcats. A second quickly followed.

"Damn, those guys are fast," Martina said.

"They may be quick to get in those things," Moondog said, "but that doesn't mean they're quick when it comes to flying them. Let's blast these bastards."

"Use your bullets first," Martina said. "Save your rockets for the station itself."

The two American pilots aimed their planes back

toward the space station. Eight small silver fighters were dashing for the Hellcats. The craft were much smaller than the space planes. Each held two rockets beneath their stubby wings.

Panther watched as the fighters raced forward. She had been in many aerial battles, but this was entirely different. In the vacuum of space the laws of aerodynamics no longer applied. The rules that governed dogfights back on Earth were null and void outside the atmosphere. All that mattered was the space plane's design. The placement and number of the thrusters were the sole determining factors in the maneuverability of the aircraft. If the Hellcats' thrusters were poorly placed, the little spacecraft would fly circles around them, destroying the American planes before they could even get a shot off.

"They aren't very well armed, are they?" Moondog said.

"Two missiles per plane," Panther said. "I don't see any guns."

"I don't remember them firing guns at us before," Moondog agreed.

"But it doesn't mean they don't have any," Panther said. "And if they can outturn us, it doesn't matter."

One well-placed shot was all it would take to destroy the Hellcats despite their larger size. If the life support system was knocked out, the plane's pilot would be killed immediately. If the craft was damaged in any other way, it might prevent the Hellcat from reentering, leaving the pilot stranded in space to asphyxiate when the plane's onboard oxygen ran out.

Panther kept her guns selected. She also armed her chaff. Satellites did not produce heat, so the rockets on the enemy craft had to be radar-guided. Along with their Gatling guns, the Hellcats were capable of carrying up to eight missiles. For this particular mission, all were rocket-propelled, radar-guided missiles, which had been modified to function in space as they did in the atmosphere.

"Let's take these fuckers out," Panther said.

She aimed her gun sight on the lead spacecraft and squeezed the trigger. A hail of bullets spat forward, racing toward the little silver craft. They slammed into the nose of the spacecraft, chewing up the front of the fuselage.

Nothing seemed to happen. The spacecraft continued to race forward. Panther pulled her spacecraft upward, nosing the Hellcat above the enemy planes. The g-forces from the sharp maneuver shoved her back down into her seat. She felt a whimper of pain from her ribs. She quickly rolled the Hellcat over so that she was looking down on the silver craft. Moondog held her place on Panther's wing, easily copying the maneuver.

The little spacecraft passed quickly beneath the two large American planes. Panther pulled back on the stick to complete the second half of the loop. Pain again shot through her chest as the g-forces hit her. The Hellcat dropped into position behind the enemy spacecraft so that she was looking directly at their tails. The eight craft immediately scattered, racing off in different directions.

"I don't think that did anything," Panther said, a hint of frustration in her voice.

"Doesn't look like it," Moondog agreed.

"I had to have hit that fucker," she cursed. "How thick is their armament?"

"Must be pretty fucking thick."

Seven of the eight fighters turned around rapidly, all diving back toward the Hellcats. The eighth spacecraft continued forward, flying further away from the space station. The little silver craft seemed to be drifting off aimlessly.

Panther swung her tail to the left, setting her sights on the fighter to the far right. She depressed the trigger, unleashing a hail of bullets at the silver craft. The ship broke off from the others, weaving away in an attempt to avoid the fire. The bullets impacted the rear fuselage. The fighter immediately stopped jinking.

The missile warning tone sounded in Panther's ear. A flash of fire ignited under the wing of the spacecraft in the middle. The rocket under the craft's left wing dropped down, racing at her plane. She instinctively pulled back on the stick, reversing her course. She gasped as the g-forces returned. Fire raced through her chest.

Ignoring the pain, she hit the button to disperse her chaff. The Hellcat released a shower of silver behind it. Panther continued to pull through, nosing down and diving away from the fight. The missile collided with the chaff, exploding harmlessly.

Three of the fighters immediately broke off, diving after Panther. The others remained in position, heading straight for Moondog's Hellcat. The Navy pilot nudged her throttles forward, racing toward the nearest spacecraft. She opened fire with her cannons as she flew over the top of the plane, riddling it with bullet holes from nose to tail.

Dashing past the enemy fighters, she caught sight of the one stray plane, still flying away from the space station. She put the Hellcat in a large arc, flipping over as she flew above the little spacecraft. Through the canopy she could see the pilot slumped over the controls, motionless.

"The bullets are working, Panther," she called as she turned back to face the remaining spacecraft. "The first guy you shot is dead. They just aren't falling out of the sky like we're used to."

On Earth, significant damage to an airplane

would hamper its ability to stay airborne, causing the plane to tumble to the ground. But wings were not necessary to fly in space. Any object would remain suspended in place no matter how bad the damage.

Panther glanced behind her to see three enemy fighters diving at her. Gritting her teeth, she smashed the stick to the side, jinking to the left and right. Pain shot through her chest as the g-forces hit her. She turned her head back. The three planes remained in position.

Panther shoved her throttles forward. Fire spouted from the Hellcat's tailpipe as the space fighter leapt away from the enemy spacecraft. Tensing the muscles in her legs and stomach, Panther pulled back sharply on the stick, flipping the Hellcat over in a sharp course reversal. The g-forces hit her, pushing her roughly into her seat. Fire danced through her chest again.

She eased the pressure off the stick as the Hellcat came over the top. Seeing the space plane racing for them, two of the fighters immediately broke off, turning away from Panther's plane. The craft in the middle remained in position, diving toward her.

She took aim at the fighter as it dove for her, squeezing the trigger. The enemy craft immediately jinked away, dodging her fire. Panther followed as the plane twisted away, training her fire on its tail. A burst of fire hit the little craft, pelting its tail with bullets.

Moondog turned back to the space station. Two of the small silver craft were racing at her Hellcat. The missile tone sounded loudly in her ear. A flash of fire filled the sky as the fighter on her left loosed one of its missiles. The projectile twisted toward her plane, fire spouting from its tail.

Moondog immediately pulled her nose up and tapped her thrusters. The Hellcat shot upward. She hit her chaff and dove back at the two small craft. The missile flew past the chaff, keeping its nose fixed on the Hellcat.

Seeing the missile gaining on her tail, Moondog nosed over. She pointed her plane directly toward the nearest enemy fighter. The little plane began to jink wildly, trying to avoid her. She kept her nose aimed directly at the craft. Try as it might, the little plane could not shake her.

Moondog continued to dive toward the silver plane, closing on it rapidly. She looked back. The missile was gaining on her. She turned her head back to the fighter ahead of her. The little craft filled her cockpit window. Seconds away from impact, she pulled her nose up, racing directly over the top of the little plane. Once clear of the tail, she immediately pointed her nose down, dashing away in the opposite direction.

The missile that had been on her tail slammed into the silver craft, which exploded in a brilliant ball of flames. The bright explosion was blinding in the blackness of space. Bits of shrapnel flew off in all directions.

The two enemy fighters turned back in toward Panther, diving at her from either side. She rolled the plane to the right, aiming her nose at the aircraft closest to her and firing. The bullets ripped through the craft, dotting the fuselage with holes from nose to tail.

The missile warning sounded loudly in Panther's ears. She saw a bright flash of flame as the remaining space fighter fired its last missile. The large projectile raced toward the Hellcat. Panther rapidly twisted away from the missile. She released another round of chaff, quickly diving away from the missile. She gritted her teeth against the pain that shot through her chest as the g-forces hit her.

She looped back toward the remaining spacecraft. Behind her the missile impacted with the chaff, lighting up the sky in a brilliant fireball. For a moment Panther was blinded by the light. Instinctively, she rolled away, pulling the Hellcat away from the fireball.

The flames immediately died out. Panther pointed her nose back to where she had last seen the enemy craft. The little silver ship had vanished. Panther quickly scanned the sky, looking for it.

After a moment, she caught sight of the enemy fighter. It was racing back to the space station, its armament spent. Panther let it go. With its missiles gone, it was no longer a threat. She turned her plane back toward the battle. Behind her the little spacecraft docked with the station.

Panther twisted her head around, looking for Moondog's Hellcat and catching sight of it almost immediately. The large space plane was hard to miss. She was racing toward the last space fighter, guns blazing. The silver craft jinked and dodged in a vain effort to escape the Navy pilot's fire. It was no use. Moondog held her position closely on his six.

In a final attempt to defend himself, the small craft suddenly reversed course, pointing his nose directly at the large fighter, and prepared to fire. Moondog heard a loud tone in her ears as his missiles locked on her plane.

She held her course and dove toward the little fighter, depressing her trigger as she did. The Hellcat swept over the enemy craft, raking it from nose to tail with bullets. Immediately the missile warning in Moondog's ears died. The ship remained still, flying away from her into the oblivion of space.

Confident her enemy was dead, Moondog pointed her plane back toward Panther's. Dodging a few of the dead fighters, she repositioned her Hellcat on the Air

Force pilot's wing.

Panther watched as Moondog rejoined her. She surveyed the sky. Several of the enemy fighters were still in sight. All hung motionless in the blackness of space, scattered about with their noses pointed at odd angles, as if they had been tossed haphazardly into the sky.

"I think we got all of them," Moondog said.

"Not all," Panther said. "One ran out of missiles and went back to the space station."

"We'd better get rid of that thing before he can get any more ammo," Moondog said.

"Right," Panther said. "Missiles this time."

The two Hellcats turned around, aiming for the large mass of metal floating in the sky a few thousand feet away. Panther switched her armament to missiles and aimed for the station. Nothing happened.

"I'm not getting a lock," she said. "Are you?"

"Not on the station," Moondog said. "My missiles want to take out that satellite at about two o'clock. Are we within range?"

"Yeah," Panther said. "They shouldn't have any problem locking onto that huge thing."

"It doesn't show up on the radar scope either," Moondog said.

"They must have made it out of radar-absorbing material," Panther said. "We'll have to shoot blind and hope they hit. Follow my lead."

She pointed the nose of her Hellcat at the large space station, flying directly toward it. Keeping her missiles selected, she depressed the trigger, firing all eight in rapid succession. Beside her, Moondog released all of her missiles. Bright trails of red fire streaked through the sky as the missiles raced toward their target.

Panther immediately pulled up in a large arc, looping over and away from the space station. She rolled through and pointed her nose back toward the large structure. She tapped her throttles into reverse, holding the Hellcat in position at a distance. Moondog stayed in place on her wing.

The barrage of missiles raced toward the station. Small blossoms of fire appeared along the structure, sparking and dying rapidly in the vacuum of space. Several hit the station directly, while others collided with the outer frame. A few of the missiles flew wide, missing entirely, only to explode beyond the station. In a moment everything was still.

"Let's check it out," Martina said.

She flicked on her gun camera and dove toward the station. A few hundred feet away she pulled up and raced along the side. She could see several large holes in the side of the station. The metal structure was bent and blackened in several places. However, human figures still appeared in the windows, moving about. The remaining fighter was docked to the station, unharmed. Despite the damage, the station had not depressurized.

"That thing is thrashed, but it isn't dead," Moondog said. The Navy pilot was still holding position on Martina's wing.

"I know. They must have designed it to be capable of surviving an ASAT attack."

"Fuck," Moondog said.

"I don't think it will be able to take another beating like that," Martina said. "C'mon, let's get the hell out of Dodge."

She pulled away from the station, positioning herself between it and Earth. She shut off the camera and hit a few buttons on the computer, calling up the next reentry window. After a moment the information she needed flashed on the screen.

"We've got a reentry window in a few minutes that will put us back at Edwards," she said. "The course looks clear. I'll call the burn."

She punched a button on her radio, switching frequencies so that she could talk to Edwards through a satellite relay.

"Edwards Control, Hellcat one," she said

"Go ahead, Hellcat," a voice responded.

"Target acquired but not destroyed. We are returning. ETA thirty minutes."

"Roger, Hellcat," Edwards responded.

Martina switched her radio frequency again. Keeping one eye on the space station, she ran through the procedures for reentry. As the clock wound down, she flipped the Hellcat over into the correct position. Moondog moved her own plane into a wider formation on Martina's right wing and put her Hellcat into the same attitude.

"Initiate burn in 3... 2... 1... Mark," Martina called.

She fired her engines. The sensation of gravity returned immediately. Beside her, she could see flames shooting from the burner cans of the second Hellcat. Slowly the two planes began to slip back toward Earth, diving away from the space station.

"Cut engines in 3... 2... 1... Mark," Martina ordered, switching off her own engines. She saw Moondog's rockets shut off. The two planes continued to slide downward, racing back into Earth's atmosphere.

Out in front of her Hellcat, a large shock became visible. The edges of the wings started to glow. The red ion haze began to creep up along the Hellcat's nose. Martina watched it lick along the metal surface, slowly tracing its way upward, covering the plane's nose and slowly engulfing the canopy, until she was completely surrounded by a red glow.

She had seen the haze in the space shuttle, but the sheer size of that craft had kept her somewhat distant from it. However, the Hellcat was small, with almost no distance between Martina and the shock created by reentry. Now, she was totally immersed in the ions. She leaned back, watching in complete awe as the plasma flow danced across the cockpit.

Through the haze she could see the large shock covering Moondog's plane. The red haze almost covered her cockpit. It wrapped around the tips of her wings and tail. It seemed as if the plane was almost completely engulfed.

Slowly the ion haze began to recede, moving back down the canopy and the nose until it vanished entirely. Far beneath the two planes stretched the vast blue of the Pacific Ocean. Above, the sky was once again deep blue. A backward glance showed that Moondog had once again dropped into a perfect formation off her wing.

Panther switched the Hellcat back into jet mode but did not bother to restart her engines. She was moving far too quickly to need them. Instead she set her course on an easy downward glide, headed directly toward Edwards Air Force Base. She watched as her altitude bled off and her speed dropped, slowing from twenty times the speed of sound, to fifteen, and then to ten.

The Hellcat had just dropped below Mach five when the California coast slid into view. Reaching forty thousand feet, Martina leveled out. She pulled her nose up, allowing herself to slow even more. As she slipped over land, she called up her flight path on the computer. She had enough airspeed and altitude to glide to Edwards if she needed to.

"Let's see if the engines will restart like they're supposed to," she said to Moondog.

The Hellcats were capable of making a power-off landing. However, having the engines running gave Martina much more control over the plane. Flying under power also gave her the ability to go around on landing if she needed to.

Quickly, she ran through the Hellcat's air start procedures. The Hellcat's airspeed continued to bleed off. As she dropped below Mach one, she hit the switch to restart her left engine. She felt a slight kick as the engine purred to life. The plane yawed to the right. Martina stepped on the rudder pedal to counter the yaw. All her engine's instruments were in the green. She quickly fired up the right engine. It started cleanly. The plane jumped forward again. She eased her foot off the rudder as the yaw vanished.

"I've got a good restart," she said.

"Both my engines are on and everything's in the green," Moondog said.

In the distance Martina saw Edwards' runway. The Hellcats dashed over the mountains to the west of the air base. Clearing the last ridge, Martina pushed her nose down and chopped her throttles back, diving almost directly toward the ground. Moondog easily copied the maneuver.

Keeping an eye out for traffic on her radar screen, she watched as the earth rushed up to meet her. The brown Mojave Desert filled her view. Only a thousand feet from the ground, she pulled back on the stick, leveling out just above the sand. Panther pointed her nose toward Edwards' strip. Moondog remained in position on her wing.

"Edwards, Hellcat one, twoship, fifteen miles west at four thousand feet inbound for full stop," she said into the radio.

"Enter right base runway two two right, Hellcat, and you have permission to land. Welcome home," the air traffic controller responded.

As the long black runway grew larger, Martina lowered her landing gear. She maneuvered her plane into position, lining up with the runway as she descended. Crossing the threshold, she sailed easily over the asphalt, pulling her nose up as she did. Her rear wheels touched gently, and she gracefully lowered her nose again, placing the front gear on the runway. The Hellcat slid smoothly to a stop at the end of the runway. Moondog landed beside her. Exiting the runway, the two planes taxied back to the ramp, stopping in front of the hangar that housed them. The Hellcats' two crew chiefs were waiting on the ramp. They marshaled the planes into their parking spots.

Martina set the brake and ran through the shutdown procedures, powering down the engines and all the other systems. Then she unhooked her oxygen mask and radio. She pulled off her helmet. A blast of warm air hit her as she raised the canopy. Martina swung her legs out of the cockpit and easily dropped the short distance to the ground.

She caught sight of Brigadier General Peters and Durant standing at the edge of the tarmac. Several ground crew members were moving to pull the planes back into the hangar. Martina began to walk toward Peters and Durant. A second later Moondog joined her. The Navy pilot was grinning broadly.

"Welcome back to Earth, ladies," Peters said as the two women approached. "Was your mission successful?"

"We found the space station," Martina said. "Whoever built that thing was expecting an attack. We blasted it with everything we had, but we couldn't completely destroy it. However, we think we damaged it pretty badly. And we took out all but one of their fighters."

"One more run and that thing will be nothing more than space debris," Moondog said. Martina nodded in assent.

"Good," Peters said. "The President wants an

official report as soon as possible. You will be debriefed while the ground crew makes sure the planes are safe to fly again. Let's get to a more secure location." He motioned to his car, waiting on the side of the tarmac.

"Yes, sir," Martina said. She flashed a smile at Durant.

"I like your plane," she said as she sauntered past. Moondog suppressed a laugh.

# ~ **14** ~

"It will take the technicians the rest of the day to finish inspecting the airplanes," Peters said as the debriefing concluded, "so you two ladies are free until tomorrow. Be back here at oh-four-hundred." The scraping of chairs filled the room as everyone stood.

"I thought they were supposed to be able to transition back and forth with minimal servicing," Moondog said.

"They are," Durant said. "However, we want to make sure they can before we try it. That's why we're inspecting them now. We don't want them to burn up on the second reentry."

"Right," Moondog said. "Let's get out of here," she said to Panther.

"I can give you two a ride back to where you're staying," Durant said as Martina put her hand on the door.

The two pilots glanced at each other. Martina shrugged her shoulders. Moondog arched her eyebrows in a way that suggested she knew there was more behind his offer.

"I guess so," Martina said.

"Beats walking," Moondog said. "It's hot out there."

"Follow me, then," Durant said with a smile. "I'm right outside."

The two pilots followed him from the room and

down the hall. As they walked through the door, Moondog nudged Panther in her left ribs and grinned broadly.

"Shut up," Martina whispered, elbowing her back. Moondog only smiled more widely.

The three stepped outside into the bright California sunlight. Durant led the way across the small parking lot and stopped by a red Ford Mustang GT convertible, sitting with the top down. Moondog's eyes lit up as she caught sight of the car.

"Not bad," she said, running her eyes along the vehicle. "I have one like it at home, except it's blue. And it's got about twice the horsepower."

"Can I drive?" Martina asked

A look of surprise crossed Durant's face. "You get to fly those planes," he said. "Let me have a little bit of fun."

Martina snapped her fingers in disappointment and flashed Moondog a look that said "drat." The Navy pilot laughed and jumped into the back, ignoring the doors. Martina slid into the front seat beside Durant. The engine sparked to life with a roar and settled into an even rumble, which made Moondog smile again.

"I do like those planes," Martina said as Durant backed out of his parking spot and turned onto the road.

"That was an incredible flight," Moondog agreed, reclining in the back with her arms stretched across the top of the seat.

"Doesn't the whole combat thing freak you out a little?" Durant asked, making a left onto another road.

"Not when you've got as many combat hours as we do," Martina said.

"When you're as good as we are, it's the other guy who gets scared," Moondog said. "Nobody can outfly the world's greatest pilots."

Martina laughed.

"Even if you're outnumbered?" Durant asked.

"We're always outnumbered," Moondog said. "Nobody's stupid enough to go one-on-one with us."

"Fighter pilots neither know, nor will they ever admit to knowing, fear," Martina explained as Durant pulled into the parking lot by the visiting officers' quarters and killed the engine.

"Thanks for the lift," Moondog said, jumping from the car without bothering to wait for a door to open.

"Can I walk you to your room?" Durant asked, turning to face Martina.

"I'll catch you two later," Moondog said, giving Martina a smug grin. Panther shot her an icy glare. The Navy pilot turned and walked toward the building.

"I guess so," Martina said, opening the door and stepping out of the car.

Durant followed her, walking beside her so that their shoulders were almost touching.

"I really do like those airplanes. I know I've said it already, but I just can't get over them," Martina said as she pushed the door open and stepped into the air-conditioned hallway. The thrill of flying, of combat, of racing along the edge of space at twenty times the speed of sound, and of speeding across the desert sands was burning inside her. The adrenaline was still pulsing through her veins, as were the sensation of flying in the clear blue sky and the stark beauty of the vacuum of space. Martina Redrick felt as if she had just conquered the world.

"I know," Durant said as they stopped outside her room.

"I was wondering," he said, leaning up against the wall and looking at Martina. "Could I buy you lunch over at the O-club?"

"I guess so," Martina said, turning to face him. "Let me get out of this flight suit and get a shower first. Meet me back here at noon."

"Okay," Durant said. He stepped forward, put his hands on Martina's waist, and pulled her to him. He bent his head down slightly, kissing her. Martina wrapped her arms around his neck and moved her body up against his, tracing her tongue along his lips.

Reluctantly, he released her and stepped back.

"I'll see you at twelve, then," he said, turning and walking back toward the exit.

Martina turned to her own door. Her head was spinning. She could remember a time when her dream of becoming an astronaut had seemed to be only a fantastic hope that she never would truly realize. Now, not only had she piloted the space shuttle, but she was flying an amazingly secret fighter with spectacular capabilities. She could not shake off the incredible thrill the day's flight had given her. Panther was a born fighter pilot. She had always been happiest in the cockpit of a plane. And the Hellcat was the most amazing plane she had ever flown.

Martina never even felt the needle pierce her skin as she reached inside the pocket of her flight suit and pulled out the card to open her door. A sudden wave of vertigo rolled over her as she lifted the key. Puzzled, she shook her head, trying to clear it.

She raised her key again and moved to slide it into the door to unlock it. The card slid to the side, completely missing the slot. Martina fell forward, grabbing the doorframe as she tried to shake off the strange dizziness that had suddenly overcome her.

It was no use. The entire world was spinning, swirling faster and faster. All Martina could do was cling to the wall, gasping for breath. Colors began to run together as everything blurred into one. Slowly the world began to fade to gray. The edges of her vision began to darken as blackness crept up, until it consumed her entirely.

Martina slumped slowly to the floor and lay motionless.

✳          ✳          ✳

Moondog stuck her key card in the slot above her door handle and pulled it out. After a moment, a small green light blinked to life. The Navy pilot opened the door and stepped inside, standing in the kitchen of the suite her new rank afforded her. While the sudden promotion had caught Moondog off guard, she had not found it difficult to adjust to her position. In the military world, a higher grade meant greater benefits and fewer people who could boss you around. Moondog smiled at the thought as she unzipped her flight suit halfway and shrugged the sleeves off so that it hung loosely around her waist.

She scanned the room. The sun was slanting through the windows in the next room, faintly spilling into the area where Moondog stood. Most of the little kitchen was dim. She stepped inside, letting the door shut behind her. She reached to the right and flicked the light switch up. Nothing happened.

Puzzled, Moondog pushed the switch back down and then up again. The room remained dark. She crossed the kitchen in two quick steps and hit the bedroom light switch. That light failed to come on as well.

*Maybe the power went out,* she thought. Her eyes immediately flashed over to the digital clock sitting on the table beside her bed. The red diodes were clearly displaying the correct time. The power was still on.

*What the fuck...?* Moondog thought, spinning on her heels. Something was definitely wrong.

Her eyes caught a flicker of motion in the dim light. She turned her head to the side, to see a small man with Asian features standing beside the wall just inside her bedroom. He lunged for her, clutching a small hypodermic needle in one hand.

Moondog immediately jumped backward, grabbing the man's wrist as she did. The man stopped in his tracks but continued to strain toward her, moving the point of the needle toward her neck despite the resistance from her arm.

Moondog flashed him a smile.

"I don't think so, fuckface," she said, grabbing his hand with her free hand and shoving his palm toward the floor behind him. Moondog felt his arm become limp as his wrist bones snapped with an audible crack. The needle fell from his grasp as he lost the ability to control his fingers. Moondog shoved him to the floor. She stepped on the needle, easily breaking the syringe in half. Several drops of clear liquid fell into the carpet.

"You ain't sticking me with anything," she said.

Suddenly, something collided the side of her face. Caught off guard, Moondog lost her balance and toppled over. She hit the ground and somersaulted backward, quickly jumping to her feet. A second, slightly larger Asian was standing in front of her, fists raised. Beside him, the man with the broken arm was climbing to his feet, anger glaring in his eyes.

The larger man stepped forward, swinging his right fist in a roundhouse punch aimed directly at the side of Moondog's head. The Navy pilot quickly raised her left arm, blocking the blow before it connected with her temple.

She moved into him, driving her fist directly into his nose. Her hand came away covered in blood as red began to pour down the man's face. He reached forward angrily, grabbing Moondog by the collar of her t-shirt and throwing her into the far wall before she could react.

Moondog crashed into the bedside table, landing in a sitting position. The table lamp toppled forward, bouncing off her right shoulder before shattering on the floor and covering the carpet with a thousand shards of glass and ceramic.

Moondog raised her head to see the man with the broken arm standing over her. She attempted to pick herself up off the floor, only to have his boot slam into the left side of her head, knocking her down. She stuck out her hands, feeling the shattered tile digging into her palms as she caught herself from falling flat on her face.

An instant later she felt the man's foot strike into her stomach. Moondog's arms gave way, and she fell face forward to the floor, doubling over to try to protect herself.

The second man stepped forward and grabbed her by the back of her collar, dragging her across the broken pieces of the lamp. She could feel the shards ripping into her flight suit and biting into her skin. A sharp pain cut into her right thigh, and another traced its way diagonally across her stomach.

The man pulled her back to her feet. Moondog glanced down. Several dozen holes dotted her black t-shirt, which was spotted with blood in almost as many places. A long, shallow cut ran across her midsection. A large piece of what had once been a light bulb was embedded in her right leg, blood seeping onto her flight suit.

The man smiled as he raised his fist again. Moondog immediately brought her left knee up, catching him squarely in the groin. He howled in pain and doubled over. Moondog raised her other leg, smashing her foot directly into the side of his head. The man crashed backward, falling into a dresser. The crackling of wood filled the room as it broke apart beneath his weight.

Moondog turned back to the smaller man just as he swung his good fist her right eye, twisting her head to the side. She turned her head back toward him, swinging her left fist into his stomach. The man stepped backward, bending forward slightly with a gasp.

A fist collided with the side of Moondog's head, hurling her into the wall. She spun around, back to the wall, to see the larger man advancing toward her. He wrapped his fingers around her neck and squeezed.

Gasping for breath, Moondog pressed her fingers into his throat. The man coughed but did not release his grip. She grabbed onto his hands, attempting to pry his fingers from her neck as the edges of her vision began to darken. He held firm.

Suddenly, everything went black. Moondog's eyes shut, and she crashed to the floor.

# ~ 15 ~

David Webster smiled as he sat down behind his desk in the Oval Office. The sun was shining brightly over the rose garden and the green lawns of the White House beyond. Above, the sky was a cloudless blue. The city was sure to heat up as the late summer day progressed, but for now the temperature was only moderate.

While the weather was pleasant, it had absolutely nothing to do with the President's cheerful mood. His happiness came from the fact that it appeared that the major crisis of his administration, the mysterious disappearance of America's military satellites, was over.

The Hellcat flight the day before had been incredibly successful. Not only had the two planes functioned exactly as intended, they had managed to almost completely destroy the foreign space station, and severely hampered its ability to function. Only two satellites had been lost since the Hellcats landed, a drastic drop from the rate before the mission of one per hour.

And while the space station was still operating, it would soon be destroyed. The Hellcats were already scheduled to be in flight, and in less than an hour the entire base would be completely obliterated. Webster's only concern would be getting the satellite network back online.

His speakerphone buzzed, interrupting his reverie.

"General Peters is calling for you, sir," his secretary said, sounding bored.

"Put him through," Webster said, picking up the phone. "Good morning, Scott. They back already?"

"No, sir," Peters said. "They haven't even taken off."

"What do you mean?" Webster asked, startled. "Why not?"

"Redrick and Ansetti have disappeared, sir," Peters said. "We can't find them anywhere."

"Do you have any idea why?" Webster asked, shocked.

"We think they've been kidnapped, sir," Peters said.

"Kidnapped!"

"Yes, sir," Peters said. "Redrick vanished without a trace, but Ansetti's visiting officers' quarters were nearly destroyed."

"As if there was a fight?" Webster asked.

"That's exactly what we think happened, sir," Peters said. "We found several spots of blood, which we identified as the commander's. There was also a broken hypodermic with traces of a knockout drug inside. Most likely whoever attacked her tried to stick her with the needle, but she fought back."

"What about Redrick?"

"Absolutely nothing, sir," Peters said. "My investigators over here think it's fairly safe to assume that whoever attacked Ansetti was after her too, only they managed to inject her before she saw them. I highly doubt she would just leave on her own."

"There's no way, General," Webster said confidently. "I've seen her file. She'd never do something like that."

"I couldn't agree with you more, sir," Peters said.

"Do you have any leads?" the President asked.

"None, sir."

"We've got to find those two, Scott," Webster said.

"I've already put every man my security police and OSI can spare on the case, sir, and alerted the local police, but I doubt much will come of it," Peter said. "Whoever has our pilots has probably already smuggled them out of the country."

"Mexico is only a few hours' drive away," Webster said, grimly. "I'll see what the CIA can do. Inform me as soon as you know anything."

"Absolutely, sir."

"I suppose we'll have to wait to get those planes airborne again," Webster sighed.

"They're useless without the pilots, sir," Peters said. "Unless you want me to train some new people on them."

"I want as few people as possible involved with those planes," Webster said. "We'll try to find Redrick and Ansetti first."

"Yes, sir."

"All right. Good hunting, Scott," Webster said, putting the phone down.

The President punched a button on his speakerphone. "Sherri, get the Director of Central Intelligence over here now," he growled.

"Yes, sir," she replied in her nasal voice, sounding as bored as ever.

Webster planted his elbows against the hardwood surface of his desk and rested his chin against his fists. Even the bright sunlight outside could not break through the dark cloud that had suddenly shrouded the President's day.

∗          ∗          ∗

The first thing she became aware of was the cold. It permeated everything, chilling her from her skin to her bones. Instinctively she curled herself into a tight ball, bringing her knees to her chest in an attempt to warm herself. But she could not shake off the icy feeling deep inside her.

The next thing she felt was the ground beneath her. It was hard and rough, and colder than the air. She could feel the stone beneath the skin on her face. It pressed uncomfortably against her body, digging into her. She was lying on her side, with her legs bent to her body and her arms across her chest. Her limbs felt strangely stiff.

Slowly Martina opened her eyes. Gray stone filled her vision, stretching in all directions. The world around her was strangely blurry. She blinked her eyes and pushed herself up with one arm. Her muscles responded slowly, with an aching stiffness.

Her vision began to resolve itself, revealing a set of vertical bars directly in front of her. Martina pushed herself into a sitting position and turned her head to the side. The other three walls and the ceiling above her were all made of the same rough-hewn rock as the floor.

She was sitting in the center of a six-by-six-foot cell, trapped. For a moment Panther simply remained motionless, staring at the black iron bars in front of her, trying to fathom where she was and how she had come to be there. The interior of the cell revealed no answers.

Martina drew her legs up beneath her and stood slowly, ignoring the protests from her sore muscles. She stumbled the two steps to the door and wrapped her hands along the bars, shaking them. The iron door refused to move.

Martina sighed and pressed her face up between the metal. She gazed to the left and right. A long, dark hall, cut from the same stone, stretched in both directions. The corridor was completely empty. Perplexed, Martina sank back to the ground.

She peered forward, noticing for the first time a

second cell directly across from the one that caged her. Beyond the vertical bars, the thin figure of a woman with shoulder-length hair was visible. She lay on her side with her back to Martina. Her flight suit had been stripped off above her waist, revealing a black t-shirt.

"Moondog!" Martina whispered. "Moondog, wake up!"

The Navy pilot groaned and rolled over slowly, sitting up. Panther nearly gasped in surprise as her friend turned toward her. Moondog's face was bruised. Flecks of dried blood surrounded her mouth and nose. A black ring encircled her right eye, which was swollen shut.

Her t-shirt was covered in small holes, several of which revealed minor cuts. A long tear ran across her stomach, revealing a bright red gash through her white skin. A large, dark red spot was visible on her upper thigh.

"Where the hell are we?" she asked groggily, blinking her good eye.

"I have no idea," Martina replied. "Last thing I knew I was at Edwards, then I woke up here. What the hell happened to you?"

"Two thugs were waiting in my VOQ when I got back," Moondog said evenly. "They jumped me."

She paused, reaching down and inspecting her right thigh.

"Think they would have had the decency to get rid of that," she muttered, wrapping her fingers around the shard of glass. A flash of pain registered across her face as she pulled it free. Moondog immediately pressed the sleeve of her flight suit against her leg to stem the flow of blood that gushed from the cut. She held up the bloody piece of glass with her free hand. It was an inch wide and about three inches long.

"That might be useful," she said, sticking it in her pocket.

"Damn," Martina said.

Moondog pulled off her shirt and began to trace her fingers along the other cuts on her skin.

"What are you doing?" Martina said.

"Looking for anything else stuck in me," Moondog said, pulling a tiny piece of ceramic from one cut.

"How did you manage that?" Martina asked.

"They dragged me through the stuff," Moondog said as she removed a second small shard of glass.

"So that's why you're all cut up," Martina said.

"Yeah," Moondog said, tracing her fingers across the long cut on her stomach. She dug a small piece of ceramic from a nick on her lower ribs, then pulled her shirt back on.

"So now what?" she asked.

"We get out of here," Martina said.

"Do you have any idea how to do that?" Moondog asked, giving her a skeptical look.

"No."

"You got your pocketknife?"

"No," Martina said. "It was in my flight bag, with my .45."

"So much for unscrewing the hinges," Moondog muttered.

"We've got your piece of glass, and I have a pen," Martina said. "If they let us out of here, we can take them down, steal a couple guns, and make a run for it."

"If they don't tie us up, or put guns to our heads," Moondog said. "And what the hell are we going to do when we get free? We have no idea where we are."

"We get out of this building, and then figure it out," Martina said.

"Panther, we could be anywhere in the world. There might not be anywhere we could go," Moondog said.

"What do you mean?"

"Think about it. We could be in downtown Beijing. You're almost six feet tall. There's no way in hell you could blend into a crowd of Asians. And what if we're in some fundamentalist Muslim nation? A couple of women in flight suits? We couldn't hide."

"We'll just have to deal with it," Martina replied. "We've got to get out of here."

"Guess we have no choice," Moondog sighed in agreement. "I'm not going to die in some fucking prison cell."

"It's the best option we have," Martina said.

"And I thought life was going to slow down when I got into NASA," Moondog muttered, lying down on her back with her hands behind her head. "This is more action than I've ever seen."

"I thought you flew in combat," Martina said.

"Many, many times," Moondog replied. "But no one ever kidnapped me or jumped me when I was on the carrier. Got in a few bar fights on shore, though."

Martina laughed. Suddenly, she stiffened. "Someone's coming," she whispered.

Moondog sat up. She could hear the faint ring of footsteps growing louder.

"You want to jump as soon as they open the door?" she whispered.

"No, they'll expect that. Wait till they bring us back," Martina whispered back. "Besides, I want to see where they take us. We might be able to learn a thing or two."

Moondog nodded and turned to inspect her right leg again. The flow of blood had slowed to a trickle. She turned her head back toward the hall. The two pilots waited in silence as the intruders approached.

A moment later four guards appeared, walking slowly down the hall. All were short, with close-cropped hair and Asian features. They wore the same unadorned military uniform and carried matching pistols, holstered at their sides.

The small group stopped in front of the pilots' cells. The lead man walked to where Moondog was caged and stuck a key in the lock, opening the door. Two of the men behind him stepped inside, grabbed the Navy pilot by her arms, and dragged her into the hall.

The man with the keys walked across the hall and opened the door of Martina's cell. He hooked the keys back on his belt as the fourth man stepped into the small room and pulled Martina to her feet. A small flicker of pain danced through her ribs as he hauled her up.

The first guard grabbed Martina's other arm, and they shoved her forward, leading her down the hall. The two other men followed, almost dragging Moondog behind them. The stiffness from the gash in her right thigh only added to that of inactivity, making it almost impossible for Moondog to use her leg. She limped behind Martina as the guards pulled her forward.

Martina kept her head up, watching her path. She was looking for anything that might be a way out, or even a useful place to overpower the guards. Neither had a very tight hold on her. She knew she could easily free herself from their grip if she chose to. But for the moment curiosity got the better of her, and she let the men take her forward.

The guards took them up a long flight of stairs into well-lit halls of cut, polished stone. They wound through the corridors, crossing other halls where men and women in uniform moved about, occasionally stopping to stare at the Americans as they moved through.

Finally, the small group approached two large

black-painted metal doors cut into the stone, which the guards pushed open. They led the prisoners inside and stopped a few feet from the entrance. The doors closed loudly behind them.

Panther and Moondog found themselves standing on a stone balcony overlooking a vast high-ceilinged room made entirely of the same neatly cut, polished rock. The room was filled with computer consoles, many with operators hunched over them. Still other technicians moved about on the floor. The walls were almost entirely covered with liquid-crystal screens displaying data printouts and thousands of satellite tracks.

A metal railing twenty feet from where the two Americans stood marked the edge of the balcony. A slender Asian woman was half sitting, half leaning where the railing met the wall on the left, surveying the scene around her impassively. Her long black hair was tied back in a high ponytail that fell halfway down her back. She wore knee-high black leather boots with heels that added two inches to her height. Instead of a military uniform, she wore dark blue jeans and a tight-fitting tank top that matched her jade-green eyes.

"There are very few people in this world who can truly appreciate the magnitude of activity that is constantly occurring in space," a voice said.

The pilots turned their heads to the center of the balcony. A short, squat man with dark hair was leaning against the rail, watching the activity below. He also wore a military uniform.

"Millions of objects, ranging in size from that of a simple bolt to something as large as the International Space Station, whizzing around this planet at thousands of miles an hour," he continued, not turning to face the pilots. "And somehow, these things almost never collide. Amazing, isn't it? Almost miraculous.

"Of course," he said, spinning slowly around and fixing his dark eyes on the two women in the back of the room, "having flown in space yourself, you are two of those individuals who can appreciate the scope of what goes on in space. Is it not so, Colonel, Commander?" he said, nodding at Panther and Moondog in turn. Neither replied.

"And being two of those individuals, you understand just how much countries such as America and her allies rely on their satellites. You use satellites for everything—weather, communication, surveillance, even figuring out where you are."

He took a few slow steps forward. "Satellites are America's eyes. And by destroying your satellites, I have blinded you," he said arrogantly.

"Who the hell are you?" Martina demanded suddenly, "and where the fuck are we?"

"I am General Sei Chin, Colonel," he said, "commander of China's military space operations center. You are familiar with America's Cheyenne Mountain?"

"I've heard of it," Martina said, almost sarcastically.

"We serve the same purpose," Chin said, "except our mountain is located where the desert meets the northern Himalayas."

"Sounds charming," Moondog muttered.

"Kinda like C-Springs without the Colorado traffic," Martina said.

Moondog arched an eyebrow at her.

"Flat and dry on one side, mountainous and cold on the other," Martina explained. "But no freeways."

"Gee, who'd have ever thought there wouldn't be freeways in the fucking Himalayas?" Moondog said.

"Shut up," Martina said.

Chin quietly studied the two Americans for a

moment, waiting until they fell silent before continuing.

"We took out America's last two military satellites this morning," he said. "All that remains of your network are those handy global positioning satellites. It is fortunate you did not attack us earlier. Your ships did more damage than I thought possible. And I must say, your flying was excellent. You are both very good pilots."

"How did you know we were the pilots?" Martina said.

"I have my sources," Chin said with a smile, turning to a second, smaller door. A tall, dark-haired man was leaning inside it. Martina's eyes grew wide with shock, only to narrow with anger as she recognized him.

"Fifty million was an offer I couldn't refuse, babe," Bill Durant said, strolling into the center of the balcony. "Never in my entire career would I make that much as an engineer."

Panther simply glared at him, anger broiling in her eyes.

"C'mon, Martina," Durant said, softening his voice. "It doesn't have to be like this, you know. All you have to do is agree to help, and you can have part of it. America is about to fall, and there is nothing you or anyone else can to do to stop it. And when that happens, China will be the world's superpower. You and I will be rich beyond our wildest imaginations. We'd get a huge mansion anywhere you want." He smiled invitingly. "I'd even buy you your own personal fleet of aircraft, every plane you ever dreamed of flying."

Martina's expression softened. "Any planes I asked for?" she said, sauntering slowly up to Durant, hips swinging as she moved.

"Anything and everything," he said, extending his

arms.

"What about a P-51 Mustang?" she said, stopping an inch away from him and staring up into his face, trapping his gaze in her glinting brown eyes. An inviting smile crossed her lips.

"Sure," he said, grinning back.

"I already have one," she said, her face darkening instantly as she drove her knee into Durant's groin.

The tall engineer gasped as he doubled over, covering his crotch with his hands.

"Who the fuck do you think I am that I would sell out the nation I swore an oath to protect at seventeen for a traitor like yourself and a couple million?" she snarled. "I wouldn't do it for all the money in the world."

She swung her fist into the side of Durant's head, her knuckles colliding with his cheek. Stunned, he crashed to the ground.

"Even if America is doomed, I would fight to my last breath to ensure she remains the great, free nation she is today," Martina said, thrusting her boot into Durant's stomach. The engineer reflexively curled into a ball at her feet.

Suddenly, something slammed into the side of Martina's head with enough force to knock her down. In an instant she was lying on the stone. She twisted to see the thin Chinese woman standing over her. The Asian placed the sole of her shoe over Martina's throat and turned to Chin.

"Let her up, Ming," he said.

The woman glared at Martina, then lifted her foot. She looked down at the pilot, flashing a sadistic smile, and tapped her foot against Martina's chest. Martina gasped in pain as a wave of fire raced through her cracked ribs. Reflexively she drew her arms up over her chest, protecting the injured area.

Ming's grin widened for a second. Then she spun

sharply on her heel and walked silently over to the railing. She leaned back against the wall and glowered at the two Americans before turning her attention back to the activity on the floor.

Before Martina could regain her feet the two guards grabbed her arms. Another shower of pain danced across her chest as they pulled her to her feet. Gripping her tightly between them, they led her from the room. The two other guards followed, dragging Moondog between them.

They wound back through the polished stone halls of the mountain, then down the long flight of stairs into the dark underground of rough-hewn rock. The two pilots were thrown unceremoniously into their cells. The guards quickly locked the door and retreated to the more inviting world above.

"Nice going," Moondog said after the soldiers had vanished. The Navy pilot was attempting to massage some life back into her right thigh.

"The son of a bitch pissed me off," Martina muttered gruffly.

"You certainly gave the bastard what he deserved."

"I'll give him a lot more if I ever get my hands on him again," she snarled. "He tries to make love to me one minute, and then sells me out to the Chinese the next. I shoulda punched him the first time I saw him."

"Punched him, fuck, you'da shot him," Moondog said. "You should have, too. Then we wouldn't have to worry about getting out of this place."

"At least we know where we are now," Martina said.

"Yeah, the fucking Himalayas," Moondog muttered. "I think I'd have preferred downtown Beijing."

"There's still a way out," Martina said.

"Yeah, the trick is finding it," Moondog said, wrapping her hands along the bars and pulling herself to her feet.

"Your leg work at all?" Martina said, watching her limp the length of the small cell.

"It's one big fucking cramp," Moondog said. "Once I get it to relax, I should be all right."

"Good," Martina said, stretching out on her back. "I'd hate to have to carry you over the Himalayas."

Moondog laughed, turning to walk the other way. "Think we can stop and summit Everest while we're at it?"

"Anybody ever tell you you're crazy?" Martina asked.

"Not nearly as crazy as you."

"Shut up and fix your damned leg," Martina said. Moondog simply laughed.

# ~ 16 ~

Ming watched as the soldiers dragged the two American pilots away. The tall engineer picked himself off the floor and staggered out of the room without a word. He slunk away like a beaten dog, tail between his legs. The balcony was deserted except for Ming and Chin, who was staring over the rail, watching the technicians at work.

Ming pushed herself off the railing and walked slowly beside it, her heels tapping the rock in a slow, even rhythm. She stopped beside Chin, running her hands up over his shoulders and pressing herself against his back.

"Why are we keeping them alive, Sei?" she whispered in his ear.

"The pilots?" Chin asked, half turning toward her.

"Yes," Ming said, stepping up to the railing. "I see no practical value to it." She idly studied her long fingernails.

"They are useful to me."

"For what?" Ming said, moving closer to him.

"As a source of information."

Ming scoffed. "You can get whatever information you need from that engineer. You certainly paid him enough for it."

"Information on the aircraft he designed, yes." Chin said. "Not on the American military or their strong points. The more information I can gain on exactly how much our destruction of their satellites hurt them, on how quickly they can replace that network and their own home defense systems, the greater chance of success I have."

"You are so naïve sometimes," Ming said, tracing her index finger from his temple to his jaw, "thinking everyone will automatically help you. Those two will not cooperate no matter how much money you offer them. They will never talk."

"I am not naïve, I am confident," Chin said. "Confident that what I cannot charm from them, you will be able to." He wrapped his arm around her waist. Ming's green eyes flashed.

"You have never failed me," Chin said.

"Let me kill them," she said softly, eyes shining.

"Not yet, my dear," Chin said, running his fingers over her lips.

He released her slowly and stepped back, leaning against the rail and studying the activity below. "If they will not cooperate with me, I will give them to you."

"And if they still refuse to talk?" she said.

"Believe me, they will talk."

Ming frowned.

"Don't worry," Chin said. "When they are no longer of use to me, I will give them to you, and you can kill them."

Ming's lips spread wide in a grin and her eyes took on a dark shine.

"But until you are told to do so, they will be kept alive," Chin said sternly.

"Then I will just prolong their suffering," Ming said, smiling.

∗　　　∗　　　∗

"Mr. President, General Peters is calling," Webster's secretary announced over the intercom. As he reached for the button, the President wondered idly if the woman ever found anything in her life interesting. To judge by the sound of her voice, she must be the most bored person in the world.

"Excuse me a moment. This may be important," Webster said to the Secretary of Defense, who was sitting opposite him. "Put him through, Sherri," he said, putting the call on speaker so the Secretary could hear as well.

"Good morning, Scott," he said. "Any news on our missing pilots?"

"We think we've identified the kidnappers, sir," Peters said. "It was the Chinese."

"You have concrete evidence of this?" Webster said.

"Yes, sir," Peters said. "It turns out the Lockheed man on the Hellcat project, Bill Durant, also vanished. We overlooked his disappearance because of the pilots."

"Damn it!" Webster said. "They managed to take the three people who knew the most about the project!"

"It gets worse, sir. That was no accident either," Peters said. "Durant was not kidnapped. He went willingly. And he gave them our pilots."

"My God," Webster said in disbelief. "Are you sure of this?"

"Yes, sir," the general replied. "Durant was staying at an apartment off base. When we discovered he was missing, I sent a couple of my OSI agents over to investigate. An inspection of the apartment revealed that he had not been attacked like Ansetti. He had packed up and left."

"Were there any clues as to where he went?"

"No hard evidence, sir," Peters said. "However, a record of his phone calls showed he had placed several calls to another apartment in town, which was inhabited by four men on Chinese visas. All of them left on the same day our pilots vanished. There was no evidence of their departure at any of the airports or docks. We think they went back to China via Mexico."

"And they took our pilots with them," Webster said.

"I'd put money on it, sir," Peters said.

"Three Americans in China would stand out," the President said. "I'll tell the CIA to have everyone over there keep their eyes wide open. Have your people keep looking for any traces of Durant or those four Chinese. I'll have the FBI send over a few agents to help you."

"Thank you, sir," Peters said.

"Good luck, Scott," Webster said, switching off the speakerphone.

"Let's see what the Chinese have to say about this," the President said, hitting the intercom. "Sherri, put a call through to the President of China. Now."

"Yes, sir," Sherri said, still sounding bored.

"Sir, do you know what time it is in China?" the Secretary of Defense asked, his expression shifting to one of slight surprise.

"I know damned well what time it is in China," Webster said, "and I don't care if I wake the son of a bitch up. I want that bastard to know how deadly serious I am about this."

The Secretary of Defense simply nodded.

"He's on the line, sir," Sherri announced. Again Webster placed the call on speaker.

"President Xiang," Webster said, "this is David Webster."

"This is rather unexpected, President Webster," Xiang said politely but coldly.

"I'm sorry to disturb you," Webster said, "but I have a rather pressing issue at hand. Two of our test pilots have disappeared from Edwards Air Force Base."

"That is unfortunate," Xiang said impatiently, "but I fail to see what it has to do with me or my country."

"We have evidence which suggests that our pilots were kidnapped by four Chinese men and taken to China, Mr. Xiang," Webster said.

"I know nothing of this," Xiang said.

"Well, should you or anyone in your government discover anything about my pilots, I trust that you will pass that information to me. And if they are found, they are to be returned to America unharmed," Webster said firmly. "Because if I discover they are being held within your nation, I will take action, and I will hold China responsible for whatever happens to them."

"I assure you," Xiang said coldly, "that the Chinese government was not responsible for the disappearance of your pilots, but if we do discover them, they will be safely returned to you."

"Good," Webster said. "I hope for your sake that my pilots are not on your soil, because I will recover them by any means necessary."

"They are not in China," Xiang said curtly.

"I hope so," Webster repeated. "Good day, Mr. Xiang."

"Good day, Mr. Webster," the Chinese President responded.

Webster switched the speakerphone off.

"What do you think?" he asked the Secretary of Defense.

"Hard to say," the other man replied. "He's either a good liar or he's ignorant."

Webster nodded. "Peters would not say the kidnappers were Chinese without the evidence to back it up."

"One of his underlings?"

"Possibly," Webster said, "although it would be

difficult to act without a superior's knowledge in that country."

"What about the North Koreans?"

"Possible, as far as the kidnapping is concerned," Webster said. "But not if we operate under the assumption that the disappearance of our pilots is connected to the destruction of our satellites. The Koreans don't have the capability to construct a space station like that. Only the Russians or the Chinese could."

"Redrick said the Chinese tried to both kill and capture them after the shuttle landed," the Secretary said.

"While the Russians helped us," Webster muttered.

"It has to be China."

Webster nodded. "But there were no records of such a project anywhere in the Chinese space agency."

"Maybe this venture is separate from it," the Secretary suggested. "To keep it secret."

"Possibly. Xiang may have commissioned someone else for this project to ensure it stays hidden from us and anyone else," Webster said. "And even if he doesn't know about it, I doubt he'll do anything to help us."

"Highly unlikely."

"I'll see if the CIA can unearth anything more," Webster said. He punched the speaker again. "Sherri, put me in touch with the Director of Central Intelligence."

"Yes, sir," Sherri replied boredly.

"That woman needs some excitement in her life," Webster commented. "Or at least some personality."

The Secretary of Defense laughed.

"Should I review the plans for invading China?" he said jokingly.

"That would be helpful," Webster said with a

smile.

"You would actually go to war to get those women back?"

"The destruction of our satellites is an act of war, and their kidnapping only adds to that," Webster said. "And I will do what is necessary to get them back and keep our planes secret. Hopefully a covert ops team will do the trick."

The Secretary nodded. "It would be hard to explain to the American public why we went to war, especially if we omit the part about the Hellcats."

"I'll worry about that when it comes to that," Webster said. "First we have to find those pilots. China is a damn big place."

"Yes, sir," the Secretary said, standing and walking to the door. "Let me know if there's anything else I can do."

"Thanks, I will."

"Good morning, sir," the Secretary said, stepping outside.

"Good morning," the President said. He planted his elbows on the desk and stared at the phone, waiting for the Director of Central Intelligence, while he wondered exactly what Xiang knew.

✳          ✳          ✳

"Hey Panther, do you really have a Mustang?"

Martina lay on her back on the floor of her cell, looking at the ceiling with her hands behind her head. Hearing Moondog speak, she rolled onto her side, carefully propping herself up on her right elbow. The Navy pilot was sitting with her back to the wall, her knees bent.

"Yeah, I really do," Martina said. "It's sitting in a barn out behind my house. Come over sometime after we get out of this and I'll show it to you."

"How on earth did you afford that?" Moondog said. "Those things go for over a million bucks apiece these days."

"It was a gift," Martina said.

"From who?"

"An old World War II pilot who lived in my hometown. He managed to get his hands on one after the war ended, and he kept it up. He used to fly it around town. I was totally fascinated by it, of course. I'd go by his place sometimes just to stare at that plane for a few minutes. When he died, a year or two after I got my wings, he left it to me. Guess he wanted to give the plane to someone who would appreciate it and fly it."

"Do you?"

"Are you kidding me?" Martina said. "If you had a P-51 would you just leave it sitting in a hangar?"

"No," Moondog said. "How does she handle?"

"She's a little tricky," Martina said, "but so much fun to fly. You got any aircraft of your own?"

"No. Just a few sports cars, a Harley, and a pickup truck. Cars are a lot cheaper and a little easier to come by."

"Too bad. If you had a Messerschmitt we could dogfight."

Moondog laughed. "I think those would cost a lot more than even your Mustang is worth, seeing as they're German. I don't have that kind of money."

"You've got to have some stashed up if you've got a bunch of sports cars parked in your garage," Martina said.

"That's 'cause I never settled down, got married, and had a bunch of kids to steal it all," Moondog said. "I've only got myself to take care of, and cars are really my only expensive taste, so I can afford to indulge myself and buy one every once in a while. Guess if I saved for a bit I could by a plane, but some other hotrod would probably catch my eye before I do. I fly enough with NASA anyway. Maybe I'll get one when I get out."

"What happens when you get married and have kids?" Martina asked.

Moondog laughed. "I'm never having kids. When I get married, I'll just take my husband's extra income and use it to get more sports cars."

Martina chuckled, rolling onto her stomach. "How come you're still single? You don't have any trouble meeting men."

"I've met plenty of men, messed around with some good-looking ones, even had a few somewhat serious relationships. But I've yet to meet anyone who could get close enough to me and who I could get close enough to for me to even consider anything long term. Guess when I meet someone I really fall for I'll marry that guy," Moondog said. "What about you?"

Martina shook her head. "I'm just cursed..." she stiffened and slowly pushed herself to a sitting position, careful not to aggravate her ribs.

"What?" Moondog whispered.

"Somebody's coming," Martina said.

"Guess Chin wasn't finished with his lecture on space," Moondog said, pulling the upper half of her flight suit on and zipping it up.

"I got enough of those in my astro class back at the Academy," Martina said, pulling her pen from her flight suit and concealing it in her right hand. "Let's skip class."

Moondog grinned broadly. "Sounds like a good idea to me," she said, sticking her hand in her pocket. Withdrawing the piece of glass, she wrapped her fist tightly around it.

The two Americans sat in silence and waited.

# ~ 17 ~

Four Chinese soldiers rounded the corner, stopping in front of the Americans' cells. Martina watched as they approached. Their movements were casual, almost lazy, as they waited for the man with the keys to open the doors. Two men stepped into each cell, pulling the pilots to their feet and leading them out into the hall.

Martina walked slowly down the long, dark corridor. It stretched ahead of her, dimly lit. The stone surrounding her was dark, the floor smooth and unpolished. In places, water trickled down along the roughly cut walls.

Two guards flanked Panther, each walking slightly ahead of her. After a moment they had released their grip on her wrists, so she walked freely between them. Behind her she could hear the footfalls of the other two soldiers. She could distinguish Moondog's steps from theirs because the Navy pilot's slight limp made her gait uneven.

Careful not to turn her head, Panther glanced at the guards beside her out of the corner of her eye. Both appeared relaxed, focusing more on the hall in front of them than on the prisoner between them. Slowly she let the pen in her hand slide downward until the tip protruded slightly from her fist.

In one fluid motion, she sidestepped, wrapping her arm around the guard on her left while thrusting the pen behind his ear and forcing it into his brain. The guard stiffened in her arms and then sank to the ground.

At the same instant, Moondog let her right leg collapse, dropping to her knee. The guard beside her stopped, twisting toward her. As he bent down to pull her to her feet, Moondog lashed out with the shard of glass in her hand. The sharp point split his neck open. Blood gushed from the cut as he fell to the ground, lifeless.

The third guard immediately spun toward Panther, reaching for his gun. The pilot swung her foot up in a high kick, striking him in the head. The soldier toppled backward, arms flailing, slamming into the wall. She stepped after him, driving her pen into his eye. The man screamed and ripped her hand away, stopping the point from penetrating through his skull. The pen remained imbedded in his eye.

Moondog jumped to her feet, twisting toward the final guard as he moved for her. He stopped just out of her reach. She stepped forward slowly, waving the sharp, bloody shard in front of her. The soldier leapt into her, grabbing her wrist and pulling her hand away from him.

Moondog moved with him, punching him in the nose. The man screamed, his hands flying to his face as blood streamed from his nose. She raised her foot, kicking him squarely in the chest. The soldier dropped to the ground.

Still covering his injured eye, the man standing in front of Panther reached for his gun with his free hand. Seeing his hand drop toward his holster, she lunged for him, throwing her body on top of his and knocking him to the floor.

Panther pulled herself up so that she was sitting on the man's stomach, facing him. He gazed up at her in surprise before frantically reaching for his gun.

She dropped her knee onto his upper arm, pinning it to the stone. She reached down with both hands, digging her fingers into his throat. Gasping for air, the soldier squirmed wildly.

Moondog stepped over the soldier in front of her, he lashed out with his foot, striking the wound on her thigh. Moondog's leg gave out and she fell backward, landing flat on her ass.

Panther leaned forward, pressing her weight through her fingers and into the windpipe of the man beneath her. Out of the corner of her eye, she saw a flash of metal, as the soldier pulled a knife from his belt. He swung the weapon up, stabbing at her arm. Panther immediately released her grip on his throat and grabbed his wrist. A sharp pain raced through her right shoulder, as the tip of knife pierced her skin. She pulled his hand away, preventing the blade from sinking any deeper.

Panther raised her right hand and brought her knuckles down across the man's temple, dazing him. She swiftly pulled the knife from his hand. In one quick slash she brought the knife down, splitting his throat open. The man went stiff beneath her as the blood gushed from his neck.

Martina pulled the gun off his body and stood, glancing back toward Moondog. The Navy pilot was sitting on the ground, watching as the final soldier crawled toward her. She drew back her left leg and drove her foot into the side of his face, twisting his head around. He fell backward, landing with his head at an awkward angle, and lay still.

Moondog stood and stepped over the man, again favoring her right leg. He was obviously dead, his neck broken. Sticking the bloody shard of glass back in her pocket, she pulled his gun from his holster and began calmly searching his body for extra ammunition. Finding none, she moved to the first man she had killed and repeated the process.

Straightening up, Moondog made sure the first gun was safe and slid it into her flight suit pocket. She quickly surveyed her surroundings. The hall was silent. The bodies of the four Chinese soldiers lay on the ground. Panther was leaning against the wall, gun in hand, watching. Blood soaked a small patch of her flightsuit on her right arm.

Moondog nodded to her. Without a word the Air Force pilot turned and began to walk toward the stairs. Moondog unsafed her own weapon and picked her way through the bodies on the floor. She limped after Panther quietly.

Silence was key to the whole operation. The two pilots knew there was no way they could possibly fight through all the soldiers based within the mountain. The only way to escape was to slip out undetected, which meant moving as quietly as possible.

There was no need to speak. Panther and Moondog had discussed their escape options at length after the guards had jailed them again and vanished. The plan was simple: overpower their escorts, take whatever weapons they could, and get out. Judging by the fact that they were trapped inside a mountain, the exit was most likely on the periphery. Unfortunately, it was also almost certain to be on the main level, which meant people.

The pilots moved slowly down the hallway, weapons at the ready. They walked as quietly as possible, alert to every sound. Periodically, Moondog checked back over her shoulder, but she saw no one. The hall remained empty except for the two escaped prisoners creeping carefully along.

After a few minutes they reached the long stairwell leading up to the main complex. Martina stopped at the bottom of the steps and craned her neck upward, watching and listening. The hall remained as silent as ever.

Panther pressed her back against the wall and slowly began to make her way up the steps, gun pointed toward the top. Moondog followed her, copying her motions. Pausing every four or five steps to listen for anyone approaching, they made their way to the main level of the mountain.

Coming within sight of the top of the stairs, Panther motioned for Moondog to remain still. Careful not to aggravate her ribs, she leaned forward so that her body was parallel to the stairs and her eyes were level with the top step. She swept her eyes to the left and to the right.

Seeing no one, she dashed up the last few steps and pressed her back against the wall, listening for signs that anyone was nearby and had heard her. Detecting none, she motioned to Moondog. The Navy pilot quickly followed her, flattening herself against the stone.

Once again the two pilots began to move, with Panther leading. They kept themselves as close to the wall as possible as they crept along, alert to the slightest sound or motion. They slipped past several corridors leading toward the center of the mountain but saw no one as they wound through the tunnel. They quickly slid by the halls and continued to move in one direction, in the hope that it would eventually lead to an exit, and freedom.

The faint sound of voices drifted to Martina's ears. The fighter pilot froze, pointing her gun down the hall ahead of her from where the sound was emanating. The voices grew louder, accompanied by the sound of footsteps. She glanced around frantically, but there was nowhere to duck into, no hiding places in sight. The two escaped prisoners simply pressed themselves further into the wall and held their breath.

The voices grew still louder as the people drew closer. Panther flicked the safety off her gun and waited for the approaching Chinese to appear. Suddenly, the voices began to diminish and the footsteps moved off. The two pilots waited stiffly until the hallway fell completely silent again.

Panther relaxed, allowing herself to breathe again. She turned to Moondog, who nodded. Slowly Panther began to move again, sliding along the walls, stopping every few feet to listen for any interlopers. Moondog crept along beside her, watching their rear.

The pilots slipped slowly by another two halls, moving cautiously. The air seemed to bear down on them oppressively. The polished corridor stretched on forever underneath the glaring lights. It seemed as if they had moved barely a few feet.

Panther paused again. The wall opposite them led into yet another hallway just a few feet beyond. The Air Force pilot waited, listening. Hearing nothing, she darted across the hall, crossing the opening. Moondog followed quickly and quietly.

Panther kept moving forward, slinking catlike through the hall. Suddenly, a metallic door in the side of the hall swung open and a small man in a military uniform stepped out, coming face to face with her.

Both the soldier and the pilots stopped dead in their tracks. His eyes grew wide in surprise, and he staggered backward, opening his mouth to scream.

The sound never escaped his lips. Instead the loud crack of a pistol filled the air, echoing down the halls. The bullet caught the man square in the chest at point-blank range. He dropped to the ground in an instant, staring lifeless at the ceiling.

"Shit," Panther whispered, listening to the gunshot reverberating through the halls. The gun in her hand was smoking. "Someone's got to have heard that."

"Let's make tracks," Moondog said.

Panther needed no coaxing. Keeping her gun pointed ahead of her, she agilely leapt over the body at her feet and took off running. Moondog immediately dashed after her, moving awkwardly. The limp in her right leg almost caused her feet to falter, but she drove herself forward, ignoring the pain shooting through her thigh and the strangeness of her step. Somehow she managed to keep pace with Panther, but only barely.

A loud shout cut through the air behind them. Moondog twisted around to see two Chinese soldiers rushing toward them. She stopped just long enough to squeeze off two shots. The first shot caught one soldier directly in the chest. The second fell an instant later.

Moondog turned back around and continued to half-run, half-limp after Panther. The Air Force pilot slowed her step for a second, allowing the Navy woman to catch up again.

"If only these damn things had silencers," Moondog muttered.

The pounding of footsteps filled the hall behind them. Moondog half-twisted around to see half a dozen soldiers rushing toward them. Her gun spoke again, dropping two more men. A third bullet clipped another soldier in the shoulder, causing him to fall back.

"Let's get the fuck out of here," she whispered to Martina.

"I'm working on it," the Air Force pilot hissed back, firing her own weapon into the crowd of soldiers. "Just keep up."

Moondog didn't reply. She turned her head back to catch a glimpse of the group behind her. Instead of decreasing from the losses the pilots had inflicted, the mob chasing them seemed only to have grown. There were now at least ten men chasing them. The Navy pilot cursed under her breath and fired off another three quick shots, taking down a few more soldiers.

The staccato pulse of gunfire filled the air behind them, causing both pilots to instinctively duck down as they ran. Dust and chips of rocks rained down on them as the bullets harmlessly hit the ceiling above them. The Chinese soldiers were aiming over them in an effort to intimidate the two women. Realizing this, Panther straightened her back, continuing to run. Moondog turned and fired off another two quick shots.

"Fuck!" Martina shouted suddenly.

Moondog snapped her head forward. A five or six soldiers were charging through the hall toward them, weapons raised, effectively trapping them. In a matter of seconds the two pilots would be in the midst of a large group of soldiers, far too many for them to overcome.

"You better find an exit damn quick," Moondog said.

"Working on it," Panther repeated tersely, through clenched teeth. She raised her gun and fired into the group of onrushing soldiers, dropping two. Her eyes darted back and forth as she ran, searching for any sign of a way out.

Suddenly, ten feet away from her, she spotted a dark metal door in the stone. The lead man in the pack in front of her could not have been more than twenty feet from her, and the distance was closing rapidly.

"Move!" she shouted to Moondog, grabbing the Navy pilot by the arm and pulling her forward, desperately racing for the door. The soldiers were a mere ten feet from her. In the blink of an eye, the distance had been reduced to five feet.

Panther threw her shoulder into the door, forcing

it open, and ran into the side hall, dragging Moondog after her. The two pilots found themselves inside another, smaller corridor. Panther released her friend without breaking stride, and they continued to dash through the hall.

Behind them the two groups of soldiers collided, only to swarm through the door a moment later in pursuit of the escaped pilots. Moondog again turned back toward them, firing the small gun in her hand. The weapon clicked empty. Cursing, she flung the pistol into the crowd behind her and focused her attention on keeping pace with Panther.

Their path twisted up another, smaller set of stairs. Panther grabbed Moondog by the collar of her flight suit, pulling her up. Panther took the steps two at a time. Moondog struggled not to trip. The Navy pilot's pace was slowing, and her limp was worsening. Reaching the top of the stairs, Panther again released her. The two dashed the remaining distance to another door, open at the end of the hall.

They rushed through the doorway. Martina slammed the metal door shut behind them, locking it, and looked around. They were in a small room, surrounded by electronic equipment. Light was streaming in from a window set high in the opposite wall. No other doors were visible.

"Fuck!" Panther spat. "We're trapped."

Moondog limped over to the window, which was less than a foot high. Outside, she could see only rocks and a few large radio towers.

"Is it big enough?" Panther asked.

"No," Moondog said, glancing around the room. "This must be where they send their signals up to that space station. They've got a huge antenna out there."

"What's that got to do with anything?" Panther said impatiently.

"I've got an idea."

Moondog reached into her pocket, pulling out the second gun and the piece of glass. She handed the gun to Panther

"Hold them off for as long as you can," she said, turning back toward the machinery and studying it. After a moment she ripped off the panel on one machine, selected a wire, and cut it in half with the glass in her hand. Quickly she stripped the covering off each end of the wire and began to tap the two wires together.

"Hope this works," she muttered.

"What the hell are you doing?" Panther said, staring at her. Outside she could hear a loud pounding on the door.

"I'll explain later," Moondog said curtly, continuing to methodically hit the exposed wires together. "Deal with them."

Panther nodded, glancing around the room again, looking for anything she could use to block the door. There were no objects present except for the machinery, which was far too large for her to move. Cursing under her breath, she pressed herself against the wall perpendicular to the door.

Outside, two loud gunshots echoed. The bullets whizzed through the door, snapping the bolt and embedding themselves in the far wall. Suddenly, the door was flung open and a soldier rushed in, only to drop to the floor a second later as a weapon cracked from inside.

Panther stepped away from the wall, turning into the crowd of soldiers. She stopped calmly behind the body, legs spread slightly apart. Her face was set in stone, and her brown eyes were ice-cold. Each hand was wrapped around the butt of a pistol, fingers curled around the triggers. The muzzles pointed directly into the crowd of Chinese.

The weapons spoke in rapid succession, dropping the first two men standing in the doorway before they could respond. Three others behind them rushed forward, only to be cut down by the bullets that flew toward them.

Realizing what was happening, a few men dropped to the ground, causing the fire to fly over their heads and take down the men behind them. Instinctively, the Chinese went for their own weapons, quickly returning fire at the American. In an instant a hail of fire was zipping past Martina. The pilot ignored it, continuing to fire into the crowd before her.

A bullet clipped the inside of Panther's right leg just above the top of her boot. A second grazed her lower left chest, only cutting through skin. She staggered backward as her guns clicked empty. Several bodies lay between her and the door. Outside, the remaining soldiers stood and charged for her.

Panther slid her right leg backward, adopting a fighting stance. She spun the guns around so that she gripped the weapons by the muzzle. She waited as the soldiers rushed toward her, the same ice-cold determination in her dark eyes.

The soldiers burst through the door. Panther brought her left hand back, swinging the butt of her gun into the temple of one man. He crashed to the ground. She stepped forward, smashing the weapon in her right hand into a second's face. A quick kick to the stomach sent a third away from her.

Something crashed into the back of Panther's legs, causing her knees to buckle. Her knees hit the floor. She rose to a crouch and swung her leg around, catching another man behind the ankles, causing him to topple over.

Despite her efforts, the soldiers swarmed over her. A boot collided with the side of her face, knocking her flat on her back.

One of the soldiers pressed his boot onto her throat, stopping just short of crushing her windpipe. She felt the pressure of a boot against each of her wrists as the guns were pried from her hands. She struggled frantically, kicking wildly. No less than five soldiers fell on her, pinning her to the ground. Panther continued to struggle, but it was no use. Try as she might, she could not move an inch.

Several soldiers moved past the crowd surrounding Martina. Catching sight of Moondog kneeling on the ground, they dove for her, grabbing her by the arms and pulling her away. She kept her grip on the wires as the men lifted her to her feet. She continued to tap them together furiously until they were pulled from her hands as the men dragged her backward.

The soldiers slowly eased their grip on Panther and pulled her to her feet. Holding her arms tightly behind her back, they shoved her forward, back into the heart of the mountain.

# ~ **18** ~

Chin looked at the two Americans standing before him on the stone balcony overlooking the control center. No less than ten foot soldiers flanked the pilots. The taller of the two glared at him defiantly despite her battered appearance. Blood was running from her mouth, nose, and three separate wounds on her body. She looked as if she was about to collapse, yet she held her head high and fixed her cold, unwavering eyes directly on him.

The smaller woman appeared to have fared the immediate fight better, but her face was still covered with old, fading bruises, and her right eye was only open a sliver. A few spots of blood appeared on her right thigh. She too stared directly at him with a defiant, almost smug look.

"I had hoped I might be able to reason with you," Chin said, leaning against the rail. "But I see now that is impossible. You will only cooperate through use of force."

"We won't cooperate at all," Martina hissed.

"I think you will," Chin said. He barked an order in Chinese. The two soldiers holding Moondog turned and dragged her from the room. Ming followed, her heels ringing on the stone as she walked. The small group disappeared from the room.

"Where are you taking her?" Martina demanded.

"My associate is going to talk to her," Chin said,

"while I talk to you."

"Divide and conquer," Martina said.

Chin laughed. "It would appear you have already been conquered, Colonel," he said.

"That's what you think," Martina replied.

"What could you possibly hope to accomplish by escaping?" he said. "There is nothing even resembling civilization for hundreds of miles. Only desert and mountains. You would be dead in a matter of days."

"I would rather die from the elements than at your hands," she answered.

"You don't have to die at all, Colonel," the general said. "If you agree to help me, I will spare you."

"I told you, I swore my allegiance long ago. Anyone who doesn't like where that lies can kiss my ass."

"In a matter of days, your country will no longer exist," Chin said, walking toward her. "I will bring America to its knees, and China will be the world's power."

"What are you plotting?" she demanded.

"Why do you want to know?" he asked.

"So I can stop you," she hissed, straining forward against the men who held her.

Chin laughed again. "You are truly a fool, Colonel," he said. "You cannot stop me. You will simply die."

"Then I'll die trying," Martina replied, continuing to lean toward Chin.

"You will die for nothing."

"Only if I fail," she said. "And I will not fail."

"I can assure you, Colonel, you will," he said.

"If allegiance means nothing to you, why are you here?" she said.

"What do you mean?"

"You aren't doing this for China, you're doing it for yourself. Why?" Martina demanded.

"Who do you think will hold the greatest power in China when I succeed?" Chin said. "Once I subdue the West, we will be the strongest nation in the world. They will give me leadership of this country, and I will be the most powerful man on Earth."

"And you think I'm a fool," Martina muttered.

"My chances of success are far greater than yours."

"You will crash and burn," she hissed. "I'll see to that personally."

"From a prison cell?" he asked. "Highly doubtful."

"If you're so sure of my failure, why won't you tell me your plan?" she said.

"That is privileged information, Colonel," Chin spat. "I have work to do." He said something to the guards, who spun Martina around and led her toward the door.

Panther glanced back at Chin as she was dragged from the room. The Chinese general was again standing at the rail, watching the people on the floor beneath. *He blinds us from space to hide something from us*, she thought. *He blinds us so he can somehow attack us, but how?* The cold stone walls of the mountain offered Martina no answers as the soldiers dragged her back to her cell.

✳            ✳            ✳

The two soldiers holding Moondog led her back down the long flight of stairs into the dimly lit corridor. Her right leg had almost stopped working altogether, forcing the men to drag her along between them, although she struggled to walk with little success. Behind her she could hear the steady, unfaltering rhythm of Ming's heels against the stone. No other footsteps echoed through the halls. Panther was not behind her.

The small group wound through the dank hallway, moving deeper into the subterranean chambers. They pushed past the bodies of the four soldiers she and Panther had killed, still lying where they had fallen. They walked silently by the rows of cells without stopping.

Moondog looked up at the soldiers holding her, almost certain they had made some mistake. But they continued forward, intent on some other destination. The sound of Ming's even gait remained behind them. Moondog lifted her head and gazed forward down the long, dark hallway stretching endlessly before her, cold and uninviting.

The soldiers dragged her onward, further into the earth. They walked in silence for what seemed like hours, until Moondog began to wonder if this wasn't a tunnel that eventually came out above ground. But no sign of daylight appeared. The long hall only narrowed and darkened, the cut of the stone becoming more and more rough.

Finally, the soldiers stopped outside a black metal door cut into the rock, similar to those in the heart of the mountain. One soldier kicked the door open, and they dragged her inside a small room, as dim as the hall outside. It was empty except for a set of shelves and the shackles hanging from the far wall. A single naked light bulb hung overhead, casting its pale light on the dark, rough stones.

The guards pulled her over to the chains. Moondog began to struggle fiercely as they spun her around, lashing out toward the men with her fists and her feet. But they managed to keep their grip on her, cuffing the metal bands around her wrists and ankles. She hung spread-eagled, her feet dangling six inches from the floor.

As soon as the last shackle latched into place around Moondog's ankle, the two soldiers spun and nearly ran from the room, vanishing back into the dark hallway. For a moment Moondog was alone, glancing slowly around the small room.

With the same even ringing of heels against stone, Ming stepped into the room. Swinging the door closed behind her, she crossed her arms over her chest and looked at Moondog. A smile crept slowly over her face as she swept her eyes up and down the Navy pilot.

Wordlessly, she crossed the room in two even steps and swung her fist into Moondog's stomach. The chains holding Moondog to the wall kept her from doubling over as a second blow collided with her body.

Ming swung her leg upward in a high kick, striking Moondog across the face and slamming her back against the rough stone wall. The pilot turned her head to face Ming, staring directly at the woman before her with a cold contempt that suggested she would tear Ming limb from limb if free.

The Chinese woman paused, studying her victim. Most people cowered from her after the first few blows, only to be screaming for her to stop after more than four or five. However, judging by the bruises already covering her prisoner's face, this was a woman who had been in a fight before and had a higher tolerance for pain.

Shrugging, Ming stepped forward, dealing a rapid succession of punches to Moondog's stomach, chest, and face, moving her fists like a boxer. The pilot remained silent as the blows rained down on her.

Ming stepped back, dealing Moondog one last sharp kick directly into the wound on her right thigh. The pilot grunted. Blood ran from her mouth and nose, and her eyes were blazing with cold fury.

"That," Ming said, "was just to soften to you up."

She walked over to the shelves, looking at the collection of implements in front of her. She studied the items carefully for a moment before selecting a bottle of yellow liquid. Picking up a needle, she drew about a milliliter of the liquid into the syringe.

Replacing the bottle, she walked back over to Moondog, sliding the point of the needle into a vein on the pilot's left wrist. Moondog continued to glare at her contemptuously as the metal pierced her skin, still straining against her chains.

"This is wonderful stuff," Ming said with a smile as she pressed the top down on the syringe, injecting the liquid into Moondog's vein. "It makes you feel as if your blood is boiling."

It felt almost as if someone had lit a fire in Moondog's arm. It started as a simple flicker of heat in her wrist, growing rapidly until her entire arm felt as if it was ablaze. The sensation spread outward, moving through her limbs like flames, until it seemed that her entire body was burning with a terrible searing heat.

"Don't worry," Ming said, flashing a grin as she pulled the needle from Moondog's arm. "It will wear off in a little while."

"Tell me," Moondog hissed, "how many people have you killed down here?"

"Many," Ming said, smiling. "Anyone who has ever countered or failed General Chin has met a very slow death at my hands." Her grin broadened as she spoke.

"You're sick," Moondog said.

Ming shrugged and walked back over to the shelves. She placed the needle on the top shelf and again contemplated other items. Selecting one from a lower shelf, she turned back to the pilot.

"Are you going to kill me?" Moondog asked coldly. Ming was surprised to see that only contempt burned in her eyes. She paused, studying the pilot before her. Strangely, she could see no signs of fear in her prisoner.

"Not yet," Ming said. "Chin wants you alive for now."

She jabbed the black rod in her hand into Moondog's lower ribs. A flash of fire shot through Moondog's body as a bolt of electricity jumped from the tip of the device into her, causing her to twist sideways.

"What were you doing with those wires?" Ming asked.

Moondog made no response. Ming raised the rod again, this time tapping it against Moondog's chin. The pilot jerked her head away as a jolt leapt from the rod and danced across her clenched jaw. She glared at Ming.

"What were you doing?" Ming repeated.

"Nothing you could possibly understand," Moondog hissed, pain evident in her voice.

Ming studied the device in her hand for a moment, slowly adjusting something on the handle. Then she pressed the tip down against Moondog's shoulder, sending a more powerful wave of electricity coursing through her body.

This time the agony was just too great. Moondog screamed, causing Ming to grin even more widely, displaying her teeth. She raised the rod, only to bring it down again on the pilot's hip. Moondog yowled again, her voice carrying down the hall, filling the air as it resounded helplessly through the long, empty, dark corridors.

✳ ✳ ✳

A slamming door pierced through the thick veil of sleep, pulling Martina back to consciousness. The sound of footsteps fading away echoed in her ears as she opened her eyes to find herself staring at the back wall of her cell. She was lying face down on the hard stone floor.

*Guess I must have passed out*, she thought, picking herself off the floor. She did not remember lying down. After the guards had thrown her back in her cell, she had inspected her wounds. The cut on her left side was merely a scrape. The gashes on her ankle and arm were larger, but neither were very deep. She could not recall anything after that.

Pulling herself to a sitting position, she quickly studied the gashes again. Blood had caked over both the graze on her ankle and the one on her chest. The slit on her arm had stopped bleeding too.

Remembering the shutting door which had first awakened her, Panther lifted her head. Her cell remained unchanged, the door still tightly locked. Across from her she could see Moondog lying motionless on her side, angled diagonally with her head closest to the door.

Moondog's flight suit had again been stripped off above her waist. Sharp red lines crisscrossed the Navy pilot's back. Her t-shirt was in tatters, showing blood on the white skin beneath. Moondog's head was tucked into her body, making it impossible for Martina to see her face.

"Moondog!" Martina nearly shouted, sliding over to the door and pressing her face to the bars. "Moondog, are you all right?"

"Let me die in peace," the Navy woman muttered, not moving from where she lay. Her voice was thick with pain.

"What the fuck are you talking about?" Martina said, in horror. "You're not dying, are you?"

"Sure as fuck feels like it," Moondog said, still remaining motionless. "Although I don't think what she did was enough to actually kill me."

"Who did this?"

"That bitch in civvies who hangs around Chin. The one who knocked you over," Moondog replied. "I'm going to fucking kill her..."

"Why?" Martina said.

"She wanted information," Moondog said tiredly.

"Let me sleep, will you?" she moaned.

"Information on what?"

"All sorts of stuff," Moondog replied. "Mostly military intel. And what I was doing with those wires. I didn't tell that fucking bitch anything, so she just hit me harder."

"What were you doing with those wires?" Martina said.

"I'll tell you later," she said softly, lifting her head for the first time. Blood covered her pain-filled face. Agony and exhaustion saturated the one eye she could open.

"Please, Martina, just let me sleep," she said softly.

Martina nodded. "Go to sleep," she said.

Moondog made no reply. She simply tucked her head back toward her chest and remained still. Only the even rise and fall of her chest indicated that any life remained in her at all.

Martina turned away from the door, pressing her back against the stone wall. She drew her knees up, folding her arms across them and resting her chin on her forearms. She stared at the dark, rough-cut rock across from her, feeling the pull of her own exhaustion.

Military intel... They were planning an attack, wanting to know what to take out, what to expect as a response. But attack how? Martina had no idea which of China's military resources Chin had at his command. With those radio towers and a space presence, he could conceivably communicate with forces around the globe.

He could position his forces for a sneak attack without America even knowing it! Without the use of their spy satellites, the United States government would have no way of monitoring every military force on Earth. The Chinese could simply slip into place and pounce. But where? And with what?

Martina sighed and leaned her head back against the wall, closing her eyes. Only one thing was certain in her mind. Somehow, she had to get out of this place.

# ~ **19** ~

"We've got something, sir!" the Chairman of the Joint Chiefs of Staff said as he strode into the Oval Office, flanked by the Director of Central Intelligence.

"What?" Webster asked, leaning over his desk. "Have a seat and tell me." He motioned to several chairs. The two men sat down.

"One of our listening stations intercepted a rather interesting signal. I think Stan could better explain it," the Chairman said, turning toward the Director of Central Intelligence.

"Have you heard of atmospheric bounce, sir?" the Director asked. Webster shook his head.

"The principle is fairly simple," the Director continued. "When someone sends a signal into space, the atmosphere deflects part of this signal back toward Earth, enabling whoever is at the point where it reflects to pick up the signal as well. The amount and direction of deflection depend on several factors, of course. We have several stations around the world to pick up signals from rival nations, which we attempt to decode as a method of intelligence gathering."

"All right," Webster said.

"We picked up an unusual signal several hours ago," the Director said. "It was encoded, but the transmission itself was broken. For some reason only bits and pieces of the signal were getting through.

"After studying this signal, our analysts realized that the breaks were actually a repetitive sequence of their own."

"A separate code?" Webster said.

"A signal within a signal," the Director said, nodding. "When we discovered this, our people attempted to decipher the embedded signal."

"And?" the President said.

"Morse code, sir," the Director said. "An S.O.S., followed by a string of nine numbers. The signal repeated for about four minutes before it ceased entirely."

"What did it mean?"

"Our analysts figured that it was a numerical identification code," the Director said. "Like a pin number or a phone number."

"Or a social security number," Webster said, slowly. "Nine digits."

"Exactly," the Director said.

"Whose?" Webster demanded.

"Commander Ansetti's, sir," the Chairman said.

"My God," Webster said, grinning. "That's a break. We have proof that she's alive."

"As of five hours ago, yes," the Chairman said.

"How on earth did she manage to get out a signal like that?" Webster mused.

"Hard to say," the Director said. "She must have come across some sort of antenna or something, and knew that if she broke into the signal there was a chance we might pick it up."

"Is there any way we can trace it back to her?" Webster demanded. "Find out where she is?"

"We can't pinpoint her exact location, sir," the Director said, "but we do have a rough idea of where the signal came from."

Webster made a come-on motion with his hand.

"Southwestern China, sir," the Director said.

"So it was the Chinese," Webster said.

"Yes, sir," the Chairman said.

"If we could get a closer look at the area, would it be possible to narrow down the exact place the signal came from?"

"Definitely, sir," the Director said. "That area of the world is very inhospitable, and as a result almost entirely uninhabited. There can't be many large antennas out there. We find some and we've found our pilots."

"Well, get some cameras over there. Take whatever pictures you need, and find that place," Webster said.

"Take pictures with what, sir?" the Chairman asked.

"Dammit!" Webster cursed. "I forgot those bastards destroyed all our spy satellites."

"And they're sure to shoot down anything else we send into orbit," the Chairman said grimly. "We'd maybe get one pass if we're lucky."

"What about aircraft?" the President said.

"Impossible, sir," the Chairman said. "A U-2 flies too low and far too slowly to survive. That plane wouldn't make it five miles past the border."

"What about a Blackbird?" the Director of Central Intelligence said. "The Chinese would never be able to touch one of those."

"An SR-71?" the Chairman said, surprised.

"Why not?" the Director said. "They fly higher than surface-to-air missiles, and they're faster than any other aircraft we have."

The Chairman shook his head. "Those were decommissioned years ago. I doubt you could find one in the entire Air Force inventory that's still in flying condition."

"What about NASA?" the Director said. "They have a few for flight testing. They might have kept them up."

"Where would these planes be?" Webster demanded.

"NASA's Dryden test facility, out at Edwards Air Force Base," the Director said.

Webster immediately punched the intercom on his desk. "Sherri, get General Peters on the line. "Now!"

✳      ✳      ✳

The F-15E pilot killed the Strike Eagle's engines and raised the canopy, replacing the sweltering air of the cockpit with only slightly cooler air from the desert. He pulled off his helmet and turned to his backseater.

"Hop on out, they're waiting for you," he said, motioning to two figures standing on the side of the ramp.

Major Richard Barker pulled off his own helmet and undid the straps holding him in the rear ejection seat. He slowly extracted his muscular frame from the back of the Eagle and swung his legs over the side.

"Thanks for the ride," he said.

"Anytime," the pilot replied.

Barker carefully climbed to the ground. Although he had spent his entire Air Force career as a navigator, this had been his first ride in a fighter. Dismounting a jet was much different than walking down the steps of a heavy.

As his boots hit the tarmac, he straightened his back, stretching to his full height of just over six feet. A broad-shouldered man whose build was just on the heavier side of medium, Barker had found the back of the fifteen incredibly cramped. Sweat slicked back his short brown hair.

Stretching his back and arms, he fixed his dark brown eyes on the two figures standing at the side of the tarmac. The first was a brigadier general, wearing blues. The second was another major, a flight suit covering her five foot eight body. Her brown hair was pulled back off her face. Although her flight suit partially concealed her figure, her long legs and thin hips and waist could be discerned. By contrast, her shoulders were rather broad. Sunglasses hid her eyes.

Barker stopped three feet from the general and gave a crisp salute. "Major Barker reporting as ordered, sir," he said.

The general returned the salute. "Thank you for getting here so fast, Major," he said. "I'm General Peters."

"Not a problem, sir. That Eagle driver was more than happy to ferry me over here at Mach two," Barker said. Peters laughed.

"And you are?" he asked the tall woman standing beside the general.

"Just call me Stang," she said, smiling as she extended her hand.

"Stang, huh?" Barker said, shaking her hand.

"My callsign," she said.

"Fighter jock?" he asked.

Stang nodded. "I'm a test pilot here at Edwards."

"You know anything about this?" he asked.

"Just that it's a black op," she said. "The general was waiting until you showed to brief us. Well, sir?" she turned toward Peters.

"Come with me," he said, walking to his car and climbing in beside his aide. The two majors sat in the backseat.

"What's your background?" Stang asked as the car began to roll.

"I'm a nav on heavies," Barker said. "Most recently AC-130s."

She smiled. "Big guns."

"Yup," he said. "What about you?"

"I flew fifteens and twenty-twos before I got

accepted to TPS," she said. "I fly all sorts of stuff here."

"How'd you get picked up for this?" he asked.

"The boss showed up about an hour ago, asked if I'd fly a classified mission for him," she said. "I didn't have much else to do, so..."

Barker laughed, catching sight of her hands. A small Academy ring with a black stone in the center sat on her finger. There was no wedding band, which he found slightly surprising. Most officers he knew were married.

"How'd they get you?" she asked.

"They asked for volunteers for a classified mission," he said. "Curiosity got the best of me. Next thing I know I'm in the back of that Eagle."

"I prefer the front," Stang said.

"We're here," Peters interrupted as the car slowed to a stop in front of a large hangar. He climbed out and walked to the hangar. The two majors followed close on his heels.

"This is NASA's facility," Stang muttered as the three officers stopped in front of the building. Slowly the doors rolled open. The two junior officers gasped in amazement as they saw what the hangar contained.

The large black aircraft's nose sat about eight feet above the ground. The front of the fuselage was thin and tapered, curving out slightly around the cockpit and then sliding back evenly for the first fifty feet of the 107-foot plane. Flat triangular wings swept out at a forty degree angle to the body, giving the craft an overall width of fifty-five feet. Two long engines with spiked cones at the front ran through the wings. A vertical tail on each was angled slightly inward.

"I don't believe it," Stang whispered. "A sled."

She pulled off her sunglasses, revealing vibrant light-green eyes.

"What?" Barker said.

"An SR-71 Blackbird. I thought they'd all been

sent off to museums," she said, turning to Peters.

"All but this one," the general said. "NASA kept it for research on supersonic and high-altitude flight."

"It can still fly?" she asked cautiously.

"They've kept her up," Peters said. "She can still fly."

"Sir, you don't mean..." Stang said.

"That's why I brought you out here."

"I don't believe it," she slowly repeated, sweeping her green eyes over the long, sleek black aircraft.

"C'mon," Peters said, walking into the hangar. "We don't have much time to bring you up to speed for this mission."

∗     ∗     ∗

Martina sat with her back to the wall, just beside the barred door. Her knees were pulled up to her chest, and her arms were crossed over them. She had found a smooth space on the wall to rest her head. She was motionless, staring at a spot just below the ceiling on the wall opposite her.

Across the hall Moondog lay on her right side, as she had for hours. The Navy pilot's arms were wrapped tightly around her chest, and her face was tucked out of view. Only her back was visible, dried blood showing through her tattered shirt. Her legs were slightly bent. The only indication she was alive at all was her slow, even breathing.

Panther had long given up trying to sleep. She had dozed off again after Moondog had returned. But now she was wide awake and completely unable to drift back off into that sweet black oblivion.

Eventually she pushed herself into a sitting position. The Chinese were nowhere to be seen, and the Navy pilot was still unconscious, leaving her alone in the cold stone cell. With nothing better to do, she had simply leaned back and let her mind wander.

At first she had tried her hand at deciphering

Chin's plans for the umpteenth time. Again she found no answers. With those radio antennas he could communicate with any type of unit anywhere in the world, making his attack options almost endless. She had no idea how many or what kind of military forces he had at his command. Without more information, she was forced to concede that she could not discern his plot.

From there her thoughts had turned to escape. The Chinese guards still left her hands unbound when escorting her. If she waited until they became complacent or distracted she could possibly overpower them again.

The Chinese obviously needed a way to get to and from such a remote base, so there had to be some vehicles nearby. If she could find those and steal one, there was a chance they could make it across the border to Afghanistan or another friendly country.

But for the moment she had no idea where the exits, let alone the vehicles, were, leaving her with nothing but a very loose plan. All she could do was wait for another escape opportunity to present itself and take advantage of it when it did.

She eventually found herself wondering what time it was. Deep beneath the mountain, the only lighting was the bare electric bulbs spaced along the ceiling, which glowed constantly. Martina had not seen the sun since being snatched from Edwards.

She still had her old battered watch on her wrist, set to California time. It was a simple analog display that did not distinguish between AM and PM, so she had no idea if it was day or night in the States. She didn't know the time difference between there and where she was. She didn't even know what day it was.

She sighed and glanced over at Moondog, who lay as still as ever. Martina silently wished that she would come around just so she could have someone to talk to. She was bored out of her mind.

There had been many times in her Air Force career when she had found herself sitting around. Hurry up and wait was inevitable in military life. Still, she had never gotten used to it. She hated being trapped in one place, and she desperately wished she could see sunlight. Or moonlight, depending on what time it was.

Panther closed her eyes and leaned her head back, wishing sleep would take her away and give her some respite. But her eyes fluttered open again after a few seconds. She was still as awake as she had been for the past hours. Giving up, she rested her head on her arms and wondered what time it was in this part of the world.

The soft, even ringing of boots on stone drifted to her ears. She lifted her head as the sound grew louder, craning her neck down the hall. A moment later two soldiers came into view. They stopped in front of her cell. One opened the door, while the other pulled Martina to her feet. They dragged her back toward the upper levels of the mountain, leaving Moondog motionless on the floor of her cell.

# ~ 20 ~

Night had settled over Edwards Air Force Base, covering the dry lakebeds with cool air. Most of the base had fallen into silence, broken by the occasional aircraft engine or the headlights of a vehicle moving along one of the airbase's many roads. The vast majority of activity had ceased for the day, leaving Edwards quiet beneath the stars.

The large, ominous shape of the Blackbird loomed into the night. The aircraft sat on the taxiway, just off the edge of Dryden's longest runway. The twin J-58 turbo ramjet engines throbbed evenly. Fuel beaded along the jet's wings and dripped to the ground beneath the plane. In flight, the metal would expand from the heat, sealing the cracks in the airframe. Until then, the droplets of fuel would form beneath the wings and fall to the earth.

Sitting high off the ground in the Blackbird's cockpit, Stang made a final check of her instruments. Everything was in the green. Her checklist complete, she took a deep breath and keyed her mike.

"Edwards tower, Habu, ready for takeoff runway two two left," she said.

"Habu, Edwards, cleared for takeoff runway two two left," the tower replied, relaying the winds. "Maintain two eight zero degrees and climb to flight level three five zero. Safe flight."

Stang released the brakes and rolled the

Blackbird slowly out onto the runway. Ahead of her the runway lights stretched into the distance. She wrapped her right hand around the stick and placed her left on the throttles. The bulky pressure suit she wore made the motions feel strange. She hadn't quite gotten used to its stiffness.

"Here we go," she called to Barker, sitting directly behind her. She pushed the throttles forward to their stops.

The two J-58's spooled up quickly, filling the black air with a loud roar. The Blackbird began to crawl forward, picking up speed rapidly as it rolled down the runway. Stang felt the controls come alive in her hands, easily keeping the large plane in the center of the strip as the airspeed indicator slipped past one hundred fifty knots.

In the backseat of the aircraft, Barker peered out the window, amazed at the rapid pace with which the buildings zipped by. The Blackbird's speed was increasing with every second, yet the landing gear remained firmly attached to the ground.

Stang eased back on the control stick, gently bringing up the nose. The Blackbird's front gear came up, lifting easily off the runway. A minute later the main landing gear followed. For a few moments the Blackbird flew level, its landing gear twenty feet off the pavement.

As the airspeed slipped through two hundred knots, Stang pulled the Blackbird into a climb, raising the landing gear. She swung the large aircraft into a westward turn, following the vectors air traffic control sent her.

Barker gazed out the window. Thousands of feet below, the lights of Los Angeles and its suburbs sprawled to the north and south, cut off abruptly by the Pacific Ocean to the west. He could spot a few lights from boats out on the water, and nothing beyond.

As they slipped over the shore, Stang again keyed the mike. "March eight one, Habu, thirty-five thousand feet, heading two eight zero degrees," she announced.

"Copy Habu," the tanker replied. The voice on the other side continued speaking, relaying a series of instructions, which Stang followed. After a few moments the lights of a KC-135 appeared directly ahead, drawing closer and closer.

Having spent her career flying fighters, a midair refueling was no new trick for Stang. Barker, however, had never seen one from this vantage point. The ride over to Edwards had been short enough to allow the F-15 to make the trip with only its on-board reserves.

He watched in fascination as the tanker grew larger, until it filled the Blackbird's windows. The tips of the Stratotanker's wings vanished from sight, so that only the large fuselage and the inside edges of the wings were visible.

From the KC-135, the operator lowered the boom. Barker watched as the end of the fifty-foot tube, marked with two small fins, drifted toward him. It passed directly over his head and slipped into a slot just behind him.

The tanker began to offload fuel. Stang held the aircraft in perfect position, flying just slightly behind and beneath the tanker. The two planes moved westward together, heading out over the inky blackness of the Pacific Ocean.

The Blackbird had lifted off with her tanks nearly empty, requiring the aircraft to be refueled almost immediately after takeoff. To Barker it seemed as if the two planes were connected for hours, as the Stratotanker dumped gallon after gallon into the SR-71's nearly dry tanks.

Finally, the operator retracted the boom. Barker

watched as it slipped over his head, moving upward to lie flat along the KC-135's underbelly once more. Thanking the tanker, Stang eased back on the throttles, allowing the Blackbird to slip further behind and below the KC-135.

"Good luck," March 81 replied, making a slow, lazy turn southward before striking back east to the coast.

Stang waited until the tanker's lights had disappeared before shoving the throttles forward and placing the SR-71 into a shallow climb. Her eyes played over her instruments. In the back, Barker focused on tracking their course.

As the airspeed crept up to Mach 0.9, Stang pushed the nose of the Blackbird down again. For all the power provided by the engines, the SR-71, the world's fastest air-breathing plane, did not have sufficient thrust to overcome the drag produced by the shock waves that formed as it reached supersonic speeds. In order to punch through the sound barrier, the Blackbird needed gravity's help.

As Stang nosed the craft down, its own weight gave it the extra momentum it required, and the Blackbird easily transitioned to supersonic flight. Stang put the SR-71 back into a climb, watching almost deliriously as her altitude and Mach number crept higher.

Glancing out the window, she could see the exhaust gases shooting from the back of the engines, forming brilliant strings of blue and red Mach diamonds in the blackness behind the aircraft. The shock cones at the front of each intake slid backward, automatically adjusting to give the engine the optimum shock configurations for its airspeed.

As the Mach number crept still higher, the turbojets lost their effectiveness. To compensate, channels opened near the front of the engine, allowing the inflowing air to bypass the compressor altogether, and turning it into a ramjet.

"We just slipped through Mach three," Stang announced, studying her instruments. She sounded slightly breathless.

"And that's eighty thousand feet," she said a few minutes later. She eased the stick forward again, leveling out the airplane.

Barker gazed out the window. Below there was nothing but blackness. Above and to all sides the stars shone with an incredible brightness he had never seen before. There was no moon, and they were far above any clouds, leaving thousands upon thousands of pinpoints of light glowing in the blackness above.

"We're on the edge of space," he said.

"Amazing, isn't it?" Stang asked. "This is probably as close as we'll ever get to space."

"Ever thought of trying to get into NASA?" Barker said.

"I wanted to be an astronaut when I was a kid," she admitted. "And I suppose it still would be nice, but flying fighters is what I really love. I don't mind if this is as close as I get. After all, how many people can say they've flown a Blackbird?"

"Or even ridden in one," Barker said. Stang laughed.

They fell silent again. Stang monitored the aircraft itself, her green eyes flitting back and forth over the instruments and gauges. She held the SR-71 in an even attitude, pausing in between checks to marvel at the sky above her for a second or two.

Behind her, Barker kept busy monitoring the Blackbird's rapid westward progress. From time to time he offered course corrections, which Stang quickly applied. Below them, the Pacific slipped by at an alarming rate.

"Hey, look at that," Stang whispered, almost halfway across the ocean.

Barker lifted his head from the chart he was studying and looked forward. To the west the sky was lightening, the stars slowly dimming. As he watched, the faint light crept eastward, fading out the fainter stars.

"What's happening?" he asked.

"We're overtaking the sun," Stang said.

In the west the sky continued to lighten. The stars above them vanished as the light filtered back into the sky. Far below, Earth's surface appeared, curving away ahead of them. The water beneath remained black.

The sky grew lighter still, turning gradually from black to deep blue. The western edge of the ocean beneath began to turn blue. Suddenly, the shimmering orange rim of the sun broke over the horizon. The sun rose gently from the western waters until it hung like an orange ball just over the water. Then it began to climb back into the sky.

"Sunrise in the west," Barker said.

"Wow," Stang said, instinctively slipping the tinted visor down over her helmet. Barker did the same.

The sun continued to rise slowly, fading back to yellow. Below, the ocean took on color, stretching vast and blue in every direction. Swirling white clouds wrapped over it in places, blanketing parts of the water. From the SR-71's altitude, they appeared far below. Around the aircraft, the sky was completely cloudless. It had turned a dark blue, slightly reminiscent of the blackness of space which had engulfed the plane earlier.

Flying along the outer reaches of the atmosphere, racing along the edge of the vacuum, the Blackbird sped westward at Mach three. It cut through the sky alone, over the desolate ocean, higher than any other aircraft flew.

"I see Japan," Stang announced suddenly.

Barker lifted his head. A long, slightly curved slope of land appeared out of the water, partly obscured by clouds. It surprised him how much of the island was visible.

He turned his attention back to his charts and focused on his job in earnest. The Blackbird continued on its course, racing over Japan. As the SR-71 crossed the western shore, he told Stang to turn south. She complied, running the Blackbird over the East China Sea between the island and the mainland.

Under Barker's direction, the Blackbird skirted along the Chinese border. Given its altitude and speed, the SR-71 was not very vulnerable to attack from other aircraft or from missiles, but the plane's crew did not want to alert the Chinese to their presence yet.

The Blackbird raced along the western Asian coast, cutting across Indochina and then dashing across the Bay of Bengal. They went feet-dry for a third time over India, racing up just inside the nation's western border.

Over Pakistan, Stang throttled the engines back and put the Blackbird into a dive. Their altitude bled off quickly, and their speed dropped gradually, placing the SR-71 at a normal aircraft's altitude and velocity as they slipped across the Afghan border. Just inside Afghanistan another tanker was waiting. For a second time Stang slid the Blackbird into position behind the other plane, and the operator lowered the boom.

Barker watched his second midair refueling in the daylight. This time the tanker appeared even closer than it had at night. The skin of the aircraft was gray, and its underbelly seemed to cover the entire sky. Again Stang held a steady course as they refueled.

"Those cameras ready?" she asked as the boom slid away from the Blackbird. The tanker turned away, heading southwest. Stang shoved the throttles forward again and began to climb.

"Ready," Barker said.

"Guide me to the target, then," she said, dipping the aircraft's nose down to throw the SR-71 past Mach one.

Barker gave her a new heading, and she quickly complied, swinging the large aircraft to the northeast. The ground began to fall away beneath them, racing rapidly by as they swept through Mach three. The terrain beneath was rough and rocky, covered with craggy mountains and patched in higher places with snow. As their altitude increased, the mountains lost their relief, and the sky slipped back to a deep, dark blue.

Stang leveled the aircraft off at eighty thousand feet just as they crossed the border into China. There was no change in the ground below as they entered Chinese airspace. The Himalayan Mountains stretched endlessly beneath, white snow marking their caps. Even from their great altitude, the roof of the world looked lonely and inhospitable. To the east, the land flattened out into brown, endless desert before curving out of view.

"We're over China," Barker reported, giving Stang another course correction.

"Doesn't look very inviting down there," she said.

"C'mon," Barker said. "I'm sure some people find mountains and desert very nice."

"What do they grow, rocks?"

"They could raise goats or something," he said. "Three minutes to target."

"Everything's in the green," Stang said, her tone instantly switching back to professional as she swept her eyes over the instruments.

"Hold this course," Barker said, checking his calculations. "It should put us directly over the target."

"What on earth is out there?" she wondered.

"That's what we were sent here to find out," Barker said.

"If I remember, we were sent here to find if something was out here," Stang said. "Why anyone would put something here is beyond me," she added, glancing down at the barren waste far below the Blackbird.

"I told you, they liked the setting," Barker said.

Stang ran her eyes over her instruments again.

"This is the first time I've flown over enemy territory unarmed," she said.

Aside from her initial flight training, and test piloting in the States, every aircraft she had flown had been armed with a combination of machine guns and air-to-air missiles. On numerous missions she had carried bombs as well. Countermeasures, flares and chaff, had always been loaded aboard as well for defense.

The SR-71 was devoid of both armament and countermeasures. The Blackbird's only defenses were its speed and its altitude. Hopefully, the sleek plane could fly too high to be reached by missiles and too fast to be caught by enemy aircraft.

So far, those defenses had worked incredibly well. In the aircraft's entire operational history, no Blackbird had ever been lost to enemy action while flying routinely over hostile territory. The SR-71 was virtually untouchable.

As the Blackbird raced toward its target, Barker made one final check of his systems. The cameras were ready, preprogrammed to shoot in sequence. He quickly checked his navigation equipment. They would be over target in a minute.

At precisely the desired moment the cameras began to fire, photographing the land beneath. Even at such an altitude the Blackbird could take very accurate pictures, with a resolution of inches. For this particular mission the cameras were set to take a series of wide-angle pictures, to cover as much earth in the region as possible. The hope was that by sweeping the ground, the photographic analysts could find exactly what they were looking for beneath the plane.

The cameras were almost two-thirds of the way through their photographic sequence when a loud alarm began to sound in the Blackbird's cockpit, making both occupants jump. Stang's green eyes immediately shifted to her instruments.

"Mark our location, now," she ordered.

"What's going on?" Barker asked, as he quickly complied with her direction.

"Someone's definitely down there," she said. "They just fired a couple of SA-2s at us. They must have some damned good radar," she added. Although not as elusive as later planes, the Blackbird was actually an early stealth aircraft, not entirely invisible, but very difficult to detect.

The warning alarm continued to blare in the cockpit. Stang pushed the nose up slightly and shoved the throttles to their stops.

"C'mon, sweetheart," she cooed as if she was coaxing a racehorse, tapping the plane's instrument panel gently. "Show us what you can do."

The Blackbird responded almost instantaneously, beginning to climb again. The Mach number crept upward as well. The SR-71 slipped through eighty-one thousand feet, followed by eighty-two thousand, and continued upward, edging up to Mach 3.2 and still gliding forward.

Stang kept her eyes riveted to the instruments as the Blackbird moved upward. She was operating the aircraft at the edge of its envelope, pushing it further with every small increase in altitude and speed. She knew the dangers of taking an aircraft past its limits, but she also knew she had to outrun the missiles beneath her. So she focused on her gauges and nudged the aircraft forward. Thankfully, everything stayed in the green as they raced upward.

"We're done photographing," Barker said as the cameras completed their filming sequence. "We're not going to lose anything, if you want to make a few maneuvers."

Stang laughed, not shifting her green eyes from the instruments.

"If I jink at this speed, it will rip the plane to pieces," she said over the blaring of the siren. The Blackbird had been designed for speed, not maneuverability. At such a high Mach number, the g-forces applied to the plane in a sudden movement would destroy it.

"Are you saying there's nothing we can do?" Barker asked.

"We can climb and run," she said, "which is exactly what we're doing now." The Blackbird was slipping through eighty-five thousand feet.

Barker checked behind him. Far below, he could see two surface-to-air missiles rushing up at them. Each was as tall as a telephone pole. They flew side by side, angled directly toward the Blackbird. Twin columns of fire marked the missiles' location against the brown earth.

"I can see them. Four o'clock," he announced.

For the first time since beginning the climb, Stang took her eyes off the instruments, turning her head back over her shoulder and watching the missiles. The SA-2s were climbing rapidly, growing larger and larger by the second. For an instant Stang was certain the missiles would collide with the Blackbird. She sucked in air, holding her breath.

Suddenly, a thousand feet beneath the Blackbird, the brilliant flame trails behind the missiles disappeared as the engines cut out. The SA-2s had reached the top of their range. An instant later both SAMs exploded. Two brilliant red flowers, as vibrant as fireworks, replaced the missiles, vanishing a second later, the broken pieces of the missiles tumbling to the ground.

Once again the sky behind the Blackbird was empty. Stang exhaled slowly, twisting her attention back to her instruments. She pulled the throttles back slightly, bringing the SR-71 to Mach three. She touched the nose down, leveling out at eighty-six thousand feet.

"I think we'll stay up here for a while," she said. "Just in case they decide to send anything else up after us."

"Sounds good to me," Barker said.

"We get our pictures?" she asked.

"We did," he said.

"Good," she said. "Let's get the fuck out of Dodge."

"I thought you liked getting shot at," he said, giving her a heading.

Stang swung the Blackbird to it, racing to the south toward the border. Either incapable or unwilling to attack, the Chinese were silent for the remainder of the time it took for the SR-71 to fly through their airspace.

The Blackbird dashed back across the Himalayas, slipping down over India and back into friendly territory. As they crossed over the South China Sea, Stang turned the SR-71 to the east, and the Blackbird raced for home.

# ~ **21** ~

Chin stood at the railing, his back to Martina, looking down at the activity beneath him. Panther knew the Chinese general was deliberately ignoring the presence of his prisoner in an effort to make her feel uncomfortable. His lack of recognition did nothing to faze her, however. Instead, she took the opportunity to survey the control center below, trying to decipher their activities.

Most of the controllers were hunched over computers or radar screens. The large displays hanging from the walls showed satellite tracks. Nothing indicated the placement of ground forces. Many people were talking into headsets, but Martina could not understand their language. All she could hear was the chatter of mingled voices.

Chin was directly in front of her. Ming stood off to his left, leaning against the rail at her usual place. She eyed Martina coldly and contemptuously. Martina ignored her. The two guards who had escorted her to the upper level of the mountain stood on either side of her. They had released her and simply waited, standing somewhat relaxed.

Finally, Chin turned to face her. He flicked his dark eyes up and down her. She stood straight and defiant, shoulders squared, staring directly at him. Cold fire roiled in her eyes. She remained silent, waiting for him to speak.

"Still unwilling to cooperate, Colonel?" he asked.

"You still ugly?" she replied flippantly.

"My reasonableness has limits," he replied slowly. "If you refuse to do what I ask, I will make you suffer."

"What are you going to do?" she challenged, her voice even. "Beat me up, like you did to Commander Ansetti?"

"Not for the moment," he said. "I told you before, Colonel, if you help me, I can make you one of the richest people in China, the greatest power in the world."

"And I told you before, I don't want your money," she said coldly. "Don't act like you're trying to help me. You're going to keep us here until we're no longer any use to you, and then you're going to kill us."

"Everyone has their price," Chin said. "Name yours, and I will give it to you, in return for the information I want."

"I'd rather retain my honor than have anything you can give me," she said.

"Strange how you cling to those values," he said, pacing back toward the rail. "You have such loyalty to a nation that will cease to exist in just over two days. Where will you place your allegiance when your country falls?"

"As long as I have anything to say about it, America will not fall," Martina said, the same defiant tone in her voice.

"Your hands are tied, Colonel." Chin said, spinning back toward her. "Your country has no idea what's coming, and you have no way to warn them."

Suddenly, the side door burst open. A small man in uniform rushed up to Chin, saluted, and began to speak in rapid-fire Chinese. Chin's face took on a look of surprise, then disbelief. He asked the soldier a question. The soldier nodded, chattering again. Chin's face paled.

Chin turned slowly back to Martina, a look of horror across his features. He took a few steps toward her.

"Something just flew over us," he said. "Twenty-four kilometers high, moving at three times the speed of sound. Do you know what this is?"

"No," Martina replied, unable to keep her lips from spreading into a grin. Her mind was racing, rapidly doing a rough calculation to shift metric into feet. Her eyes began to dance as she realized the aircraft's true altitude.

"Liar," Chin accused fiercely. He snapped something in Chinese. The two guards lunged forward, grabbing Martina by the arms. The American remained motionless as Ming walked up to her and smashed her fist directly in Martina's face, splitting her upper lip. Blood began to trickle down the pilot's bruised face.

"What just flew over us?" Chin demanded.

"I don't know," Martina replied, smiling widely, her teeth covered with blood.

Ming shoved the palm of her hand into Martina's cracked ribs. The American gasped, staggering backward until she collided with the far wall. The two guards moved with her, unwilling to release their hold on her. The Chinese woman moved forward as well, continuing to apply pressure to the injured area, smiling as she did.

The wall pressed harshly into Panther's back, and the force against her cracked ribs sent tongues of fire dancing through her chest. Despite the pain, she remained motionless, her smile twisted from the agony in her body.

"What was it?" Chin said, stepping closer to her. Anger flared in his eyes. His infuriation at her defiance only seemed to please the American more.

"I don't know," Martina repeated, the pain in her

voice unable to hide the excited glittering in her eyes.

"It's no matter," he said, curtly. "We've already launched against it. In a few minutes whatever is up there will no longer exist."

Ming scowled and removed her hand from Martina's ribs, stalking back to the railing. The soldiers released their grip on her. Martina straightened her back and moved forward, away from the wall. The guards moved with her, staying six inches on either side of the pilot.

"Sir!" the soldier who had first reported to Chin called in Chinese. He was standing over the railing, speaking to someone below. "The SA-2s missed. It was out of range."

Chin cursed, turning to face him. "Launch fighters," he ordered.

"It will be out of our airspace by the time they get airborne," the man replied. "It's moving far too fast for any of our planes to catch it."

Chin cursed again, twisting back to face Martina. The anger in the Chinese general's face was more pronounced.

"Too high for your SAMs?" she said, flashing her bloody grin.

Chin did not reply. He barked at the guards, who grabbed the pilot by the arms and spun her around. They marched her silently out the door, back through the stone hallways, and down to the lower level of the mountain.

They stopped in front of her cell. One man pulled the door open, allowing the second to shove her inside. As she stumbled forward, the first soldier closed the door behind her, locking it. The two men spun on their heels and disappeared down the hall.

Martina sank slowly to the ground, still smiling to herself. Across from her, Moondog lay exactly as she had for the past several hours. She had not stirred when the soldiers returned with Panther. Martina didn't know if she remained where she was because she was too deeply asleep to notice or because she simply did not want to move.

Martina sat motionless for a few minutes after the soldiers' footsteps had faded down the hall before sliding herself over to the door and pressing her face through the bars. She looked at Moondog for a moment, noting that she was still breathing.

"Moondog," she called softly. "Moondog, wake up."

"What?" the Navy pilot moaned. She rolled over slowly so that she faced Martina, lying on her stomach. She raised her head off the floor but did not lift herself any further. Martina could still see evidence of pain in the one eye she could open.

"Something just flew over us," she said. The Air Force pilot was grinning wildly despite the blood running from her upper lip. Moondog's face remained impassive.

"It was flying Mach three at eighty thousand feet," Martina continued.

"Mach three at eighty thousand?" Moondog said, incredulous. "That's not possible." Her facial expression shifted to one of surprise.

"There's only one airplane in the world that can do that," Martina said, still smiling broadly. "An SR-71."

"A Blackbird," Moondog said in disbelief.

"Whatever you did worked," Martina said. "They're looking for us."

"Hopefully they found us." Moondog paused. "How could it be a Blackbird?" she said. "Those were decommissioned years ago."

"Apparently not all of them," Martina said. "Chin launched a couple of SAMs against it. The plane was too high. They couldn't touch it. It had to be a Blackbird."

"That's the best thing I've heard since we got here," Moondog said, the hint of a smile creeping across her face.

"I see you've still got some life left in you," Martina commented, leaning back against the wall beside the door.

The Navy pilot grinned. "They ain't finished off old Moondog yet."

     &#42;        &#42;        &#42;

Richard Barker's boots hit the tarmac at Edwards. He took his hands off the ladder leading to the SR-71's cockpit and stepped back. Beside him, Stang was gazing up at the jet, sweeping her eyes over its long, black body with an almost wistful look on her face.

The Blackbird sat silently on the ramp outside its hangar. A series of lights illuminated its sharp frame in the darkness. Its engines were silent. The cockpit was opened into the cool night air, with the ladder trailing down to where the crew stood. A strange sadness surrounded its silhouette, once more confined to the ground.

Already Dryden's ground crew was rushing from the hangar, surrounding the Blackbird. They quickly prepared to pull the plane back into its hangar, remove the film from its cameras, and service the aircraft. Once they had finished, they would put her back into waiting until NASA or the Air Force called for her service again.

"It's a shame," Stang said, studying the airplane. She kept her eyes fixed on it, wanting to absorb every ounce of the sleek craft. "They were meant to fly, not to sit on display at museums. We still have use for them, and they're still the fastest thing around."

Barker realized that she did not want to leave the large plane behind. As a pilot, she was happiest at the controls of an aircraft. Flying the Blackbird had been one of the most incredible experiences of her life. The thought of being unable to fly the SR-71 again saddened her.

"Major!" someone shouted. Barker turned his head. Stang sighed and twisted away from the Blackbird. Brigadier General Peters was approaching.

"Mission successful, sir," Stang said, saluting. The bittersweet expression vanished from her face, turning to one of business.

"Excellent," Peters said, returning the gesture.

"There's someone there, sir," she continued. "We flew right over an SA-2 site. They launched two SAMs at us."

"Any damage?" he asked, concerned.

"They couldn't reach us, sir," she said, grinning wryly.

"That's good," he said. "What did you think of her?"

Stang shook her head slowly. "That plane is incredible, sir. I'd fly her again in a heartbeat."

"I'm sure you would," Peters said. He dug into his pocket, producing two small objects, which he held out to the Blackbird's crew.

"Mach three plus pins," he said. "You've flown it. You earned them."

"Thank you, sir," Stang said, picking up one of the pins and studying it with a grin.

Peters handed the second pin to Barker.

"Thank you," the navigator said, taking the pin.

"You're welcome," Peters said. "Of course you can't tell anyone how you got those." The two majors grinned.

"I've arranged for you to have the day off tomorrow, since you've already busted crew rest," Peters said to Stang. "Go home and get some sleep."

He turned to Barker. "You can catch a ride back to your base tomorrow. In the meantime just get a lift to the VOQ. Thank you again, major." He extended his hand.

"Not a problem, sir," Barker said, shaking it.

"Good morning, I guess. Carry on," he said, turning and leaving the two junior officers standing on the tarmac.

"That was interesting," Barker said to his frontseater. "Want to grab a beer?"

"I don't drink beer," she said.

"You don't?" he said, slightly surprised.

"Nope," she said. "Don't like it. I am kinda partial to tequila, though, if you want to get a margarita."

Barker laughed. The two majors turned back toward the hangar, leaving the Blackbird to the technicians.

# ~ 22 ~

The photographic analyst snapped to rigid attention as Brigadier General Peters walked into the room. Seeing him suddenly stand, the two men sitting across the table also rose. Turning to face the general, they too came to attention.

Both men were Navy SEALs, based at Coronado, on the California coast. The shorter of the two was a lieutenant junior grade named Mike Hawk. He was of medium build, standing a few inches short of six feet. His hair was shaved close to his head, making it impossible to determine its color. Thick muscles wound through his bare arms. His battle dress uniform covered the rest of his trim, muscular body.

The second man, Andrew Kennedy, also wore a battle dress uniform. Like Hawk, he was trim and muscular, but his build was lighter. In contrast, he stood just over six feet. His thick black hair was cut short. He studied Peters through a pair of dark eyes set in a tanned face.

"Carry on," Peters said.

The photographic analyst nervously settled back into his seat, not completely relaxing. The SEALs joined him, appearing more at ease. Unlike the analyst, they did not seem to be alarmed by the presence of the general. They were too focused on the information in front of them.

The table itself was covered with large

photographs taken by the Blackbird just hours earlier. One particular shot sat on the top, and all three men were studying it. The analyst moved his pen over the picture and began pointing out its contents to the SEALs.

Peters crossed the room, stopping just to the right of the SEALs. The analyst glanced up at him nervously as he paused. The general remained silent. He leaned over the table slightly, looking at the large photograph.

"This is the Chinese base," the analyst began, sounding a little uneasy. "You can see several large radio antennas here." He pointed to the large structures with his pen. "There is a SAM site here, and a radar antenna here." He moved his pen across the photo as he spoke, indicating each aspect of the picture. The SEALs followed his motions intently.

"This is a road," he said, pointing to a long, thin strip winding across the photo. "It leads to a runway a few miles away, equipped with several hangars. He shuffled through the pictures, selecting another and dropping it onto the table.

"This is the airstrip," he said, indicating a large paved area with three buildings sitting beside it. The frames of airplanes were visible alongside. "The contingent is small. Four MiG-29s," he said, indicating a group of aircraft, "and two transports." The analyst pointed to the large aircraft.

"The road continues off this way," he said, "back toward eastern China."

He slid the second photo back underneath the first.

"Here, it leads into the mountain," he said, pointing to a cavern in a large mountain. "There are two secondary entrances to the mountain, here and here." He placed his pen on each. "We believe the Chinese base is inside the mountain itself."

Finishing his speech, the analyst leaned back, glancing nervously toward Peters again. The two SEALS continued to study the photograph for several more minutes. Neither spoke as they intently pored over it.

"Is there anything else out there?" Hawk said finally, lifting his head and fixing his eyes directly on the Air Force man.

"No," the analyst said. "Not for hundreds of miles. It's all desert and mountains."

The SEAL nodded and turned his attention back to the photograph. The room remained silent for another few minutes.

"Well, what do you think?" Peters asked the SEAL.

"It's suicide, sir," Hawk said plainly, turning to Peters. Kennedy leaned back and looked up at the Air Force general but said nothing.

"How so?" Peters said.

"We have no idea what we're up against," Hawk said. "For all we know there could be only two soldiers with AK-47s guarding your pilots, or a whole regiment down there. That mountain could have one little cave, or miles and miles of tunnels."

Peters frowned.

"Basically, all these pictures show is that there is something in the mountain, but we can't tell just what," the SEAL continued. "We'd be going in completely blind. We could wander down there for days and not find your people."

"If we had a plan, or a map of some sort, we could do it," Kennedy said, his voice deep and even. "But we need to know exactly what's there."

"A map, huh?" Peters said, straightening his back. "I'll see what I can do. In the meantime, do as much as you can without one."

"Yes, sir," the SEALs said in unison.

"Carry on," Peters said, turning on his heel and

walking quickly from the room.

✳      ✳      ✳

Li Won lifted her head as the door to her office opened and her boss stepped inside. Zhan Chow's face was nearly expressionless. He scanned the room slowly, as if lost in thought, smiling when his eyes fell on Li.

"How did the meeting go, sir?" she asked, returning his smile.

"Decent," he replied. "Everything's on schedule for the most part. Of course, there are always one or two things that are lagging..."

"Always," Li agreed.

"Any messages for me?" Chow asked.

"No, sir," Li said.

"I'll be in my office, then," he said, walking through her small office and pulling open the door that led to his own. He disappeared through the door, closing it softly behind him. Li could hear him walking to his desk.

As her boss vanished, she turned her attention back to her own work. A master schedule for the agency was sitting on top of her screen. Li minimized it and pulled up a second window, showing a running search.

The program was currently probing every computer on the Chinese space agency's network and the Chinese military's network, rapidly scanning for the inputs Li had entered. Although it was running off her work computer, she had disguised the code to make it appear as if it was an external hack, and a very undetectable one at that. The search was about three-fourths of the way through and had yet to produce any results.

Li scowled, minimized the search window, and called up the calendar again. Grumbling, she went back to work on planning and reorganizing the schedule to her boss's specifications. It was a mind-numbingly simple task, but it was something she had to accomplish in order to maintain her posting at the agency. As of yet, she had not failed to complete anything assigned to her, giving Chow every reason to value her work.

After about twenty minutes her search engine pinged, the computer emitting a faint chime very similar to the noise her email program made when a message was received. Hearing the sound, Li quickly minimized the calendar in front of her and pulled up the search engine.

The search was complete. It showed three separate results to her query. All were remote radio stations China used to communicate with its satellites. Li immediately called up the information her search had uncovered.

The first site was located along the coast, in a densely populated area. Li frowned, immediately dismissing the site. She had been told the station would be located inland, far away from any towns or villages.

Closing the results for the first site, she called up the second. This site looked more promising. It was located in central northern China, just beneath Mongolia. There were very few people located in the region.

Smiling, Li called up the site plans. The map showed three large antennas and two satellite dishes. A medium-sized building sat beside the antennas. A quick scan of the information revealed that four men, working in teams of two, manned the station. There was also a brief floor plan, showing living quarters and a control area.

Li frowned again. The location fit the description, but the site was far too small to match what her controller wanted her to find. Whatever her boss in the Central Intelligence Agency was looking for, this site did not have it.

Dismissing the second location, she closed the information she was looking at and pulled up the data for the final site. It was located in the southeastern part of the country, on the edge of the northern Himalayas. That part of the world was almost entirely uninhabited, making the site another possibility.

Li called up the rest of the information on the area. Instead of revealing the site plans, as the second site had, the words "ACCESS DENIED" flashed on her screen, with "CLASSIFIED" appearing directly beneath.

Li stared at the flashing words. For some reason, the information about this place was being kept secret, while the other two sites were easily accessible. Someone was trying to hide something about this particular location.

Li grinned. This was almost certainly what her controller wanted her to find. Closing the "ACCESS DENIED" window, she set to work bypassing the mechanisms that kept the information secure. Her fingers flew rapidly across the keyboard as she attempted to unlock the information on the radio station.

The plans themselves were deeply encrypted. It took Li almost twenty minutes to successfully hack through the security devices hiding the information. However, the site plans finally revealed themselves to her. Li's eyes grew wide as she scanned the data in front of her.

The information revealed that the control facilities for the site were actually buried within a nearby mountain. Three separate layers had been dug out. The lowest level contained mostly storage areas. The middle section was by far the largest, housing a vast satellite control area and many smaller work stations. The upper level served as a housing area.

The data revealed that a hundred technicians were stationed within the mountain. Fifty soldiers served as guards. A dozen antennas and receiving stations marked the northern side of the mountain, beside a large door leading inside. Several smaller channels led out in other directions.

The plans further revealed an airfield to the northeast, equipped with a small contingent of MiGs and several larger cargo planes. Several surface-to-air missile sites dotted the area, providing an even stronger defense.

Li leaned back in her chair, exhaling slowly in astonishment. Whoever had built this facility had done so in absolute secrecy. Even the director of the space agency did not know about it. If he had, Li would have too. She shook her head slowly. This had to be what the Americans wanted.

She reached into her handbag and pulled out a small disk, which she slipped into the computer's drive. She quickly downloaded all the available information on the third site onto the disk. Once the download had been completed, Li slid the disk back into her purse.

She closed the information about all three sites, then shut down the search engine itself. Making sure there was no remaining evidence of the search on her computer, she again called up the calendar she had been working on.

Li checked the clock on her wall, which indicated it was ten minutes to noon. Slipping her purse over her shoulder, she stood and walked to Chow's door. Raising her hand, she rapped twice on the wood.

"Yes?" Chow called from the other side of the door.

Li cracked the door open and stuck her head inside. Her boss was sitting at his desk, bent over his work. He smiled when he saw her.

"I'm going to go and grab some lunch in town," she said. "Would you like me to get you something too?"

"Certainly, thank you," Chow said.

"I'll be back in about half an hour," Li said, stepping back and shutting the door behind her.

She made her way down to the ground floor and out onto the streets of Beijing without so much as a glance from the space agency's other employees. They were used to seeing the director's secretary running all sorts of errands for her boss.

Li moved quickly along the sidewalk, winding expertly through the crowded roadside, dodging businessmen, vendors, and the homeless. She made her way quickly back to her apartment building and up the stairs to her own small room.

Dropping her purse on the desk, she unlocked the drawer, removing her laptop and cellphone. She opened up the laptop. As the computer booted up, Li dug the small disk from her purse. She inserted it into the laptop's drive.

Flipping open the satellite phone, she dialed a number from memory and held the phone to her ear. She heard a single ring. The CIA's carefully hidden satellite communications network had yet to come under attack, as it was disguised as a European satellite phone network.

"Section A control center," a voice said.

"This is Dragon Lady," Li said. "I'm secure."

"Do you have it?" the controller said.

"I do," Li said. "I'm uploading it now." She hit a few strokes on the computer, transmitting the site plans over a secure link to the control center.

"We've got it," the controller said after a moment. "Thank you, and carry on."

"Dragon Lady will comply," Li said, snapping the

phone shut. She hit another series of keys, wiping the information from the disk. Then she removed the small object, placing it back in her purse. She powered down the computer.

Locking the laptop and the cellphone back in the desk, Li slung her purse over her shoulder and slipped out of her apartment, back to the streets. Stopping to buy lunch from a local vendor, she made her way quickly back to the space agency.

✳        ✳        ✳

"Can you do it?" Peters asked.

The two SEALs sat in front of him, poring over the schematics for the Chinese base. They had been intently studying the information for the past fifteen minutes, whispering quietly to themselves occasionally.

"Absolutely, sir," Kennedy said, straightening up.

"This is the lowest level of the mountain," Hawk said to Peters, pointing to the top piece of paper. "It's mostly just used for storage, food, supplies, and the like."

Peters nodded.

"These small rooms over here are jail cells," he said, indicating one area. "That's most likely where your pilots are. Fortunately, most of the Chinese activity occurs on the upper level. We can sneak in, at an entrance here"—he pointed to another spot on the map—"grab your pilots, and sneak back out. Very easy."

"And since it's the bottom level, we could plant charges and bring the whole mountain down after us," Kennedy added evenly.

"Excellent," Peters said. "I'll be back in a minute. Carry on."

He stepped from the room, leaving the two SEALs to study the plans. Walking quickly, he entered his own office, picked up the phone, and punched in a number. Staring out at the base through his window, he waited to be connected.

"What have you got, Scott?" David Webster asked as he came on the line.

"They can do it, sir," Peters said. "They can bring the entire place down if you want."

"Outstanding," the President said. Peters could sense him smiling. "Do it. Give them whatever they need."

"Yes, sir."

"And Scott," Webster added, "I want them over there immediately."

"Yes, sir," Peters repeated. "Good morning, sir."

"Good morning," the President said.

Peters set the phone down and strode quickly from his office back to the small conference room. The two SEALs were still bent over the plans. They turned around and came to their feet as the Air Force general entered.

"The mission is authorized," Peters said. "Get our pilots out and destroy the place. You will be given all the resources you need, and you will go as soon as possible."

"Yes, sir," Hawk said. He turned to Kennedy.

"Let's go to China," he said to his second in command.

The dark-haired SEAL simply grinned.

# ~ 23 ~

The guards escorting Panther and Moondog pushed open the large double doors leading to the central command center. Silently, they led the two prisoners inside, stopping just beyond the door. The two men standing in the rear closed the door.

Martina slowly scanned the room. As always, the area beneath the balcony was a constant buzz of activity. Controllers scurried about the floor busily, while others hunched over their desks, fixated on their work. She could hear the faint hum of their mingled voices, chattering in Chinese.

She raised her eyes to the screens. They remained the same as before, displaying only satellite tracks and data. A brief scowl passed over Martina's face. There was still nothing that hinted at Chin's plans.

Slightly discouraged, Martina turned her attention to her immediate surroundings. Ming stood in the far corner of the balcony, leaning against both the wall and the rail. As always, she glared angrily at the two Americans.

Bill Durant stood off to Martina's right. Catching sight of his tall figure, she fixed her fiery eyes on him, her lips curling upward in a snarl. Her fierce expression suggested she would lunge at him if not for the two men by her side. Seeing the sudden shift in her face, Durant stepped back abruptly, eyeing her warily.

Chin stood in the center of the room, leaning over the rail. As the door shut, he turned around, studying his captives. Smiling broadly, he stepped forward, stopping about five feet from Martina. She immediately shifted her gaze to him. Free of her cold stare, Durant relaxed slightly, moving farther away from the pilot. He kept his eyes fixed cautiously on her.

"In less than an hour, Colonel, you will see the fruition of my plan," Chin said, spreading his arms broadly.

"And I suppose you still won't tell me this plan," Martina said coolly.

"You will see soon enough," Chin said. He turned sharply, fixing his eyes on Ming.

"They're all yours," he said to her. "Kill Ansetti, but bring Redrick to me, alive and conscious. Put her in so much pain that she is unable to move."

"With pleasure," Ming said softly, a sadistic grin spreading across her face. She pushed herself off the rail, drawing up to her full height. She crossed the room in a few broad, easy strides, brushing past the two pilots.

Durant gazed toward Chin, relaxing slightly as the general spoke. He cautiously turned his gaze back toward Martina. If the tall pilot had heard the order, it had not registered on her face. Her gaze was as cold as ever.

Ming barked something in Chinese to the soldiers standing beside the pilots as she moved by them. Shoving the large doors open, she strode outside, head held high and eyes fixed straight ahead of her. Her pace did not slow as she disappeared from the room.

The soldiers standing beside Panther and Moondog grabbed the two women by the arms and spun them around. Quietly, they marched the pilots out of the room, following the thin Chinese woman. The doors swung shut behind them, closing loudly. In an instant the constant hum of activity that permeated the control room vanished, leaving a heavy silence in its place.

The sharp ringing of Ming's boots filled the hallways, followed by the steady footfalls of the guards and their prisoners. The long stone corridors were completely devoid of any other life. Everyone else inside the mountain was manning their posts in anticipation of the coming strike.

Ming led the way through the polished halls of the upper level and down the broad stone steps to the lower chambers. The light dimmed as they moved beneath, to the rough-hewn rock of the lower passages. Martina picked her head up as they moved past the jail cells, wondering exactly where they were being taken. The small group continued down the narrowing hall, moving through the tunnel for what seemed like miles.

Finally, Ming turned and pulled open the door to a small room. She walked smoothly inside. The soldiers followed, seemingly hesitant. Martina moved warily up as they pulled her inside, alert for any opportunity to free herself. Moondog simply snorted in disgust.

Martina scanned her surroundings. The room was small and dimly lit. A pair of shackles hung from the far wall. Beside them, three wooden shelves were filled with various implements, ranging from brass knuckles to needles. Martina stared at the devices in horror. The small room was nothing more than a torture chamber.

Ming stood to the other side of the shackles, her sadistic grin broadening. Even her eyes seemed to shine. The Chinese woman was once again back in her element. She fixed her cold gaze at the soldiers holding Moondog's wrists and barked something at them in Chinese. Martina shuddered involuntarily as she realized the woman actually found some sick pleasure in all this.

The two men moved almost immediately, pulling the Navy pilot forward. Moondog made no attempt to resist. Spinning her around, the soldiers lifted her up, cuffing her wrists and ankles into the shackles. Moondog had an almost bored expression on her face, like a student forced to sit through the same lecture for the third time.

Clasping the cuffs around Moondog's ankles, the two men turned rapidly and fled the room, brushing quickly past the soldiers holding Martina. The door shut behind them. She could hear their quick footfalls fading down the hallway. After a moment the sound of the two men racing away vanished completely, leaving the room in complete and utter silence.

Ming walked slowly in front of Moondog, studying her with a menacing smile. The Navy pilot's face retained the same tired expression as the Chinese woman looked her up and down. For a moment, neither budged, as Ming pondered her first move.

Panther slowly turned her head, glancing at the soldiers standing on either side of her. Both men were looking forward, their attention focused entirely on Ming. They had released their grip on Martina's arms and were standing as if they were made of stone, nearly trembling. Their terror was so strong that she could smell it, feeling their emotion surrounding her.

Martina smirked. Their fear of Ming had almost completely immobilized them. Neither was even aware of the tall American standing between them. They were too focused on the terror before them, having completely forgotten their charge.

Slowly, Martina raised her left hand, placing her fingers on the holster the soldier to her left wore. Barely touching the holster, she ran her hand up along it until she felt the cold metal of his gun. Moving very cautiously, she curled her fingers around the butt of his pistol and carefully extracted the weapon. The man was too petrified by Ming to even notice Martina move.

In an instant she had unsafed the gun. Raising the weapon, Martina squeezed off a shot. The bullet smashed through the soldier's temple, exploding out the left side of his head. His eyes rolled back into his skull, and he toppled over backward, lying in a heap on the floor.

Martina rapidly twisted around, firing a second shot just as the soldier on her right turned to her. The bullet caught the man squarely in the chest at nearly point-blank range. He staggered backward as blood flowed from his chest, and collapsed to the ground. Satisfied both men were dead, she quickly transferred the weapon to her right hand.

Hearing the shots, Ming turned around sharply, only to find herself looking down the muzzle of a pistol. The tall Air Force pilot stared down the weapon, her expression cold. Her eyes blazed with an icy fire as she fixed her gaze directly into Ming's eyes. To either side of her, the soldiers who had guarded her lay dead.

"Don't move," Martina hissed.

A sharp wave of rage raced over Ming's cold face at this new atrocity. She glared angrily at Martina for a brief moment, furious that the pilot would attempt to subdue her. Almost instantly, she stepped forward, rapidly swinging her right fist directly at Martina's face.

The blow never collided. The pilot merely sidestepped, allowing Ming's fist to sail harmlessly past. Martina drew the pistol back and lashed out with the weapon. The muzzle caught Ming directly across the face. The force of the blow was more than enough to knock her down. She dropped to the floor in a heap.

Martina stepped over her, legs slightly apart in a shooter's stance. The Chinese woman stared up at her, fear and surprise replacing the rage in her eyes. Slowly, Ming slid backward until her back collided with the far wall. Suddenly trapped, she glanced around hysterically, looking for any way out, as Martina slowly advanced toward her.

"Not so easy when the other person fights back, is it?" Martina said, grinning coldly. Her eyes were hard and merciless.

Ming said nothing. She looked up at the muzzle of the pistol, pointed directly at her heart. She was trembling. She had never encountered someone bold enough to stand up to her. Even the soldiers cowered away from her. But the woman in front of her was no victim, and she was clearly in control of the situation. One look at her stony eyes told Ming that she would not hesitate to pull the trigger if Ming made any sudden moves.

"Get up," Martina snapped. Moving obediently out of fear, Ming scrambled to her feet and stood rigidly, staring at Panther in terror.

"Release her," Martina ordered, nodding toward Moondog. The Navy pilot had watched the preceding events calmly. She was smiling coldly, watching Ming shake with fear. The Chinese woman could see the same hardness in her face.

Fearfully, Ming moved along the wall. Martina followed her, keeping the pistol pointed directly at her. The Chinese woman cautiously bent down and slowly unshackled Moondog's ankles. Glancing over her shoulder at Martina, she stood and freed the Navy pilot's wrists.

As she undid the last cuff, Moondog turned on her. Grabbing the Chinese woman's hand, she cuffed her arm in the shackle. Shoving Ming's body against the wall, Moondog trapped her other wrist. Finding herself in the place of her numerous victims, Ming's eyes grew wide with horror. She attempted to struggle, kicking out at Moondog.

Without even blinking, Moondog smashed her fist into Ming's temple, momentarily dazing her. The Chinese woman stopped fighting immediately. Bending down, Moondog clasped the lower shackles around Ming's boots.

Moondog straightened her back, then swung her right fist into Ming's stomach with as much force as she could muster. The Chinese woman cried out in pain. Moondog flicked her eyes over Ming and stepped back slowly, glancing at Martina.

The tall woman shrugged, casually lowering her gun and crossing her arms. Ming shifted her gaze back and forth between them, her eyes filled with panic. Every muscle in her body was tense, but she was too petrified to struggle. Instead she simply trembled. She was trapped, with no way to fight back, and she knew it. Fear ran through her face.

Moondog walked coolly to the wooden shelves. She paused for a moment, studying the items that lay on top, her eyes slowly playing over everything. She slipped the brass knuckles over her fingers and studied her hand. Shaking her head, she slid the implements off and replaced them. Ming began to tremble uncontrollably.

Moondog bent to the second shelf, picking up a whip. She unwound it, looked it over for a moment, and swung the end across the room. The whip cracked loudly in the thick air. Ming flinched at the sound, twisting her head away from Moondog.

Moondog shook her head again. She curled the whip back up and laid it back where she had found it. Straightening her back, she scanned the shelves again. After a moment her eyes feel on a bottle of yellow liquid. She picked it up, studying it silently.

She grabbed the largest needle she could find. Inserting the tip into the top of the bottle, she pulled the plunger back, completely filling the syringe with the yellow fluid. She calmly studied the needle in her hand for a moment before setting the bottle back on the shelf and walking slowly to Ming.

"I'm sure you remember this stuff," Moondog said coolly. "It makes you feel as if your blood is boiling."

"But that much is lethal!" Ming nearly screamed, her eyes fixed in terror at the full syringe in Moondog's hand. Her fingers had curled tightly around the chains above her wrist, and she was unconsciously pulling herself upward.

"I know," the pilot replied nonchalantly. "I'd really like to take my time and give you a death fit to avenge everyone you've made suffer, but unfortunately we have to go stop your boss, so this will have to do." Her voice took on an icy edge as she spoke.

"I hope Satan gives you his worst, 'cause it ain't going to be anything compared to what I'm going to do to you when I get to Hell," Moondog snarled.

She stepped forward, plunging the tip of the needle directly into Ming's neck. She smoothly injected its entire contents into her body. Snapping the point off inside her flesh, Moondog stepped back, throwing the remainder of the syringe onto the floor.

Ming screamed as the fire began to race through her body. Her eyes grew wide with pain. Her body began to shake violently, wracked by spasms. The veins in her neck and arms bulged out, her heart racing uncontrollably.

For several minutes her agonized howls filled the

small room, accompanied by the stark ringing of the chains holding her to the wall. Her limbs flailed uncontrollably, her body writhing in the shackles. Suddenly, the Chinese woman let out a final, terrible, pain-filled wail and fell silent, her body instantly going limp. Her head sagged downward, her eyes staring lifeless at the floor.

Moondog and Panther looked at her body in silence for a second, then turned slowly to face each other.

"Grab a gun," Martina said slowly, nodding toward the dead soldiers on the floor. "Let's take Chin down."

Moondog nodded, bending down quickly over the body of the soldier to her left. She pulled his pistol from his holster and armed it. Working her hands quickly over his body, she searched for any extra ammunition. The search produced a small knife, which Moondog slipped into her pocket. Finding nothing more, she stood, turning back toward Martina.

"Thanks," she said.

"Don't mention it," Martina said. "Let's go."

She stepped quickly over the guards' dead bodies and walked out into the hall. Moondog followed her. As she stepped from the room, the Navy pilot pulled the door shut behind her. The door closed, leaving Ming's lifeless body hanging limply from the wall in the darkness and silence of the small room.

Martina paid little attention to the sound of the door closing. She began to walk back toward the stairs leading to the upper level. Moondog followed, catching up to her in a matter of seconds. Panther simply acknowledged her with a nod.

Keeping their guns at the ready, the two women moved quickly down the hall, scanning the area for any approaching soldiers. Fortunately, none appeared as they raced back toward the center of the mountain. The lower halls were completely deserted.

"Do you know what Chin's plotting?" Moondog whispered as they made their way through the rough stone corridor. The Navy woman moved awkwardly, half-limping, half-dragging her injured right leg behind her.

"No," Martina said simply. "But I still think I know how to stop him."

"How?" Moondog asked.

"He has to communicate with his attack force," Martina explained. "To do so, he's using something based in space. If we destroy the communication link from here to there, he won't be able to order the strike."

"Those antennas," Moondog said.

Martina nodded. "Do you think you can find your way back to that room with the transmission equipment?"

"Easily," Moondog said.

"Good. Get up there and do whatever you can to disable those things."

"You want me to go alone?" Moondog asked, slightly surprised.

Martina nodded.

"What are you going to do?"

"Distract Chin," Martina said plainly.

"How?"

"I'll think of something."

"We've got more firepower if we go together," Moondog said. "And we've got a much better chance of getting out of here alive."

"I know," Martina said. "But when those soldiers don't take me back up there, Chin's going to get suspicious. He'll send someone to get us, and when he finds us missing he'll start combing the place for us. With any luck, if I show up in front of him he might just forget about you."

"And I can shut him down without him even knowing I'm there," Moondog said.

Martina nodded.

"But why can't you take out the antennas?" Moondog said. "I can distract Chin as well as you can."

Martina shook her head. "It won't work. Chin told that bitch to kill you. If you show up he'll know I'm still alive, and somewhere else. But if it's me he just might think you're dead, and not bother to go looking for you."

"You got some sorta plan?"

"No," Martina said blankly. "Just show up and see what he does."

Moondog gaped at her in astonishment.

"It'll work," Martina said.

"All right," Moondog said reluctantly. "But as soon as I wreck those antennas, I'm coming back and pulling you out."

"Okay," Martina nodded. The two women had reached the steps leading to the upper level. Slowing their pace, they cautiously made their way up, moving as silently as possible, listening for any indication of life above.

Reaching the top step, Martina leaned forward, glancing to either side. The hall was as silent and empty. Drawing herself up to a standing position, she stepped out into the corridor. Moondog followed.

Martina turned toward her.

"Go," she said. "Good luck."

"Same to you," Moondog said. "Be careful."

"Don't worry about me," Martina said, smiling. Her eyes took on a wild sheen. "Those bastards won't hurt me."

She darted forward, almost running through the hall, holding her gun ahead of her. Moondog watched her for a brief second before twisting to the right and rushing away, moving as quickly as her injured leg allowed. For a moment their footsteps echoed through the halls, the corridors slowly falling silent again.

# ~ **24** ~

The interior of the C-130 Hercules was dark and cold. The throbbing of the four turboprop engines filled the cargo bay. The cabin was not insulated, magnifying the noise of the air rushing around the fuselage. Pale red bulbs cast an eerie, dim light through the cabin.

Andrew Kennedy sat along the C-130's cold bulkhead. The back of the Hercules was nearly empty except for the eight men waiting in the mesh cloth slings that served as seats. The men rode in silence. Some were asleep; others were double- and triple-checking their gear. The rest merely looked forward, their blank facial expressions not revealing their inner thoughts.

Kennedy stared at the far wall of the aircraft, running over the mission in his mind for the umpteenth time since takeoff. He had been flying on various airplanes for what seemed like days as the team was ferried from the United States to Afghanistan. There they had boarded the Hercules for the flight into China.

On the earlier flights the tall SEAL had slept. Leaving his gear in one corner, he had found a seat or a patch of floor, and dozed for hours. Most of the team had done the same. But this close to the mission, Kennedy found it impossible to rest. Adrenaline was already flowing through his veins, heightening his senses. His gear was now strapped to his back, digging into his shoulders. He ignored it, focusing on the task at hand.

Kennedy checked his watch, pressing a small button on the side to illuminate the face. The green hue from the watch lit up the dim interior of the cabin. Seeing the glow, the man seated next to him glanced over. Kennedy lowered his wrist. They were over Chinese airspace by now. The go signal would come at any minute.

His muscles reflexively tensed slightly. The adrenaline coursing through his veins was increasing as the tall SEAL mentally prepared himself for the mission. He silently ran through his gear checklist in the back of his head, assuring himself that everything was in place.

Out of the corner of his eye Kennedy caught a glimpse of motion. He turned his head slightly to see the crew chief moving toward the back of the plane. The noise from the engines drowned out the sound of his boots.

Kennedy followed the crew chief with his eyes as the man walked the length of the plane. He stopped beside the SEAL sitting at the far end of the door, bent down, and said something to him. Even though he nearly shouted, the roar of the turboprops muffled his words.

Mike Hawk simply nodded to the crew chief. The SEAL rose to his feet. He shouted to his men, who also stood, grabbing hold of the bulkheads as they did. The crew chief turned, walked back to the front of the aircraft, and vanished back into the crew cabin.

There was a flurry of activity among the SEALs as they checked each other's gear for the final time. Each slipped a full mask over his face and turned on the flow of oxygen. Completing the tasks, they turned toward the back of the plane and stood motionless.

Kennedy felt the weight of his pack on his shoulders as he stared at the heads of the seven men in front of him.

After a few moments, a thin white line appeared along the rear bulkhead of the C-130. An incredible wind immediately filled the cargo cabin, tugging at the SEALs and fluttering the straps of the plane's seats.

The line widened slowly, flooding the back of the Hercules with light. Blue sky appeared beyond. The rush of air and the roar of the engines grew louder as the rear ramp slid open, moving at an agonizingly slow pace.

Kennedy gazed up at the light to the side of the door. It was burning bright red. He turned his head forward, watching as the cargo ramp slowly slid to its full open position and stopped. The tall SEAL could see the brown of the earth below as well as the sky above. He looked back at the light, fixing his eyes on it. The bulb was still red.

Suddenly, the red bulb switched off, and a green bulb beneath blinked on. At the head of the column, Hawk started to run, vanishing almost instantly. As the leader of the team, he saw it as his duty to jump first, placing his second in command at the back of the line.

Without hesitation, the column of SEALs charged forward after their leader, rushing from the plane. Kennedy watched the men in front of him disappear one by one. His boots pounded against the cold metal of the C-130 as he raced ahead.

The man directly in front of Kennedy vanished, leaving only the gaping sky before him. Suddenly, the floor fell away beneath his feet, and he felt himself tumbling through the air. Reflexively, he stuck his arms out and arched his back. Instantly he stabilized in flight. He immediately yanked his rip cord.

His parachute came streaming out of his pack almost instantly, rapidly filling with air. Kennedy felt a sudden, strong jerk upward as his downward velocity slowed. He glanced up. The canopy was fully inflated above his head. Instead of rapidly rushing toward the ground, he was now floating slowly downward, hanging underneath his chute. Reaching up, Kennedy gripped the risers of his parachute.

Ahead of him, Kennedy could see the seven other members of his team silhouetted against the sky, all under canopy. The SEALs were strung out in a straight line, floating gracefully through the sky. Kennedy straightened himself, following the man directly in front of him.

The jump was known as a HAHO—high altitude, high opening. The jumpers deployed their chutes almost immediately after leaving the aircraft and would cover about forty miles over the ground as they descended. The height they jumped from was so great that they would lose consciousness almost immediately if not for their oxygen masks.

Settling into an even glide, Kennedy allowed himself to relax slightly. He kept his eyes focused on the jumper directly in front of him, steering to stay near the others. Occasionally he checked the altimeter strapped to his wrist. The small device was slowly winding downward.

From this height, the ground looked very distant. The earth did not appear to be moving at all. The only indication that he was descending came from the altimeter. The air whistled by him, tugging at his limbs and rippling the fabric of his clothing. Kennedy easily held his position, closely following the others as they descended.

The C-130 turned and headed back toward friendly territory as soon as the last SEAL departed the plane. The whine of its engines faded away, disappearing within a few moments. The only sound was the whoosh of the wind zipping past Kennedy.

The ground was coming closer. Kennedy glanced at his altimeter again. The features of the earth below were becoming more and more defined. Kennedy calmly watched the terrain below him pass by, enjoying the feel of the air flowing around his body as he slowly descended

More and more land features began to materialize. The terrain was mountainous. He could pick out the black strip of a road winding over the brown earth. A large group of antennas and satellite dishes sat off to the right of the road, stretching hundreds of feet into the air. The scene appeared almost identical to that in the Air Force's photographs. They were on target.

In front of him, he saw Hawk's feet hit the ground. A second later the team leader's parachute deflated behind him. One by one, the other SEALs touched down beside him. Kennedy expertly steered himself to the small group of men as he floated through the last few hundred feet of the jump.

Kennedy's boots skimmed over the rocks as he glided toward the others. His feet touched the ground, and he took a few steps to bleed off his forward velocity. He came to a stop beside Hawk. His parachute deflated slowly, falling to the earth behind him.

Wordlessly, Kennedy slipped off his parachute harness, discarding it beside the chute itself. He reached across his back and unslung his M-16. Chambering a round, Kennedy rested the weapon across his hands, muzzle pointing forward and down. He looked at the others. All were armed and ready. Kennedy nodded to Hawk.

"Let's move," Hawk said.

∗     ∗     ∗

General Chin stood at the railing of the balcony,

watching the activity beneath him. Beside the small Chinese man, Bill Durant leaned over the rail, studying the technicians with mild interest. The people on the floor took no notice of either. A eight soldiers stood against the far wall, appearing very bored.

"Soon, Mr. Durant, you will witness the fall of the United States and the rise of China," the general said, turning toward the engineer. Durant moved slightly sideways to face Chin, leaning against the rail with his right hand.

"I'm curious to see how you plan to bring America to her knees," Durant said.

"It's very simple," Chin said proudly. "I have placed a missile submarine off the Atlantic coast. On my order, it will fire two missiles, one aimed at New York, and the other at Washington, D.C. Both America's economy and government will be destroyed. Without them, the nation will collapse. The submarine simply awaits my order to fire."

"Amazing," Durant said.

"The beauty of it is, they will never be able to trace the attacks back to us," Chin said. "And even if they do, America will no longer have the strength to retaliate. I will defeat the world's greatest nation with one swift blow."

"You've thought this out," Durant said.

"Completely," Chin said, smiling. "Nothing can stop me."

He turned back to the railing, watching the bustle of activity beneath him. He briefly checked his watch.

"I wonder what's keeping Ming," he muttered, turning toward the door. "She should be here by now with Redrick."

"I swear, that woman wants to kill me," Durant said, sounding slightly apprehensive.

Chin laughed. "Don't worry. Ming will subdue her.

Your friend will be in so much pain that she won't be able to move."

Durant smiled.

"Good," he said.

"Once she gets here I will give the order to attack," Chin said, turning back to survey the control center.

Suddenly, a soldier burst through the side door. He ran up to Chin and saluted. The general returned the gesture.

"Sir," the soldier reported in Chinese, "radar picked up an aircraft flying sixty kilometers to the west, just inside the border. The signature suggested it was a cargo plane. It flew a few kilometers into our territory, then turned back into Afghanistan. Altitude and airspeed remained constant the entire time."

"He was probably just lost," Chin said. "Seal the doors, just to be sure. And post guards at every entry to the room."

"Yes, sir," the soldier said. He saluted quickly before spinning on his heel and vanishing back through the door. A few moments later he appeared on the floor below, barking orders to the controllers in Chinese.

"It's nothing serious," Chin said to Durant in English, seeing the puzzled look on the American's face. "I'm having them close the doors just to be sure. They can only be operated from here, so we'll be locked inside, safe from anything that might be out there. We'll be able to reopen them when Ming returns."

On the floor, a controller moved to a small box separate from the satellite controller's console, and pulled a lever. A series of locking mechanisms in every door in the room latched shut, sealing off the control center.

As the controller spun around, a gun exploded loudly. The bullet caught the man square in the chest, knocking him over backward. The entire room instantly fell silent, the controllers staring in horror at the body.

A tall woman stepped from the shadows. Without breaking stride, she bent down and snatched a cigarette lighter off the dead man. Spinning around, she flipped the pistol over in her hand and smashed the butt into the door controls, breaking open the box. Flipping the lighter open, she dropped it inside.

Tendrils of white smoke began to curl up from the box, accompanied by the smell of burning plastic. An instant later flames began to shoot from beneath the metal fixture as the wires inside caught fire, frying the inner workings.

Panther turned to face the balcony. Standing with her legs spread slightly apart, she spun her gun so that her fingers again curled around the hand grip. She placed her hands on her hips, squaring her shoulders. Tossing her head back, she glared up at Chin and Durant. The corners of her lips curled upward in a cocky smile.

"Nice of you to shut the doors for me," Martina shouted to Chin. "It makes everything so much easier."

"What!" Chin bellowed in surprise, his fingers tightening into fists around the rail. "How did you get free?"

Beside him Durant's face paled, a slight trace of fear appearing in his eyes.

"Your guards are fairly useless," Martina said, stepping forward, "and very quickly overpowered."

"Where's Ming?" Chin demanded.

"Paying her respects to the devil," Martina snarled.

Chin's face went white with rage, his eyes growing large.

"Don't worry, you'll soon be joining her," Martina

said, stopping directly in front of him. "I'll see to that personally."

The Chinese's general looked as if he was about to explode from rage.

"I know what you're planning, Chin," Martina taunted. "I heard everything!" she called, throwing her arms into the air.

"Kill her!" Chin snapped to his soldiers, anger roaring his voice.

The soldiers standing near the wall behind Chin rushed forward. Standing at the edge of the rail, they raised their weapons and sighted directly at Martina. A moment later they opened fire, bullets flying toward the fighter pilot.

Martina immediately dove to the side, away from the stream of gunfire. She vanished behind a row of consoles. A bullet grazed her right hip as she leapt away, cutting a small gash in her flight suit. As she disappeared from sight, the soldiers ceased firing. Half of them ran for the stairs leading to the lower level.

Panther landed on her left side, immediately swinging herself into a sitting position. Raising her own gun, she looked to her left and right. Several Chinese controllers sat on either side staring at her, unsure how to react to the American in their midst.

Panther slid her back up against the side of the console, glaring threateningly at the Chinese. Her hip was burning. She glanced down at the wound. The cut was shallow, trickling blood onto her flight suit. Ignoring it, she twisted her attention back to the Chinese.

Martina turned, crouching behind the consoles. She quickly scanned the area again. Seeing no one, she stood, peering over the row of consoles. Another group of controllers sat on the opposite side. Beyond was only the stone of the mountain, sloping upward to form the balcony, ten feet in the air. Martina placed her hands on the console closer to the balcony and jumped, vaulting over the computers.

Gunfire again filled the air as the soldiers standing above her caught sight of their quarry. She hit the ground, immediately tucking her body into a ball and rolling forward underneath the balcony. She drew herself up onto her haunches, gun at the ready. The shooting ceased immediately.

Suddenly, something impacted against Martina's back with enough force to send her sprawling on her stomach. Landing on the ground, she rolled over, raising her gun. Before she could find her target, a boot kicked the weapon from her hand.

Panther lifted her head. One of the Chinese controllers was standing over her, grinning. He drew his foot back, smashing his boot into her left side. She grunted and rolled with the blow, tumbling over backward like a gymnast and leaping to her feet. She drew herself up to her full height, dwarfing the man in front of her.

The man continued to advance, swinging his fist at the pilot's head. Martina quickly sidestepped, dodging the blow. She moved forward as she did, driving her own fist into his stomach. The man gasped and doubled over. Martina kicked him in the face. The man flew backward, landing flat on his back.

Martina quickly turned her head. Four Chinese soldiers were approaching her, each aiming a pistol directly at her chest. She moved her eyes over them, studying each in turn. All were smaller than her in stature, closing in on her steadily.

Martina lunged for the soldier standing directly in front of her, grabbing his wrist before he could fire his pistol. She stepped behind him, placing his body between hers and those of the three other soldiers, who were again aiming their pistols toward her.

The Chinese soldier tensed with surprise as Martina grabbed him. Before he could react, she twisted his arm upward, pointing the gun, still in his hand, directly at the side of his head. Wrapping her finger over his, she squeezed the trigger.

The gun exploded in the man's hand. The bullet shattered his head as it penetrated his skull, splattering brains and blood. The soldier went limp, sagging slowly to the ground. Martina pulled the gun from his grasp as he fell, immediately slipping her hand around the butt and looping her finger through the trigger.

She instantly raised the pistol, firing at the soldier directly in front of her. Seeing her lift the weapon, the man dropped to his knees. The bullet missed his head by inches. Martina stepped forward, firing again. This time the soldier was not fast enough. The small projectile penetrated into his chest, killing him instantly.

Suddenly, a hand grabbed Martina's left wrist. A second later she felt a sharp point jab her in the ribs. Martina twisted her head sideways. One of the two remaining soldiers was standing beside her, pressing a knife into her side. The tip of the blade pressed against her skin, but did not draw blood.

Angrily, she swung her gun toward the soldier. Before she could bring the weapon in front of her body, a second hand gripped her right wrist. An instant later the pistol was yanked from her fingers. The second Chinese soldier immediately twisted her arm behind her back, causing her shoulder to scream in pain.

The man to Martina's left lowered the knife and grabbed her arm with his hand. The soldier to her right eased the tension on her other arm. She began to struggle fiercely as the two men dragged her forward out of the shadow of the balcony. Stopping, they spun her around so that she faced the upper level.

Chin leaned over the railing, smiling broadly. Beside him, a wave of relief washed over Durant's face, turning slowly to a grin. Martina glared up at them, lips curling upward in a snarl. Her eyes blazed like a caged animal's as she struggled against the men who held her. The cold rage in her face suggested that she would destroy the two men above her if she were free.

"Is that the best you can do, Colonel?" Chin laughed, smugly victorious. "You haven't accomplished anything."

Panther snarled, straining forward against her captors. Neither man loosened his grip. Her boots slipped against the stone, but she did not move.

"Order the attack!" Chin called.

# ~ **25** ~

Moondog raced through the polished stone corridors. The uneven pounding of her boots rang through the halls. The sound of her footfalls filled her ears, drowning out all other noises and making it almost impossible for her to hear anyone approaching.

She moved awkwardly, almost dragging her right leg behind her. Her thigh was stiff and sore, the muscle nearly refusing to work. A wave of pain shot through her leg every time her foot hit the ground. Moondog ignored it, forcing herself to move forward.

Her eyes darted from side to side as she ran, looking for the slightest motion. Every few steps she checked back over her shoulder. She kept alert for any sign of someone approaching as she moved. She held her gun in front of her, knowing that she would most likely have only a second's warning if someone was to appear. The weapon was raised and ready.

But the hallways were completely deserted. Moondog neither saw nor heard another living soul as she hurried forward. Despite the lack of life, she continued to sweep the hall with her eyes, aware that a soldier could appear at any moment. Her time as a fighter pilot had taught her never to let her guard down, a lesson she was not about to forget.

After what seemed like ages, the familiar small metal door appeared in the side of the wall. Moondog slowed her pace as she moved toward it, slightly relieving the burning sensation in her right thigh.

She stopped in front of the door, reflexively shifting most of her weight to her left leg. Pointing her pistol directly at the door, she wrapped her free hand around the door knob. As soon as her hand landed on the cold metal, she yanked the door open.

The door swung wide, revealing the smaller hallway beyond. The narrow corridor was completely empty. It stretched forward before Moondog, silent. The light bulbs that ran along the top were spaced further apart, making the side tunnel dimmer than the main ones.

Moondog slid slowly through the door, pulling it shut behind her. The door closed quietly. She stepped forward, walking as quickly as she could down the hallway. Her right leg threatened to give way with every step.

Dismissing the pain rushing through her thigh, she forced herself to move. Despite her awkward gait, the distance closed quickly. She reached the small flight of stairs after a minute. Placing her left hand on the wall, she hauled herself up the steps.

Moondog nearly tripped as her foot hit the top step. She teetered forward, catching herself just before she lost her balance. A sharp wave of pain raced through her leg as her foot hit the stone. Muttering a string of curses under her breath, Moondog straightened her back and fixed her eyes on the door a few feet in front of her.

The Chinese had removed the broken metal door that hung from the hinges when she and Panther had first discovered the little room. A thin sheet of plywood had taken its place. The only metal visible in the new door was the handle. Moondog gripped it and tugged at it. The door refused to budge. It was locked.

Moondog glanced at the weapon in her hand. Putting a bullet through the bolt would be the quickest way to open the door. But a shot she used now would be one shot she didn't have later, when the small projectile could mean the difference between life and death.

Moondog sighed and lowered the weapon. She stepped back and flung herself into the door. The wood emitted a loud crack as her shoulder hit it. A sharp pain danced through her arm. Moondog stepped backward, rubbing her shoulder. Steeling herself for the blow, she again rushed toward the door.

The plywood split in half with a loud crack. Moondog crashed to the floor on the other side of the door in a shower of splinters. Her left shoulder slammed into the stone floor, followed a second later by the rest of her body.

Moondog raised her head, half lifting herself up off the ground. Two soldiers were seated at a table directly in front of her, staring wide-eyed at the American. For a brief second neither moved. Then both jumped rapidly to their feet.

"Fuck," the Navy woman spat.

The soldier nearest Moondog charged toward her, stomping his heel into her right shoulder. Moondog immediately rolled flat onto her back. The soldier stepped over Moondog, he kicking the gun from her hand.

The second man snatched a radio off his belt and began to shout into it. Hearing his rapid-fire Chinese, Moondog lifted her head, her eyes growing wide. The man looked back at her, continuing to chatter into the radio.

Moondog rolled away from the first soldier and jumped to her feet. Ignoring the man directly in front of her, she ran past him, tackling the soldier with the radio.

The man crashed to the floor beneath her. The

radio flew from his grip, shattering as it landed on the stone a few feet away. Lying flat on his back, the soldier looked up to find Moondog straddling his chest.

Moondog placed her hands on his neck, digging her thumbs into his throat. The man gasped, flailing beneath her. The pilot simply leaned forward, sinking her weight through her hands and into his windpipe.

Suddenly, something collided with the side of her head, knocking her off the soldier. He scrambled to his feet as Moondog tumbled backward across the stone. She landed a few feet from him, half on her back.

Drawing herself into a crouch, Moondog lifted her head. The two soldiers stood in front of her, closing slowly. Behind her was a row of transmission equipment. Rapidly, Moondog stood, balancing uneasily on her left leg.

The man standing to her right stepped forward, angling his fist toward her nose. Moondog twisted to the side as he did. His hand hit her left shoulder, sparking an incredibly sharp pain, which spread like fire through her shoulder.

Moondog staggered back, landing hard on her right foot. Her knee immediately sank down as her leg gave way. Her hands shot outward, her fingers brushing the cold metal of boxes lining the wall. She braced her palms against the metal and pushed upward with her arms, stopping herself from falling downward.

Slowly, Moondog pulled herself back upright, shifting her weight onto her left leg once more. She watched the two Chinese men moving toward her. Pain and fire danced in her eyes. The corners of her lips curled upward in a twisted, maniacal grin.

The first Chinese soldier stepped up to her, kicking her directly in the cut on her right leg.

Moondog grimaced in pain as her leg moved with the blow, her foot coming off the floor. Her body dipped, but she managed to keep herself upright, using her arms to steady herself against the wall.

He swung his fist toward her face. Moondog moved her head to the side. The soldier's knuckles collided with the metal casing just to her left, leaving a deep depression in the equipment.

Before the soldier could recover, Moondog drove her left hand into his gut. He stumbled backward, doubling over as he did. Grabbing hold of the top edge of the tall box behind her with both hands, Moondog raised her good leg, thrusting her foot directly into his chest. The man flew backward, landing sprawled on the floor in front of Moondog. Dazed, he rolled to the side and moaned.

The second soldier launched himself at her, shoving her back into the wall of transmission equipment. Her leg gave way and she fell to the ground. Pinning her against the large metal boxes with his body, he pressed his fingers into her throat.

Moondog could feel the pressure of the two points digging into her neck and closing off her windpipe. She gasped, finding herself unable to draw any air into her lungs. A slow, burning sensation began to spread through her chest, growing in intensity. The corners of her vision began to grow dark, closing in slowly.

Suddenly, the man in front of her went rigid. His eyes grew wide, his face frozen with shock. Slowly, his fingers fell away from Moondog's throat as his body sagged downwards. He crumpled on top of her and lay still.

Moondog pulled the small, bloody blade out from beneath his right ear. Shoving the dead body upward with her right hand, she kicked him off her with her good leg. The corpse flopped to the floor beside her.

She lifted her head to see the second soldier pick himself up off the floor. With one swift motion, she flung the knife across the room. The blade flew through the air, sinking deep into the soldier's chest. He dropped to his knees, then fell flat on his face and lay motionless.

Moondog leaned her head back against the metal transmission equipment and shut her eyes, gasping for air. After a moment she raised her right hand, gingerly running her fingertips over her left shoulder. Her collarbone was broken. She could feel the fracture beneath her skin.

There was little she could do about the break. Lowering her hand, she surveyed the room. Both Chinese soldiers lay on dead on the floor. The door was wide open, but the room was silent. For the moment no one was coming.

Moondog spotted her pistol lying in the far corner. Slowly, she managed to pull herself to her feet. She limped over to where the small weapon lay. Bending over, she picked up the gun and straightened her back.

Curling her finger around the trigger, Moondog turned her attention to the task at hand. The transmission equipment was contained in several tall silver boxes that covered three of the four walls. A series of lights along the top indicated that the equipment was in operation. Moondog paused, considering her options.

All the boxes were very large, and therefore probably very heavy. Moondog could scarcely stand, and she doubted she would be able to move even the smallest one an inch. To cut the wires that connected the equipment to the antennas, she needed to get behind the boxes.

That option obviously wasn't available at this point. She looked down at the dead soldier in the middle of the floor. A knife hung from his belt. She could pry open the front covers with the blade and rip the wiring out. It would take a little time, but it would work.

Moondog sighed and moved toward the first box of equipment. As she did, she caught sight of a thick cable running out of the stone a few inches above the ground. The wire disappeared behind the row of equipment.

Moondog stopped in her tracks, studying the thick coil. The cable had to be a power source of some sort. If she severed the wire, all the equipment would be inoperative in an instant, saving her precious time.

She looked at the knife again. The handle was plastic, wrapped in rubber to provide a solid grip. She could use the blade to cut the power wire, hopefully shutting down all power to the equipment.

She walked over to the body and pulled the knife from its sheath. Quickly walking the remaining distance to the wall, Moondog dropped to her knees beside the cable. Setting the gun on the floor by her right leg, she transferred the knife to her right hand and stuck the tip into the fabric of her flight suit, just below her left elbow.

Pulling the knife blade through the cloth, Moondog tore through her flight suit, ripping the lower part of her sleeve off. She wrapped the green material around the hilt of the knife. The rubber hilt shouldn't conduct electricity, but she wanted to be safe. Gripping the cable with her left hand and the knife with her right, she began to saw through the wires inside.

The tips of the cable sparked as the knife slipped through them, parting coil after coil of wire. The metal was hard, separating slowly, but gradually the knife slid deeper and deeper. Finally, the cord snapped through completely. The end of the wire fell to the ground, sending a small shower of sparks onto the stone. Moondog immediately raised her head, surveying the equipment. Every light on the metal boxes had blinked off.

Grinning, Moondog dropped the knife. Picking up the pistol, she pulled herself slowly back to her feet. As she turned toward the door, her ears caught the sound of boots on stone, rushing rapidly forward. Moondog tensed. They were coming for her.

✳     ✳     ✳

The SEAL team moved quickly over the brown rocks. They walked silently, weapons raised, holding a rough formation. They covered the terrain in seconds, approaching the slope of the mountain. A small hole was cut into the rock, a metal door separating the inside of the mountain from the elements. The SEAL team rapidly positioned themselves on either side of the door, weapons pointed toward the entryway.

Hawk stepped forward, placing his hand the doorknob. The door swung open freely. He advanced slowly, pointing his M-16 into the mountain. A long, dark tunnel stretched before him, completely empty.

"Smug little bastards," he said to his team with a grin, "thinking no one can touch them in there."

"Not very smart," Kennedy added, smiling.

Wordlessly, Hawk turned and walked into the tunnel. The other seven SEALs followed him, Kennedy bringing up the rear. They moved in single file, all following Hawk's lead. None spoke as they slipped beneath the earth.

The tunnel was carved into the rock. The floor was even, but the sides and ceiling were rough stone. Scattered light bulbs lined the top of the tunnel, connected by a strand of wire. They cast a dim light off the dark stone.

The SEALs slipped quickly along the side of the

wall, every man alert to any sign of human life. They kept their rifles raised. Each man watched the one in front of him out of the corner of his eye as he scanned for approaching enemy soldiers.

The hall stretched on endlessly, winding deeper and deeper into the mountain. The walls were solid, unbroken by other passages or doors. Eventually the tunnel began to widen. More light bulbs appeared overhead, brightening the area.

A series of barred doors appeared in the walls. Jail cells had been carved into the rock on each side. There were ten small chambers in all. The SEALs quickly dashed between them, peering into every cell in turn. All were empty.

"Fuck," Hawk cursed. "They must have taken them above." He turned toward Kennedy.

"Plant the charges," he said. "Let me know as soon as you're done."

Kennedy nodded.

"Come with me," Hawk ordered, pointing to three of the men.

The SEAL turned and began to move again, heading for the upper level. The other three soldiers followed him. Kennedy turned back to the three remaining men.

"Let's go to work," he said.

# ~ 26 ~

Chin raised his arms above his head and repeated the order, this time in Chinese. His voice echoed triumphantly off the high stone walls. Curling his hands around the rail again, he leaned forward, grinning victoriously.

Martina's eyes blazed. She stopped struggling, staring upward at the general. A sinking feeling filled the pit of her stomach as her expression shifted from one of rage to one of horror. She had failed. She hadn't been able to stop Chin from ordering the attack. Now thousands of innocent people would die.

Suddenly, the large display screens lining the wall went blank. The satellite tracks disappeared in an instant, leaving only the curving backdrop of Earth. The telemetry data simultaneously vanished off the computers. The controllers started shouting, filling the air with chatter. They began rushing frenziedly back and forth, trying to get the information to come back up. The screens remained empty, only causing the panic to increase.

Chin's mouth dropped open in shock. "What's happening?" he bellowed in Chinese.

"We've lost communications with everything," a soldier standing on the floor shouted up to him. "Both transmission and reception."

"How?" Chin demanded.

"I don't know," the man stammered.

"Get us back in contact again!" the Chinese general demanded.

"We're trying," the soldier said, shaking his head. "Nothing's working."

Martina grinned as she watched the ensuing panic surround her. Every piece of equipment had suddenly gone inoperable. Controllers were moving about rapidly, trying to get the computers to work again, to no avail.

Chin stood on the balcony, his face a mixture of horror and anger. He was shouting to a man below in Chinese. Martina could not understand what was being said, but one glance at Chin's expression was enough to tell her that the attack order had not been transmitted.

Panther's grin broadened. She had succeeded in buying Moondog the time she needed to shut down the radio antennas. No matter what the controllers did, they would not be able to get their data to reappear. In order to do so, they would need to repair whatever equipment the Navy woman had destroyed.

Martina quickly shifted her attention to the two men gripping her arms. Both were caught up in the confusion, watching the people rush around them instead of paying attention to the woman standing between them. They had loosened their grasp on her wrists when she stopped struggling.

Panther twisted to the side, slamming the sole of her right boot into the leg of the man standing beside her. The blow hit him directly behind his knee. The soldier's legs buckled, and he fell to the ground, releasing his grip on her as he did.

Panther turned toward the man on her left, stepping forward and smashing her right fist directly into his face. The man stumbled back. She wrenched her hand free of his grip as he fell. He reached for his gun. Seeing his hand drop to his holster, Panther lunged for him, knocking him over onto his back.

Panther grabbed for the weapon. His hand landed on top of hers as her fingers curled around the butt of the weapon. Quickly the soldier wrapped his other hand around her wrist, attempting to pry her grip off the pistol with his fingers.

Behind Panther, the second soldier climbed slowly to his feet. He walked over to where the American sat, anger blazing in his eyes. He raised his foot, smashing his boot into her shoulder and knocking her off his comrade.

Panther rolled with the blow, landing half on her side. The gun slid out of the soldier's holster. She raised the weapon, pulling the trigger. The bullet caught the soldier standing in front of her in the chest, knocking him over.

The soldier beside her grabbed her wrist, stopping her from turning the gun on him. He smashed his free hand into her face. Panther felt warm, wet blood trickling down her face, accompanied by the sharp taste of it in her mouth.

Flicking her wrist, she tossed the gun toward the far wall. The pistol landed a few feet behind the soldier, clattering on the rock. The man immediately released Panther's arm and turned toward the weapon.

Panther raised her right leg, jamming her heel into the side of the soldier's face with as much force as she could muster. The blow spun his head around, breaking his spine. The man's body went limp, and he crumpled to the floor. His head twisted awkwardly to the side, his vacant eyes staring at the far wall.

Panther climbed to her feet. Stepping over the body, she reached down and retrieved the pistol. Straightening her back, she looked at the balcony above her. Chin stood at the rail screaming at his controllers. He did not seem to notice that the

American was free.

Panther gazed to either side. The controllers were too caught up with the sudden computer system failure to pay any attention to her. They continued to rush frantically about, doing everything in their power to restore the telemetry data. No soldiers were visible on the main floor.

Panther turned toward small door cut into the rock. Quickly making her way past the bodies on the floor, she walked to the door, placing her hand on the knob. The handle turned freely, and the door swung open.

A small flight of stone stairs led upward, curving back toward the balcony. Panther charged up the stairs, her boots ringing against the stone. The steps ended in a small landing. A second door sat at the opposite end.

Panther kicked the door open. It swung wide, revealing the large open area of the stone balcony. Seeing Martina, the four soldiers standing on the upper level immediately raised their weapons and began to fire. The sound of gunfire instantly filled the air.

Panther ducked back behind the rock. The swinging door hit the far wall and bounced back. She grabbed the door as it swung toward her, allowing it to close part way so that there was only about an inch of space between the door and the wall. The bullets bounced harmlessly off the door and the rock surrounding it.

Sticking her head through the door, Panther fired off two quick shots. The first caught the closest soldier in the chest. He toppled to the floor as the other soldiers released another barrage of fire toward the American. She quickly ducked back behind the door to avoid the bullets that flew toward her.

Hearing shooting directly behind him, Chin

twisted around in surprise. His guards were unloading their weapons at the staircase that led to the floor beneath. Bill Durant stood against the far wall, watching them. The tall engineer's eyes flicked back and forth between the Chinese soldiers and the small door, unsure how to react.

Panther appeared in the side of the door, rapidly shooting again. The pilot was amazingly accurate with a pistol. Another of Chin's nearest soldiers fell to the ground. The other men loosed another volley just as the American disappeared from view. Chips of rock and dust flew from the far stone wall, and dents appeared in the metal door, but none of the bullets touched the pilot.

"Kill her!" Chin screamed at them. "Kill her!"

The two remaining soldiers rushed for the door, jerking it open. The American stood in the center, legs spread slightly apart. Bright red blood covered her right hip. Her flight suit was tattered and stained dark red in several other spots. She held her head high, sighting down the barrel of the pistol. Cold fire blazed in her eyes.

Her gun barked twice in rapid succession before either of the soldiers could react. A bullet caught each of the two guards directly in the chest. Both men fell backward, landing on the floor flat and lifeless. Martina stepped over their bodies and stopped. Keeping her gun raised, she surveyed the room slowly.

The bodies of the other two Chinese soldiers lay strewn about the floor, blood pooling around each. Chin stood to her left against the rail, face ablaze with rage. To her right, Durant was pressed against the wall. The tall American's eyes were fixated on her, reading her cold glare. Slowly, fear began trickling into his own eyes. Panther turned toward him, locking her gaze on him. She leveled her gun directly at his heart and pulled the trigger.

The weapon clicked empty. Cursing, Panther flung the useless gun away. Durant exhaled with relief as the pistol hit the ground on the opposite end of the balcony. It landed with the sound of metal against stone, skidding to a stop far from her reach.

Angrily, Chin crossed the room in a few quick strides, watching as Panther tossed her weapon away. Stepping forward, he smashed his right fist into the side of her head. He swung at her a second time. She ducked, crouching down beside one of the dead soldiers. Keeping her eye on Chin, she ran her hand along the side of the soldier's leg, her fingers touching the hilt of the knife that hung from his belt. Panther yanked the weapon free.

Chin grabbed her by the collar and pulled her to her feet. Despite the fact that she was taller than him, the general had the advantage of weight, and easily lifted the American. She stared down at him with her steel eyes, shoving her knee upward into his groin. The general shouted in pain, nearly going limp.

Panther thrust her arms up, breaking his grip on her. Reaching across his throat with her left forearm, she grabbed the left side of his collar, hauling him upward. She pushed him back, stepping into him as she shoved his back into the far stone wall. She held his body against the rock, pressing her arm into his neck as she did.

Suddenly, a muffled explosion shook the room, coming directly from the floor. Rock dust floated from two large metal doors that led into the lower level of the control room. Panther turned her head, looking down at the floor. The doors remained solidly on their hinges, closed fast.

Panther turned her head back toward Chin. The Chinese general was grinning.

"My soldiers, Colonel," he said, flashing his teeth. "In a few minutes they will have broken through the doors. Then they will kill you."

"They'll be too late to save you," Martina said. Raising her right hand, she angled the knife in her grip directly toward Chin's neck.

The loud crack of a gunshot echoed through the high-ceilinged room. The bullet grazed Panther's right shoulder, cutting through her flesh and imbedding itself in the rock in front of her.

Panther turned her head around. Durant stood against the far wall, clutching a pistol in his hands. The muzzle was pointed directly at her back. Slowly, the engineer readjusted his aim and squeezed the trigger a second time.

Panther immediately released her grip on Chin and dove to the ground. She tucked herself into a tight ball as she hit the floor, every injury in her body crying out as she crashed into the rock. Panther ignored the pain as she rolled over smoothly, allowing her forward momentum to carry her back onto her feet.

She stepped forward into Durant, knocking his hand back as she did. Both his back and his arm hit the stone wall behind him. Taken by surprise, he released his grip on the gun, the weapon falling to the floor.

Panther curled her left hand around his throat and raised her right. A flash of light glinted off the silver metal of the knife. The engineer wriggled against the stone, trying to free himself, but her grip was too great. She touched the tip of the blade to his throat.

"You son of a bitch," she hissed, cold eyes flashing.

Durant thrust his left hand directly into her lower right chest. Panther gasped as a wave of pain washed through her broken ribs. She staggered backward, her hand falling to her side. Her heels caught the body of a Chinese soldier and she toppled over, landing hard on her back.

Durant stepped over her, dropping onto her chest. Another wave of pain raced through her ribs as his weight crashed onto her. He straddled her, pressing his knees into her chest. Panther inhaled sharply, her face twisted with agony.

"Don't hate me, Martina," he said. "I simply took advantage of a good deal."

Panther grimaced, glaring up at him with a pain-filled snarl. She gritted her teeth, unable to speak because of the constriction on her lungs.

"I'm sorry," he said, leaning forward and wrapping his hands around her throat. "But I won't let you kill me."

Panther lifted her right arm off the ground, plunging the dagger in her hand directly into Durant's thigh. The engineer howled with pain. She yanked the weapon free and jabbed the blade into his side just below his rib cage, eliciting another wail.

Panther pulled the knife from his skin again and raised her hand, stabbing the blade directly into the side of Durant's throat. The silver tip protruded from the other side of his neck.

The engineer gasped, his eyes growing wide. His body went stiff and he fell to the ground, blood gurgling from his throat and spilling from his mouth and both ends of the knife. For a second he stared frantically at Panther, then his eyes shut and his body went limp.

Panther pulled the knife from his throat and stood slowly. She straightened her back, glancing slowly around the room. Her breathing was deep and quick as her body attempted to recover. Fire was still dancing through her lower chest. She held the knife out to her side, halfway up her body.

Before she could catch sight of him, Chin moved

toward her, striking her across the face. Panther staggered back. The Chinese general grabbed her wrist, smashing her hand into the rock. Caught off guard, Panther dropped the knife. It clattered to the floor beside her feet.

Chin grabbed her by the collar, shoving her backward. Panther winced as her shoulder slammed into the rock. The Chinese general pressed her body against the wall. Panther glared down at the little man, fury mixed with pain filling her eyes.

"You are indeed foolish, Colonel, thinking you can stop me," Chin said. "I will still topple your country."

"With what?" Martina hissed through clenched teeth, her lips twisted upward in a pain-filled grin. "Your communication equipment has been destroyed. You're cut off and isolated from the rest of the world."

Chin laughed. "Are you so shortsighted as to think I didn't have a backup plan?" he asked.

Panther's eyes grew wide in shock.

"There is a nuclear missile silo adjacent to this facility," he said. "I need no antennas to launch my intercontinental ballistic missiles. It is not nearly as surreptitious as a submarine, but they will still do the job. All I need to do is give the order, and America will be destroyed."

Raising his voice, he shouted loudly in Chinese.

✳     ✳     ✳

Moondog limped slowly toward the door. Cautiously, she stuck her head around the shattered remains of the plywood sheet, peering down the long, thin hallway. At least a dozen soldiers were charging straight for her.

Catching sight of Moondog, they immediately opened fire. She stepped backward, flattening herself against the stone wall beside the door. The bullets flew across the room, hitting the transmission equipment opposite her.

Moondog gazed at the pistol in her hand. The clip was full, but it still did not contain enough ammunition to stop all the approaching soldiers, even if every bullet scored a kill. Maybe if she could get her hands on one of the soldier's guns...

Moondog shook her head. The chances were very slim. Most likely the soldiers would cut her down before she could even empty her pistol. She realized she probably would not make it out alive. Her eyes narrowed. She knew her chances were of survival slim, but that didn't mean she wasn't going to try to fight her way out.

Moondog stepped backward, moving alongside the wall. She stopped several feet from the door and turned back into it. Leaning against the stone for support, she raised her pistol and aimed directly at the door.

A second later a soldier leapt through the broken plywood onto the floor of the room. Moondog squeezed the trigger. The gun in her hand barked, and the soldier dropped to the ground, blood pooling around his dead body.

Two more men burst through the door. Rapidly, Moondog adjusted her aim. The first shot caught one man in the back. Hearing the gunfire, the second twisted around, only to be struck by a bullet in the chest.

Another soldier rushed into the room, two more close on his heels. Moondog grinned. The door was acting as a choke point. The break was so slim that only one or two men at a time could fit through. She could hear the other soldiers pounding against the door, trying to break the plywood and enlarge the gap.

Moondog readjusted her aim and squeezed the trigger three times in rapid succession. The two men in the lead dropped immediately, shot through the chest.

The third bullet caught the last Chinese in the right shoulder. He dropped his pistol as the bullet embedded itself in his arm. Ignoring the gun as it clattered to the stone, he lunged at Moondog. The Navy pilot was unable to move quickly enough to get out of his way.

The soldier crashed into Moondog, knocking her to the ground. She landed half on her side, back against the wall, with the soldier on top of her. He grabbed her hand, pulling the gun from her grasp. The man tossed the weapon onto the stone a few feet from her and struck her across the face with his good hand.

Moondog raised her left leg, thrusting her knee into the man's crotch. The soldier rolled off her, landing on the floor. She lunged for him, grabbing the knife off his belt and plunging it into his lower chest before he could react. The man went stiff.

Moondog kicked him away and leaned back against the stone. She quickly snatched up the gun lying next to her. She knew she could not regain her feet before the next few soldiers rushed into the room, so she simply raised her pistol and waited for them to appear.

The chatter of automatic weapons suddenly filled the room. Moondog's stomach knotted. She was done for. She had one or two shots left at the most. The rifles would cut her down before she could even try to retrieve another weapon.

Another Chinese soldier rushed inside. Moondog reacted quickly, squeezing the trigger on her pistol. The bullet caught the man in the side of the head, and he went down. The sound of automatic fire grew louder.

A second soldier darted into the room. Moondog shifted her aim and pulled the trigger. The gun clicked empty. Tossing it aside, she scanned her surroundings, searching desperately for the nearest weapon.

The Chinese soldier twisted around. Catching sight of Moondog, he turned toward her, raising his gun and aiming directly for her chest. The soldier grinned as he wrapped his fingers around the trigger and squeezed.

A burst of automatic fire shook the room. The bullets cut through the soldier, and he crumpled to the ground. Moondog watched the body fall in surprise, turning her head slowly back toward the broken plywood door.

A man dressed all in black leapt into the room, stepping quickly over the dead body. He stood a few inches short of six feet. His shoulders were broad, and his head was shaved. He clutched an M-16 in his hand, fingers curled around the trigger.

Three more men rushed into the room after him. All were identically dressed and carried M-16s across their chests. Moondog's eyes grew wide with surprise as she realized that all four were Americans.

The lead man stepped over the dead bodies, walking toward Moondog. As he approached her, he let his rifle swing downward so that the muzzle pointed toward the floor. He stopped in front of the pilot and lowered his hand. Moondog grasped his wrist, and he pulled her to her feet.

"Commander Ansetti?" he asked.

Moondog nodded, looking up at him as she rested her weight against the wall to keep her leg from collapsing. He stood two or three inches above her.

"Who are you?" she asked.

"Lieutenant Mike Hawk, ma'am," he said.

Moondog stared at him for a second, then gazed at the other three men behind him. They stood beside the door, guns aimed down the hall.

"You're Special Forces," she said.

Hawk nodded. "Navy SEALs," he said. "We've come to get you out of here."

Moondog smiled. "Thanks," she said.

"Let's go," Hawk said. He stepped forward, slinging his M-16 across his back. He gently took hold of Moondog's right hand and pulled her arm over his shoulder. He wrapped his free hand around her waist and began to lead her toward the door.

"Wait!" Moondog said. "Martina!"

Hawk stopped, turning toward her.

"You know where Colonel Redrick is?" he asked.

Moondog nodded.

"Tell me," Hawk said.

# ~ 27 ~

On the floor of the control room a man began to move, pulling a key from his pocket. He walked to a small console in the center of the room, apart from the many rows of controllers. He slid the key into a slot. As he turned the key, the panel in front of him lit up, data appearing on the screen.

Martina watched in horror as the man began to type on a keypad on the console. Mustering as much force as she could, she swung her fist into Chin's stomach. The Chinese general doubled over slightly, his grip on her loosening.

Panther raised her leg, driving her foot into his side. Chin toppled backward, landing flat on his back a few feet from her. Panther glanced around desperately, looking for any type of weapon. Her eyes landed on a pistol lying on the floor a few feet away.

Panther lunged for the gun. Her fingers curled around the butt of the weapon as she tumbled over, her body again crying out in pain as she hit the floor. She came up in a kneeling position. Her eyes danced quickly around the lower room before her.

Almost immediately her gaze locked on the soldier standing at the keypad. Panther raised her weapon, aiming directly toward him, and fired off two quick shots. Both bullets caught the soldier in the back, and he slumped forward over the console.

Chin picked himself off the floor and rapidly

crossed the distance to where Panther knelt. Swinging his foot up, he kicked the pistol from her hand. The weapon rattled to a stop on the balcony twenty feet away.

Chin reached down, grabbing the back of Panther's collar and pulling her to her feet. He pushed her back into the railing, twirling her body around so that they were again face to face. Blood covered the American's mouth and nose. Pain was rampant in her icy eyes, but her lips still curved upward, revealing her bloody teeth.

"I'll kill you myself," Chin hissed as he leaned into her, pressing her back over the balcony.

With a loud crash that reverberated through the room, the metal rail broke free beneath their combined weight. Both Martina and Chin toppled backward. They fell fifteen feet through the air to the hard stone below.

Panther's entire weight came down on her left foot. She heard a cracking sound as her boot hit the floor, followed by a sharp pain in her shin. Her leg immediately buckled and she fell backward, landing hard against the stone. An instant later Chin crashed onto her, her body breaking his fall. A wave of pain washed through Panther's whole body as his weight slammed into her. She gasped for air but found herself unable to breathe.

Chin drew himself up slowly on all fours, then climbed to his feet. He peered down at the American below him. Martina was staring at the ceiling, face awash with agony. Her lips moved slightly, but she made no sound. The pilot coughed, rolling onto her side. Ignoring her, Chin turned his attention to the console which housed the controls to launch his nuclear missiles.

Panther pulled herself to a sitting position. Her lower left leg was throbbing. Blood was soaking through her pant leg. Several white shards of bone pierced through both her skin and her flight suit.

Wincing, Panther rolled over onto her stomach. She didn't try to stand, knowing her leg would never be able to hold her weight. Instead she drew herself onto her hands and her right foot, and launched herself at Chin. She caught the general around the waist. He crashed forward.

Chin rolled onto his back. The American pulled herself on top of him, holding him against the ground with her body weight. She wrapped both hands around his throat and squeezed with all the force she could muster.

The Chinese general gasped for breath. He raised his right hand, punching her in the jaw. Panther grunted in pain but held her grip, digging her fingers deeper into Chin's neck.

Chin thrust his hands under her chest. Planting his fingers on her rib cage, he pushed her upward. Panther's face immediately twisted in pain. Chin shoved her sideways. She rolled to the stone beside him, landing on her side.

Chin stood, brushing the dust off him. He stopped in front of Panther, jabbing the toe of his boot into her left shin. She wailed as his foot collided with the broken shards of her bone. Instinctively curling into a ball, she pulled her legs to her chest and wrapped her hands around the wound.

The general planted his foot on Panther's right shoulder, rolling her onto her back. He stepped over her and dropped down. Panther exhaled sharply as his weight landed on her chest. Chin wrapped his fingers around her throat and leaned into her.

"You can't stop me, Colonel," he said with a grin, tightening his hands around her neck. "I will kill you as soon as I have destroyed your precious America."

Releasing his grip on her neck, Chin climbed to

his feet, leaving Panther gasping for air. Turning, the general walked over to the nuclear missile launch console. He pulled the dead soldier off the controls, flinging the man to the floor behind him. Chin studied the display panel for a moment, then rapidly began to type on the keypad.

Slowly, Panther rolled onto her stomach and pushed herself on her hands and knees. She lifted her head, blood running freely down her face. She spit blood to the side and glared up at Chin, her eyes blazing with cold rage.

Using her hands and her good leg, she began to crawl slowly over the stone. She dragged herself toward where Chin stood, rapidly programming his nuclear missiles. Her left foot trailed behind her at an awkward angle, leaving a small path of blood across the stone.

Inputting a final keystroke into the pad, Chin twisted around, grinning triumphantly. The American was crawling across the floor toward him. He laughed, watching her creep slowly over the rock, moving like an injured dog.

"You don't know when to give up, do you, Colonel?" he called to her. "Look at yourself. Do you really think you can stop me?"

If Martina heard him, she gave no indication of it. She simply continued to pull herself forward over the stone, teeth gritted with pain and determination.

"It's over," Chin crowed. "I've won. All I have to do is push one more button, and your nation will be wiped out."

He spun slowly back to the console, dramatically raising his right hand above his head.

Panther threw herself forward, landing beside the body of the dead Chinese soldier. Her hand immediately fell to his waist. In one swift motion, she pulled the knife from the sheath on his belt and flung the weapon toward the Chinese general.

The knife flew through the air, tumbling end over end. The tip of the blade sliced through Chin's biceps, and the dagger dropped to the floor beside him. Chin's arm fell as the knife ripped through his muscle. The general yelped in pain, and he spun around angrily, his eyes searching for the tall American pilot.

With all the power in her arms and her good leg, Panther flung herself at Chin, tackling him from the side. The general toppled sideways, landing on his shoulder on the hard stone beside the console with Panther half on top of him.

Chin swung his left fist upward, catching her in the side of the jaw. Panther swayed slightly to the side. Planting his hand on her shoulder, he shifted his weight beneath her, throwing her body off his. She crashed into the console, landing on her left side.

The Chinese general climbed to his feet. Slowly, Panther drew herself up on her hands and knees. As she did, Chin kicked her across her midsection. She fell back to the ground, arms sprawling wide. Her fingers touched the hilt of the knife, her hand reflexively curling around it.

Chin stepped over her, moving back to the console. Panther rolled onto her back as he reached for the launch button. She raised her right leg, slamming her shin across the back of his legs. Chin's knees buckled, and he dropped to the floor. His hand fell away from the launch controls, curling around the edge of the console.

Martina pushed herself back to a sitting position just as Chin lifted himself off the ground. The general lunged for the controls, fingers outstretched. She threw herself at him. He grinned as his fingers touched the launch button.

Panther collided with Chin, knocking him to the side. His hand swung away from the launch controls as the pilot knocked him backward. A sharp pain raced through his lower chest as he landed on the floor in a sitting position.

Chin glanced downward. Panther's right hand was jabbing his lower left side. Slowly, she drew her arm away from his body, pulling a six-inch knife from his flesh. The long silver blade was covered in blood.

Chin's eyes grew wide with shock as he stared at the bloody dagger. He lifted his gaze up to the American. A smile crept slowly over her face, her eyes turning to ice. The Chinese general froze, his gaze fixated on her.

Panther jabbed the blade into his side again, this time sliding the tip beneath his lower ribs. Chin's body went rigid as the blade pierced his heart. Air hissed slowly from his lungs as he fell backward, lying motionless on the floor.

Martina rolled off Chin and slowly dragged herself across the floor on her hands and knees. Reaching the console that controlled the missile launch, she gripped the edges with her hands. Careful not to let any weight rest on her left leg, she pulled herself up on to her right foot and studied across the launch controls.

Leaning against the console for support, she reached across it and pulled the key from its slot. In an instant the entire console went dark. Martina twisted around, lowering herself back to the floor with her arms and her good leg. As she sat back on the floor, she pressed the tip of the key into the stone, snapping it in half.

Tilting her head back, Martina leaned against the console. She cast her eyes around the room. A dozen Chinese controllers stared at her, unsure how to react. The whole control center was spinning slowly around her, colors whirling and fading. Still, she could make out some of the Chinese moving cautiously toward where she sat.

A wave of exhaustion washed over her. Martina shut her eyes. Her body felt as if it was on fire, every little scratch on her skin crying with pain. The adrenaline that had coursed through her veins moments earlier was quickly leaving her bloodstream, making it impossible to ignore the agony washing through her body.

Suddenly, a loud explosion shook the room. Martina opened her eyes again, her gaze locking on the large doors leading into the control center. The metal doors were wide open, their edges twisted back. Martina exhaled. Chin's soldiers, coming to kill her.

Almost immediately, automatic fire filled the room, cutting down the Chinese controllers who stood around Martina. Those who were still alive dove to the ground, flattening themselves against the stone to avoid the flying bullets. Many scurried away, diving down behind the consoles out of the path of fire.

Four men rushed into the control center. All were dressed entirely in black and carried M-16s, which they fired across the room, causing the Chinese to remain flattened on the ground. They were larger than the Chinese, both in build and height. The lead man was at least six feet tall. And their features were distinctly American.

Andrew Kennedy stopped a few feet inside the room. It appeared to be a massive control center with an incredibly high ceiling. Rows and rows of computers filled the floor. All were completely blank. Many large, empty display screens hung from the walls. The bodies of at least a dozen Chinese soldiers littered the stone floor.

Off to his left, a tall American woman sat with her back against one of the control consoles. Her body was nearly limp, large patches of crimson staining her green flight suit. She held her head up slightly, looking at the group of SEALs.

"Keep me covered," Kennedy ordered.

He stepped forward, slinging his M-16 over his shoulder as he moved. He quickly stepped over the bodies of the dead Chinese soldiers littering the floor and stopped a foot in front of Martina. She turned her head toward him as he approached, gazing up at the tall SEAL questioningly through half-glazed eyes.

Wordlessly, Kennedy bent over, sliding his arms underneath her. Gently, he lifted her battered body into his arms. The pilot offered no resistance. She let him raise her up to his chest, all the while staring silently at him through her glassy eyes.

Spinning around quickly, Kennedy turned back toward the door. He picked his way carefully over the bodies on the floor. The other three SEALs stood beside the door, leveling their weapons at the Chinese controllers.

Holding the pilot tightly in his arms, Kennedy hurried through the twisted metal doors, past another group of dead Chinese soldiers lying just outside the control room. The three other SEALs turned to follow him as he raced out into the hall. They immediately went into a rough formation around him, pointing their M-16s down the hall and watching their back. Their fingers rested on their triggers as they searched for any life around them.

Martina watched the hall slip by as she lay limply in the SEAL's arms. Everything seemed to move at a slow, surreal pace. She saw lights flashing by overhead, one by one. They hung above her for minutes at a time, only to be replaced by long stretches of dark rock. The sounds of the SEALs' footsteps echoed distantly in her ears. She could feel the footfalls of the man who held her, his boots hitting the ground at long intervals.

She sensed that something about these men was

different from the Chinese soldiers who had kept her prisoner, but she could not fathom what. She tried to reach back into her memory and recall what it was that made her think so, but her mind refused to work.

Slowly, Martina turned her head back to the man who held her. His hair and eyes were dark, and his tanned face was set with determination. She saw his features clearly enough, but her brain could not process more than what her eyes received. All she knew was that he was carrying her; she did not know where or why.

Suddenly, brilliant sunlight flooded over them, accompanied by bright blue sky. The SEALs rushed from the mountain out onto the uneven, rocky terrain beyond. Another group of four men appeared to their left, all identically dressed and armed. They dashed over the rock toward Kennedy and the others. Moondog hobbled along between two of them, her arms flung over their shoulders. They supported her as she ran forward.

The thumping sound of rotors filled the air. Kennedy lifted his head. Two MH-53 Pavelow helicopters were flying through the sky above them. As the tall SEAL watched, the two helos descended, touching down on the wide stretch of road not twenty feet in front of the small group of Americans.

Off to Kennedy's left, Hawk and the others moved to the chopper nearest them. The SEAL team commander helped the second pilot into the helicopter. As she vanished inside, he and the other three men climbed on board. Immediately, the Pavelow lifted off and began to climb, turning toward the west.

Pulling the woman in his arms tightly against him, Kennedy ducked beneath the rotors of the second Pavelow. Still holding her, he sat on the side of the helicopter and swung his legs inside, leaning his back against the far wall. Slowly, he lowered the pilot in his arms so that her upper back lay across his legs. She moved her glazed eyes slowly around the interior of the Pavelow and then returned her gaze to Kennedy.

Kennedy reached into his pocket and removed a small transmitter as the three other SEALs quickly jumped into the helicopter, finding spots inside the small cabin. They lowered their weapons and began to settle down for the ride. The Air Force crew chief who sat in the front shouted something into his headset. Slowly, the Pavelow began to move, lifting off from the rock and climbing into the air.

Kennedy gazed outside as the ground fell away beneath him. He depressed a button on the transmitter in his hand, holding his finger against it for several seconds. Far below, he heard a low rumbling, growing louder with time. The mountain seemed to shake, dust billowing out from all the tunnel entrances. Kennedy smiled to himself. The charges he had planted had worked, destroying the interior of the base.

Replacing the transmitter in his pocket, Kennedy turned his head back to the cabin of the helicopter. The pilot dipped the nose, flying over the ground to the west after the first Pavelow. In a moment Kennedy could see the other chopper flying through the air beside them as the two aircraft pulled back into formation.

The helicopter's crew chief moved past Kennedy, closing the doors to the helo. The loud noise of the wind vanished, and the thumping of the rotors diminished. The cabin grew darker as the sunlight decreased. The crew chief walked back to the front of the helicopter and sat down, scanning the SEALs with mild disinterest.

Kennedy glanced down at the pilot. Two of the

other men had moved beside her. One was squatting down by her legs, splinting her shin. The second crouched directly across from Kennedy and was quickly bandaging the wound on her right hip.

The pilot stared at the two men. She neither moved nor spoke as her gaze wandered slowly between the SEALs. She winced with pain as the man by her feet touched her broken leg, pulling the splints around her bone together. Despite the agony that registered across her face, she remained still, relaxing after an instant.

Kennedy turned to the man across from him, who had just finished applying the dressing to her hip.

"Lift her up, gently," Kennedy said.

The man nodded and slid his arm under Martina's back, easily pushing her into a sitting position. He moved closer to her, placing both his hands on the uninjured area below her neck to hold her up. She turned her head to look at him, then slowly moved her eyes back to Kennedy, a look of utter incomprehension on her pale face.

Kennedy shrugged off his gear, tossing it on the floor beside him. Quickly he found his small medical kit and pulled a pair of scissors from it. Raising the scissors, he cut away the right shoulder of Martina's flight suit. Reaching back into his bag, he pulled out a bandage and pressed it against the wound.

He nodded to the man across from him as soon as the dressing was in place. Slowly, the other SEAL lowered her again, laying her back down across Kennedy's legs. He quickly flicked his eyes over her body, evaluating her condition. All of her serious injuries were bandaged, leaving only a few small cuts and bruises. The other two SEALs moved away from the pilot, leaning against the bulkheads of the helicopter to unwind after the mission.

Kennedy stared down at her. She was still looking

up at him, slowly following his motions with her half-dead eyes. From the dazed, quizzical look on her face, he could tell she did not understand what was happening around her. Slowly, he reached down and laid his fingers against her neck, feeling for a pulse.

Kennedy raised his head back up, looking at the Air Force crew chief.

"Hey," he called, "you got a med kit on this thing?"

"Yeah," the crew chief shouted over the pounding of the rotors.

"It got a blanket?" Kennedy asked.

"Yeah," the man repeated.

"Give it to me," Kennedy shouted. "She's slipping into shock."

The crew chief turned and pulled the med kit out from where it was stored. Opening it, he removed a large gray blanket and tossed it across the cabin to Kennedy. The tall SEAL stuck out his arms, easily catching it.

He unfolded the blanket, draping it over the pilot's body. The man seated by Martina's feet moved forward and pulled the cloth over her boots, covering her legs. Kennedy tucked the blanket around her shoulders so that it completely covered her body. She continued to gaze up at him through her glassy eyes, uncomprehendingly.

Kennedy leaned down over her, locking his eyes on hers.

"Hey, it's all right," he said, his voice deep and even. "We're Americans, we've come to take you home."

Martina gazed up at him for a second longer. Then she nodded almost imperceptibly and closed her eyes, her tall body relaxing completely. Only the even rhythm of her breathing indicated that she was alive at all.

# ~ **28** ~

The members of the cabinet and the Chairman of the Joint Chiefs of Staff all came to their feet as David Webster entered the large conference room. The President crossed to the head of the table, dropped a small stack of papers on top, and sat down. The others immediately took their seats.

"Good morning, gentlemen," Webster said. The other men present all responded with nods or good mornings.

Webster reached forward and punched a button on the desk in front of him.

"Sherri, are we in touch with Edwards?" he asked.

"Yes, sir," his secretary replied, her usual bored nasal tone coming over the intercom. "General Peters is on line one."

"Thank you," Webster said, reaching over and pushing another button.

"Good morning, Scott," he said.

"Good morning, sir," Peters' voice came over the speakerphone.

"What's the news?" Webster asked.

"The mission was successful, sir," Peters announced. "The SEAL team landed at one of our forward bases in Afghanistan a few hours ago. Both Colonel Redrick and Commander Ansetti were with them."

"Excellent," Webster said, smiling. "And the

Chinese base?"

"At least partially destroyed, sir," the Air Force general reported. "The SEALs planted charges on the lower level, which fired successfully. Unfortunately, we have no way of determining the extent of the damage."

"Understandable," Webster said. "What about our satellites?"

"According to what Commander Ansetti passed on to me, the entire operation was being controlled from inside that mountain, sir," Peters said. "It's highly possible that with the destruction of the base the Chinese will be unable to continue to man their space station, but at this point I can't say for sure."

"Any word from the Chinese, Gordon?" Webster asked the Secretary of State.

"Nothing, sir," the Secretary said. "It's possible they might just cover up the whole thing, call it an earthquake."

"Let me know if you hear anything," Webster said.

"Yes, sir," the secretary replied.

"Where are our pilots now, Scott?" the President said into the speakerphone.

"They received some basic medical treatment at the forward base in Afghanistan. They're being med evaced back to the United States as we speak," Peters said. "They should arrive early tomorrow morning."

"What shape are they in?"

"Commander Ansetti was pretty beat up. She's covered in cuts and bruises, but fortunately no serious injuries. Apparently the worst of it was a broken collarbone and a nasty gash in her right leg that's making it a little difficult for her to walk. She was fully conscious when they landed in Afghanistan," Peters said. "As soon as the doctors finish patching her up, she's going to send me everything she knows on the Chinese operation."

"Forward that to me, please, Scott," the President said.

"Yes, sir," Peters said.

"What about Colonel Redrick?"

"Colonel Redrick was barely conscious when the SEALs reached her," Peters said. "Apparently she passed out on the helicopter flight from China, and as of yet hasn't come to. The doctors at the forward base figured it was most likely from blood loss. She had a couple minor gunshot wounds and a bad fracture of her left leg, as well as some smaller abrasions. They think she should be all right once she gets proper medical attention."

"Keep me posted," Webster said. "I want to know when that plane lands."

"I will, sir," Peters said.

"Thank you, Scott," the President said. "I think that about covers it. Unless anyone has anything to add?"

He surveyed the room. The various members of the cabinet all shook their heads. Webster turned back to the speakerphone.

"I think that just about closes the book on that one," he said. "I'll let you get back to running your base, Scott. Thank you again, and have a good morning."

"You're welcome, sir," Peters said. "Good morning."

The line clicked dead. Webster reached over and turned off the speakerphone. He looked back toward the papers in front of him. Lifting his head to face the cabinet again, the President smoothly moved to the second item on his agenda.

*        *        *

THREE MONTHS LATER:

Edwards Air Force Base sat in silence in the early morning light. The dawn quiet was interrupted only by the occasional car or jet engine. A light breeze blew a few grains of sand across the desert. The sky above was pale blue, lightening in the east. The stars had faded, but the sun had not yet appeared above the horizon.

Two aircraft moved slowly from a small hangar, crawling single-file along the taxiway to a remote runway. To a casual observer they appeared to be simply F-22 Raptors, but a closer inspection revealed that these aircraft were actually very different.

The two planes were smaller than Raptors. There were subtle alterations in their bodies. Black tiling coated the aircraft's underbellies, creeping up around the tips of the wings and the tail. The black surface completely covered the nose up to the edge of the cockpit. Small holes appeared in the tiling at odd intervals along the body.

The strange aircraft moved smoothly along the taxiway. They stopped briefly beside the asphalt strip to perform a few final pre-takeoff checks before crawling into position just on the side of the runway.

"Edwards tower, Hellcat One, holding short of the active ready for takeoff."

"Good morning, Hellcat," the tower replied. "You are cleared for takeoff."

The air traffic controller quickly relayed the winds, instructing the pilot on the initial course to take.

"Safe flight," he concluded. "See you back here in a few hours."

"Cleared for takeoff, Hellcat One," came the response.

The two aircraft maneuvered out onto the runway, turning side by side. As they swung onto the strip, the pilots pushed the throttles forward. The Hellcats' dual jet/rocket engines roared to life, breaking the silence of the morning like thunder. The noise increased as the engines came into full afterburner, fire streaming from each plane's twin exhausts.

They surged down the runway in a tight formation, rapidly picking up speed as they raced along. The planes rotated simultaneously, their nose wheels lifting into the air as one. A second later, both planes' main landing gear came off the runway.

The two planes began a gentle climb, raising their landing gear. As they reached the end of the runway, the Hellcats made a sweeping turn to the east. They leveled out a few thousand feet above the airbase and began to pick up airspeed, racing toward the rising sun.

As the Hellcats reached their maximum velocity, they pulled nose up, flying completely vertical. Earth rapidly dropped away beneath them as they raced toward the sky, trading every bit of airspeed for altitude.

The planes slowed as they reached the top of their climb, until they were barely moving forward at all. Just before the aircraft slipped into a stall, the rocket engines kicked in, increasing the fire shooting from their exhausts. The Hellcats leapt forward, streaking toward space.

"Hellcat one, Hellcat two," the shortwave radio between the two planes crackled. "How your ribs feeling, Panther?"

"Good as new, Moondog," Martina Redrick said, grinning beneath her oxygen mask as she felt the familiar sensation of g-forces pushing her down into her ejection seat. "No pain at all."

Martina twisted around. Off to her right, she saw Rachel Ansetti's Hellcat climbing on her wing in perfect formation. Two bright plumes of flames shot from the tail of the aircraft as it raced skyward, nose pointed directly toward the heavens.

Martina glanced at her own six. She was not checking for bogeys. She knew no other aircraft would be there. They were far above where even a Blackbird could fly. Instead she stared at the two brilliant columns of red-orange fire that spewed from her own tail, forming a long series of Mach diamonds. She watched the ground grow smaller and smaller behind her.

Martina gazed forward. The sky around her was growing darker by the second, fading from light blue to deep blue to black. Stars appeared as faint pinpoints of light, growing brighter as the Hellcat climbed.

Martina checked her heads-up display.

"Cut engines in 3... 2... 1... Mark," she called, reaching up and shutting off her engine.

The roar of the rockets died away instantaneously. In their place, only silence remained. Martina felt herself being lifted up against the straps that held her in her ejection seat. She gently pushed the stick forward.

Small bursts of flames shot from the thrusters, moving the Hellcat's nose forward. Another set fired as Martina leveled the plane in its orbit. Behind her, Moondog slid perfectly into position on her wing. Earth curved away beneath the two aircraft, a vivid swirling mass of blues, greens, browns, and whites.

On all other sides, the Hellcats were surrounded by the blackness of space. Thousands of stars shone as pinpoints of light, and the sun blazed yellow. Dozens of silver satellites floated by at different speeds, passing both above and below the planes. Sitting in complete silence, surrounded by the emptiness of it all, Martina felt as if she herself was completely engulfed in the vacuum. The sheer size of it all was incredible.

She grinned beneath her mask.

"Hey Moondog, let's see what these things can do," she called.

"Guess you want to get your ass kicked, huh?" Moondog replied.

"You'll be the one getting your ass handed to you," Panther replied. "Let's dogfight!"

High above Earth's atmosphere, the two space planes locked in combat.

Now Available From Karla K. Goodhouse

# FIREBIRD

A test flight in the Hellcats, the Air Force's new Top Secret fighters, plunges Martina Redrick and Rachel Ansetti deep into the midst of a deadly terror plot.

When an armed B-1 bomber makes a mayday call, Martina and Rachel are diverted to intercept the aircraft. Once the bomber is on the ground, they make a shocking discovery. The crew is dead and at the controls is a young F-22 pilot, Vince Carlton. Carlton claims he snuck on board to prevent a shadowy terrorist organization from hijacking the bomber for their own evil purposes, but evidence suggests he was actually the culprit.

The attempted theft is only the beginning. A mysterious figure is sneaking around the Hellcats, trying to learn their secrets. The terrorists are now targeting Martina and Rachel, hoping to steal their jets instead of the bomber. And when someone tries to kill Carlton, it becomes clear that things might not be what they seem.

With the terrorists plotting a devastating attack on U.S. soil, it's once again up to Martina and Rachel to stop their diabolical scheme, and the fate of the nation rests in their hands.

# About the Author

Karla K. Goodhouse grew up in rural New England. A natural storyteller, she was fascinated by all things air and space. She graduated from the US Air Force Academy in 2005 with a degree in Aeronautical Engineering. While at the Academy, she also studied martial arts. Today, Karla is a maintenance officer in the US Air Force Reserve and a commercial pilot.

Hellfire is the first of three Martina Redrick novels written to date. Karla is currently working on a fourth.

Visit her website: www.karlakgoodhouse.com.

# Glossary of Military and Aviation Terms

**Afterburner** aka **Burner** – The section of a jet engine behind the turbine where fuel can be injected and ignited to produce extra thrust.

**AIM-9 Sidewinder** – A heat seeking missile. Designed to lock onto the heat from an enemy aircraft's engine exhaust.

**AIM-120 AMRAAM** – Advanced Medium Range Air to Air Missile. A radar guided missile. Designed to lock onto the radar signature of an enemy aircraft.

**Bogey** – An unidentified aircraft.

**Burner Can** – An aircraft's tailpipe.

**C-21 Learjet** – A small aircraft used for VIP transport.

**C-130** – A cargo transport powered by four turboprop engines.

**Chaff** – Countermeasures used against radar guide missiles.

**F/A-18 Hornet** – Navy fighter jet.

**F-15 Eagle** aka **"15"** – A tactical fighter jet.

**F-15E Strike Eagle** – A multi-role fighter jet.

**F-16 Fighting Falcon** aka **"Viper"** aka **"16"** – A compact, multi role fighter jet.

**F-22 Raptor** aka **"22"** – A multi role stealth fighter jet, capable of supercruise, or supersonic flight without the use of afterburners.

**Flares** – Countermeasures used against heat seeking missiles.

**G-suit** – A garment worn by fighter pilots to prevent loss of consciousness due to G-forces. When the g-force on a pilot increases, the g-suit inflates, putting pressure on the pilot's legs and preventing blood from rushing to his or her feet.

**Guard Frequency** – The emergency frequency used by military aircraft.

**HAHO** – High Altitude High Opening. A parachute jump from a high altitude, usually around 40,000 feet MSL. The parachutists open their chutes almost immediately after exiting the aircraft. They can travel distances of up to 40 miles before reaching the ground. Special Forces teams conduct HAHO jumps to reach their targets undetected.

**Immelman** – A course-reversal maneuver executed by pulling back on the stick, so the aircraft climbs. The back pressure is maintained until the aircraft is on its back at the top of a loop. Then the pilot rolls the aircraft upright, completing the maneuver.

**In the Green** – Within safe operating limits.

**J-58** – The turbo-ramjet engine used in the SR-71 Blackbird.

**Jink** – To maneuver erratically in an attempt to shake an enemy aircraft.

**KC-135** – An aerial refueling aircraft also used for cargo transport.

**Light Bird** – A Lieutenant Colonel.

**Mach** – The measurement of an aircraft's speed as a ratio relative to the speed of sound.

**MH-53 Pavelow** – A large helicopter.

**MiG 29 Fulcrum** – A Russian made multi-role fighter jet.

**MiG 31 Foxhound** – A Russian made interceptor.

**NORAD** – North American Aerospace Defense Command. The agency which oversees U.S. and Canadian airspace.

**O-4** - Officer pay grade equivalent to the rank of Major in the Air Force, Army or Marines and Lieutenant Commander in the Navy.

**OSI** – Office of Special Investigations. An Air Force agency similar to the FBI.

**Over the Top Maneuver** – Any aerial maneuver in which an aircraft executes a pull up to inverted flight.

**SR-71 Blackbird** – A spy plane used by the U.S. Air Force capable of flying Mach 3 at 80,000 feet MSL. Now retired.

**TPS** – Test Pilot School.

**Transponder** – A device used to identify an aircraft to air traffic control.

**Wilco** – Short for will comply. Used by pilots to inform controllers that they will follow the instructions given.

**VOQ** – Visiting Officer's Quarters. Lodging on a military base for officers who are there for a short stay.

**Zoom Climb** – A maneuver in which an aircraft pitches nose up, trading all excess speed for altitude very rapidly.